Family

Kaylid Chronicles Book 5

Mel Todd

Bad Ash Publishing

Atlanta, GA

Copyright © 2019 by **Melisa Todd**

All rights reserved. No part of this publication may be reproduced, distributed or transmitted in any form or by any means, without prior written permission.

Melisa Todd/Bad Ash Publishing
Powder Springs, GA 30127
www.badashpublishing.com

Publisher's Note: This is a work of fiction. Names, characters, places, and incidents are a product of the author's imagination. Locales and public names are sometimes used for atmospheric purposes. Any resemblance to actual people, living or dead, or to businesses, companies, events, institutions, or locales is completely coincidental.

Book Layout © 2017 BookDesignTemplates.com

Family/ Mel Todd. -- 1st ed.
ISBN 978-1-950287-03-1

In the end, my family, natural and chosen, are why I survive.

I'll destroy the world before I let my children get hurt.

—TONAN DIAZ

CONTENTS

Chapter 1 – Moments in Time 1

Chapter 2 – Human Dragons 10

Chapter 3 – Other Realms 19

Chapter 4 - Waiting Game...28

Chapter 5 - Watching the Show 36

Chapter 6 - Project Management............................44

Chapter 7 - Restrictions...55

Chapter 8 - Money Buys Nothing 65

Chapter 9 - Parks...76

Chapter 10 - Backlash 86

Chapter 11 - Fear 100

Chapter 12 - Goodbyes 112

Chapter 13 - More Questions.................................122

Chapter 14 - Consequences 131

Chapter 15 - Home?..139

Chapter 16 - Grass is Greener 147

Chapter 17 - Complications....................................156

Chapter 18 - Path Less Traveled 164

Chapter 19 - Plans Realized 173

Chapter 20 - More Visitors 180

Chapter 21 - Other Worlds 192

Chapter 22 - Cultural Differences 202

Chapter 23 - Pivot 211

Chapter 24 - Imprint 220

Chapter 25 - Paths Chosen 229

Chapter 26 - Dinner Display 238

Chapter 27 - Offer Made 248

Chapter 28 - Circus is in Town 257

Chapter 29 - Wrench in the Works 265

Chapter 30 - Tipping Point 272

Chapter 31 - Green Light 279

Chapter 32 - Trouble 287

Epilogue 304

Chapter 1 – Moments in Time

Who will win, the animal or the human? More and more people are asking these questions after a few more attacks by rabid Shifters. If you shift will you de-evolve into your animal form? What does this mean for the protections that were rushed into law? People are starting to wonder if this new ability might come with more downsides than just invading aliens. Already people are asking if we would be under this level of danger if Shifters weren't here. ~TNN News

Toni's life was a series of moments forever branded into her mind, heart, and soul.

The day Jeff asked her to marry him.

The day she found out she was pregnant with twins.

The day the officer knocked on the door and she knew before he said anything, her husband was dead.

The day her children were born.

The day she turned into a jaguar.

The day her children turned into jaguars.

The day her children were captured, driven away in a bus, and she could do nothing.

The day her children returned to her, a naked McKenna Largo watching with haunted eyes.

The day she woke up in the jungle, once again away from her children.

All those moments were seared into her mind, every detail perfect. And none of them compared to watching the Drakyn walk out of the wormhole and speak to McKenna. She'd been focusing so hard on what McKenna was saying to the soldiers, that between her, not to mention Perc and JD's, worry and stress something had changed. She needed to be there to see what they were seeing, to figure out if the transmitter was a trap. An ally that might save their world. That was vital. For the first time she'd regretted staying behind with the kids. Something clicked in her brain and her vision grayed out then brightened to reveal a scene from her dreams.

In front of her a portal resolved, swirling and silvery, but with colors she'd only seen in fragments of memory.

This must be through McKenna's eyes, but how?

Something one of the twins said flickered through her mind, an offhand comment she hadn't paid attention to then. The consequences of being a working mother, you ignored anything that didn't seem world-ending at that moment. And given everything seemed literally world-ending, she had paid little attention.

The figure walking out of the portal ended any wool-gathering and she stopped breathing as a red and gold dragon man appeared on the grass in front of her best friend. Wings glittering and moving as a head swiveled and seemed to peer into her soul.

Oh shit, he's real? How can he be real?

The spike of adrenaline driven by her sudden panic broke the visual connection just as McKenna spoke to the being. His words rattled in the mind-space, and an awareness of all of them resonated back through into her mind.

Toni fought to breathe when she wanted, needed, to curl up and cry and scream at the same time.

"Mom? Who's Kenna talking to? JD said it's a worm. What's a worm?"

She forced open her eyes to see Jessi standing in front of her, a frown on her face. While her eyes were pure Toni, bright emerald green, Jessi's face structure reminded Toni of Jeff every time she looked at her. Jamie too, both living reminders of the man she still ached for at night. Breathing helped get oxygen back into her brain, and she shoved the image of a living Drakyn into her private thoughts, hard.

"Remember the not-dreams you told us about, where you're out fighting and killing creatures? They were kinda lizard-like?"

By this time Jamie, Charley, and Nam had shown up. She could hear Carina in the kitchen, blissfully ignorant of her panic.

Why she wants to be changed like us I don't know.

Though she did know, she just didn't want to admit to the incredibleness of it all. Not when she lived with the terror that her children, all their children, might be killed or captured. It did strange things to a parent when each time you looked at the ones you loved; you wondered if it was the last time. And when you had to live with the knowledge you might be unable to protect them.

Charley nodded. "Yeah. The whole game thing, but I didn't like killing them. They were pretty. And it just felt icky."

Nam said nothing, but she didn't look surprised either so Toni let it go.

Protecting the innocent my ass. These kids know more than I do, and I wish they didn't but what's done, is done.

"I think from what JD told me and a few things from my own not-dreams, the Drakyn can become bigger, like dragons. And I think it's wyrm," she spelled it out for Jessi, "an old word for dragon."

"There's no such thing as dragons." Jamie protested. "It's gotta be a sort of dinosaur or something. Dragons aren't real."

"Why not?" Jessi's instant response told Toni an argument was about to ensue.

"Stop. You want to argue, go downstairs. I'm not getting in the middle of it." Toni stood, stopping the nascent reason to blow off steam. Four sets of lips pouted at her. "Don't pout at me. You want to go argue, go downstairs where you won't disturb anyone."

Or make enough noise someone on the street might hear you.

They all sagged but went tromping downstairs. Though Nam grabbed a quick hug before she headed after them. In her wake she left a soothing feeling of calm. Toni smiled. That little girl charmed everyone she met. Shaking off the mood and hoping to think about memories from dreams she'd almost convinced herself were long in the past, she started towards the kitchen, when McKenna asked her if she minded company.

Keeping her mental voice cheerful she replied with an affirmative and verified the details. Her family was coming home. But they were bringing with them government officials and someone that couldn't exist.

"Carina, we have incoming," Toni announced as she entered the kitchen. Carina froze, looking at her, eyes wide. "No, sorry. Not that kind. McKenna and the others are coming back and bringing important guests."

The tension bled away from Carina's body and she glared at Toni. "Are you trying to give me a heart attack? At twenty-two I shouldn't be having heart attacks!" The glare she gave Toni mixed admonishing and teasing. For a moment there Toni saw Carina's grandmother, Marissa Watkins, the family friend that had babysat Toni when she'd been a little girl.

"My bad. No, just the rest of our motley crew asking for food and drinks." She moved over, throwing some of the cherished supply of cider into the freezer for a quick chill and pulling out the whiskey bottle. Since getting drunk was all but impossible, it had become something to savor and enjoy the memory of drinking more than anything else.

"Oh good. The kids will be delighted. Do they know?" Carina finished what she was doing, slicing up the block of cheese so they could use it on sandwiches.

Toni tilted her head, thinking and probing the mindspace. "Not yet. They weren't listening when McKenna asked. If they knew I'm sure they'd be up here bugging me every thirty seconds. I'll tell them when she gets closer." Toni heaved a mock sigh. "I think my kids like her better than me."

"No, she just doesn't yell at them and they don't see her every day. More the favorite aunt thing." Carina bent over and pulled out ingredients to make some simple food. The grocery stores were on limited hours and provisions, but the house had been well-stocked, and a full freezer provided before the invasion began, so they were still doing well. If it kept up for another two weeks, that would change.

"That works. Kinda how I feel about her. The sister I never had. Oh well. Let's get ready for our own invasion."

It didn't take long before she could feel McKenna getting close while Carina had some food in the oven. Just feeling her family getting nearer helped. Hourly Toni found herself checking to make sure they were all still alive and well. The loss of Caroline reminded her they could die. Immortal they might be. Impossible to kill they weren't.

~Kids?~ she said, knocking on their mental walls. Normally they stayed in their own space and none of the adults felt like they needed to be in their space, but they had the freedom to come into the public space at any time.

She felt them flood up into it, bright little bricks of essence in her mind.

~What, Mom?~ Jessi again, her little hellion. She would be a handful when she reached her teens.

Please by all living things let her reach her teens, free and happy.

But her tone wasn't disrespectful, just distracted. Which meant Toni probably didn't want to know what they were involved in.

~Oh, nothing. I just thought you might like to know McKenna will be here in a few minutes.~ Her voice purposefully nonchalant. Moms knew how to be pains too.

~YES!~ She flinched at the mental yells and then the thunderous pounding up the stairs as the four of them burst through the door led by Charley.

"She's coming home? Where is she? Is she here?" His almost desperate need cut at her, and the look on Nam's face wasn't any better. Though when Jamie reached over and hugged Nam to him, she swore Carina was cutting onions.

"In a few. If you watch from the windows by the door you should see them pull up. If they get out of the cars without guns you can go meet them. Be quiet." The last two words fell in an empty room as all four of them had sped to the windows and were peering out.

I swear if they were in animal form all their tails would be twitching like crazy.

She checked back in with Carina, but of course the wonderful girl had everything under control.

"Remind me to give you a raise."

Carina glanced at her dark braids jangling as she laughed. "You don't pay me; you just pay my bills. But a new phone when this is all over wouldn't be amiss." The grin on her face eased some of the tightness in Toni's chest.

"That might be possible," Toni said, grateful once again for this young woman.

"They're here!" Charley didn't quite yell, but his voice was loud enough both Carina and Toni cringed. Living with it so quiet, even moderate noises seemed loud. "McKenna got out and they're looking around. It's clear."

The military term sounded odd from him, but he'd been through as many dream simulations as she had. At this point it probably seemed normal.

"Go."

The door flew open as she headed that direction and Charley and Nam disappeared from her sight. To her bemusement, Jamie and Jessi stayed at the door, letting her go through while they hung back. Toni cast them glances as she walked out, but scanned the area looking for a dragon. He wasn't there.

Am I glad or not about that?

"You were attacked? Why didn't you say anything?" McKenna voice rang in the quiet afternoon. Toni followed her eyes to the scorch marks and shrugged.

"Because you couldn't do anything, and it would have only stressed you out. I handled it. We're fine." Toni looked around the area, though for the dragon or danger she didn't know. "Though we shouldn't stay out here much longer. People are noticing."

She slipped back in and headed for the kitchen as McKenna got people moving. It felt strange to be outside, so exposed. And that very feeling made the shivers worse. From the conversations in the room more people had come in, a few voices she didn't recognize filled the living room, but she didn't worry about it right now. She stayed there where it was safe until McKenna pinged her.

~Hey. You okay? Any reason you're hiding in the kitchen?~

Crap. I guess I can't hide in here forever and I can't keep them with me.

~I missed you guys. And I'm fighting the temptation to pull all of you into my arms and never let you go again. It hurt not having you here,~ Toni admitted. She didn't ever want them to leave.

~Good. 'Cause we felt the same way. I thought our not being here would keep you safer. Apparently, I was wrong.~ The stress and edge of fear in her voice cut at Toni and she straightened. Too many people around right now, so she settled for words.

~Kenna, no one is safe right now. But I took care of it, left the bodies in the street and sent a text for a body pick-up. Which is the strangest thing ever to say.~

~Why don't you and Carina come out and meet the dragon.~

Oh dear gods, he is here. Is it really him? It can't be. Those were dreams. It can't be real.

~Sure. Want a cider?~ Toni offered, trying to not let her mental voice shake at all.

~Yes, please.~ The need in McKenna's thought made Toni smirk. She grabbed the drink and walked out, handing out the drinks. Only then did she let her eyes drift to the man who wasn't a man in the living room.

He talked to the kids, but she could barely process the words as his wings and tail appeared, leaving the creature that had haunted her waking memories since she was a child standing there in front of her. His colors seemed off, wrong somehow, but she had no doubt it was the same being she'd once played with in fading dreams.

"I saw, but I didn't believe. It is you." Toni didn't mean to say those words, she didn't mean to think them, but they fell into the suddenly quiet room.

Chapter 2 – Human Dragons

Body disposal services have sprung up fast. With a simple text message, they will come get the body, log it, and dispose of it. If it has ID on it, they will notify the next of kin, otherwise DNA is being recorded and attached to all the containers for later examination. The cynic in you might wonder how many murders are being committed and will never be brought to justice. But given the actions of the Hamas and gangs in some areas, maybe it is worth it for a few people to disappear and no charges being pressed. Sometimes killers kill the right people. ~ Op Ed piece in SacWasp

"Toni? Are you okay?" McKenna asked, a spike of worry in her voice.

Toni tried to get her emotions under control but as the Drakyn's eyes fastened on hers, she had to resist falling into that swirl of light.

Everything cascaded into her brain, the dreams she'd thought were just childhood fantasies, faded over time, now reappeared vibrant and clear in her mind. She fought to not dive back into her dreams, but instead revel in the old friends. The stories her parents had told her that she'd forgotten when she grew older, fresh and new again. Plus the sense of rightness that made no sense at all.

"I, no, yes, sorry, just," she forced the words out, but they were just a jumble of sounds. Her friends,

FAMILY

her family, looked at her, worry clear on their faces. Noise of another car parking saved her. "You deal with that; I'll be in the kitchen." She shoved the words out and fled, needing time to come to terms with the memories and emotions.

The stories of her parents, about their ancient, royal heritage, descended from the gods. She'd barely remembered it when researching stuff for JD. The legend of the jaguar goddess hadn't matched what she barely remembered from her parents' stories. But seeing him, the scales, the colors, the wings, brought all of her long-ago dreams rushing to the forefront.

It can't be real. But it is real. The dragon from your dreams is standing out there. It can't be any crazier than everything else going on. Turning into a jaguar, aliens invading, why not dragons?

That thought helped to steady her emotions. Closing her eyes, she leaned against the kitchen counter. She breathed in and out, ordering her heart rate to slow and breathing to calm.

"Everything going well in the living room?" Carina asked. "Hey, are you okay? You look like you've seen a ghost."

Toni stayed where she was for a few more heartbeats, making sure she had control of herself before responding. The new voices coming from the living room told her she didn't have long. So once again she pushed back the memories and focused on the here and now. Something she'd perfected when Jeff was killed. You focus on this minute, this hour. Everything else will wait until it's time. If she had her way, the dragon would wait a very long time.

She opened her eyes and smiled; it wasn't as forced as it seemed. "Seeing a dragon is memorable and it shook me a bit. But we have more guests. Things ready?"

Carina gave her a doubtful look, but let it slide and they worked bringing drinks and making sure everyone was taken care of. It gave her something to do, plus monitoring the kids mentally once they were shooed back down to the basement.

Whoever picked this house knew what they were doing. It's been perfect to keep us all safe. Yet give the kids space to play without feeling like they're prisoners.

She checked on the argument in the basement, about dragons again, and helped with the kitchen. Normally not her favorite place, but avoiding the dragon, Rarz, apparently had priority over everything else. Her actions generated more questioning looks from McKenna, and Cass checked in on her but she'd learned in the months and years after Jeff's death to act as if you were just fine. No matter how fragile your hold onto sanity might be.

The sudden decision and the move to a military base caught her off guard. One minute they were going to be there, the next they were being shipped someplace else, without any chance to argue. She headed up to deal with moving and packing again. Anger at once again the kids being at risk, at the fact that she needed to leave them, and the mystery of the dragon. That didn't even add in the fact there were people out there trying to kill them. Rage, fear, confusion, and worry all mixed into a stew of emotions she couldn't even sort out. Her actions were on automatic, her mind focused on the kids and definitely not on the dragon, when McKenna called her name.

"Toni?"

She tried not to cringe. She didn't want to lie, so she redirected to other viable worries.

"I know, I know. This is the best hope we have. That if I stayed, we would probably all die. And by all, I mean all humans. I know that I'm being silly. That they will protect the kids to the best of their abilities. I know all of that!" Her voice broke on a sob, but it was more rage than sorrow. "And I still don't want to go. They are changing so fast, becoming people in their own right, not just my kids and I'm terrified that I'll miss it. I'm terrified something will happen and I won't be here to take care of them, to hold them, listen to them sleep. And I can't do anything about it, and I didn't choose any of this."

McKenna pulled her into a hug and Toni went, needing the feeling of someone else holding her. She realized her face was wet, and the fact that she was crying let her cry even more. Some of the stress bled off and she tried to remember the last time she had let herself cry. Much less had someone else hold her while she cried. She couldn't remember and that had a strange pain also. Finally, she pulled away from the comfort.

"Thanks. I guess I needed that. I'll be okay."

"You're one of the strongest women I know. Of course, you'll be okay. But that doesn't mean you can't hurt."

"Pot, Kettle?" Toni responded, fighting back a full-blown smile. "I know how you feel about Charley and Nam. Don't tell me this isn't killing you also."

"It is. I want to be here with them. She's so young, so I get it. But not being here hurts. However, if I don't try to do something and we all die?" McKenna shrugged. "I'm torn so I'm doing what I can."

Why is there never a tissue when you need it?

Her nose was running, and she swiped at it. "You're doing fine." She finally gave in and used her t-shirt. "Okay, enough emotions. We have stuff to do, then an enemy to kick out of our solar system."

"You sure you're okay?"

"No. But I'll make it. Trust me, compared to Jeff dying, this I know I can handle. I just needed that cry I guess." She turned to look at the laundry that needed to be done, including her now dirty t-shirt.

"Good. Next question – what's up with you and the Drakyn?"

Shit, shit, shit, what do I say? I can't even begin to explain anything right now.

"That obvious?"

"Just weird. You don't usually react like that. So what's the issue?" McKenna didn't stare at her, instead helping to pack, which made it easier to respond.

"When I saw him walking out of that portal I almost choked. It was like my dreams had been made real."

"How did you see that? You weren't there."

"No, but we heard the comments you made, and I was stressing. I wanted to see what was going on, especially with Perc and JD muttering, like whispers in the mindscape. I just wanted and suddenly it was like I was there, but the view was odd. I could see it through your eyes. Everything in color. It lasted only for a minute or two, but I couldn't focus on anything except him."

"We can do that, too," Charley said softly.

Toni jumped and stared at him.

I need to pay more attention to who is around when I talk.

"Do what?" But that vague comment about seeing through others' eyes resurfaced in her mind.

"See through each other's eyes. I mean I can only see through Jessi's. But Jamie can see through hers also. We haven't tried with Nam. She's still too new to the group. But yeah, we found that out." Charley shrugged. "Just heard you talking about it and thought I'd tell you. But it is kinda cool occasionally. We're all packed up. So where are we going now?"

Those little stinkers. I wonder how often they do that?

McKenna was hugging Charley, and Toni wished hers were here to hug, but they were good at adapting. Too good. "You guys okay with all this change?"

"Sure. This is fun. Dragons, aliens, army guys, invaders. It's like being in a movie." His excitement made Toni want to laugh and scream. This wasn't a game but having them scared wouldn't help either.

"If you say so. Go get your stuff downstairs. I think we're moving to a base." McKenna's voice was light, but Toni figured she had to be stressed, too.

"Ooh, will we get to stay in barracks? That would be awesome." The boy's excitement made Toni snort. If only it were that simple.

"Maybe. I'll ask. Now get." McKenna shooed him off. "I think I'm jealous they think this is fun. But I don't want to disabuse them of that idea," McKenna commented as she watched them trot down the stairs. "But now," she said turning back to Toni. "Rarz, spill."

"Dammit, I was hoping you'd been sidetracked." She made it a light tone, but the words carried more truth than not.

I don't know what to tell her. And the truth doesn't make sense to me.

"Not so lucky. Spill, but do it in my bedroom so I can pack."

Giving into the inevitable, Toni followed McKenna to her room.

"So yeah, the dragon walking out of a big shiny portal was a bit of a surprise, but nothing like the fact that I recognized him."

"What?" Toni smirked at the look of surprise on McKenna's face.

"All my life I dreamed of dragons. Both as humanoid and on all fours. Honestly when I shifted, I was surprised I didn't turn into a dragon. But who tells people that stuff? I just pushed it away and focused on being a kid, then being an adult, then a mom. It was silly dreams and not like I had them every night. I'd almost forgotten them and haven't had them in the last few months. The dreams on the ship pushed them to the side, I guess. So when he walked out, I almost choked."

"Huh. What do you think it means?"

"No clue, other than me being weird. But really there are only so many ways dragons can look. I doubt I dreamed about him specifically. Probably just a weird parallel thing. I mean a dragon and aliens and Shifters."

An alien you apparently share DNA with? That raises more questions.

"Personally, I think it would be stranger at this point if they weren't linked. Besides, he keeps looking at you funny also. As if he knows you." McKenna pointed out, amusement on her face.

Toni groaned. "I hate it when you're right." She looked around focusing on anything other than the thought of the Drakyn. "That looks like everything. I'll talk to him later. If we survive it might matter. Now? I'll try to quit freaking out every time I see him. But he looks wrong without the wings."

McKenna grinned. "Agreed. But still, it was getting a bit claustrophobic with them, he uses them the way I use my tail in both my forms."

"That he does. Anything else?"

They fell into organizing everything else. To her relief in the resulting chaos, the subject was dropped, and Toni stayed in the background of all the activity. She focused on the kids and made sure she didn't get left alone with Rarz. She saw him looking at her a few times and occasionally there was a brush of a question against her mind, but she pushed it off. It didn't matter right now.

All too often she felt like the fifth wheel on a double date. JD and Cass were cute enough to spike your blood sugar. Then there was McKenna and Perc. She was tempted to lock them in a room with a bed and some porn to see if maybe they would get over whatever their issue was. They danced around their attraction, but it was clear neither of them had done anything about it yet. She wanted to tell McKenna life was short, take your chances when you can. But McKenna didn't need a reminder, she knew. Instead Toni kept her mouth shut and let them be.

Most of the plans seemed to treat them all as afterthoughts, but she didn't know enough to argue. She went with the flow, paying little attention to anything but the kids, always present in the back of her mind. Watching Rarz change into a dragon in that dark warehouse, the menace in the shadows, the shape of him, the power that rolled from him, made her want to react. But in fear or joy she couldn't say.

Chapter 3 – Other Realms

The attacks continue and various countries have all but come to a standstill. There are reports of riots in Paris over food and the invaders. More and more old weapons are making appearances from where family had stashed them after World War II. At least ten deaths are blamed on old ammunition causing backfires, but then most people don't care. Death seems to be the currency of the day and either you will be taken or killed if you get in the way of these invaders. Better to go out in a manner you control ~ TNN Talking Head

The next forty-eight hours turned into a blur of action. Practicing, training, meeting so many people she gave up trying to track names, and always being aware of Rarz. The day they stormed the spaceship, the dreams returned to her during her nap. She'd not had time to process anything between the training, walking through portals, learning call signs. Everything felt like it was coming at her a million miles an hour and her ability to cope had been pushed to the brink. Toni had fallen asleep the minute her head hit the pillow on the cot in an Army tent. She found herself in the world she'd almost denied had existed.

Bright and clear as if she had stepped into a high definition film. Unlike the not-dreams they had been sent, this time she had control over her body, and it was hers, not some other person's.

She turned slowly, smiling at the strange yet familiar double moons in the lavender sky. Her throat caught at the sight.

I hadn't realized how much I had missed that view. I thought it was all a dream.

"You came."

Toni spun at the voice, terror beating in her throat and she fell, foot slipping on the dew damp grass. Sitting on her ass, she found herself looking up at the Drakyn. The one from Earth. The ones from her dreams.

His red and gold scales appeared more purple and pink in this light, more right. Her eyes locked on his and once again his whirling colors pulled at her, coaxing her to dive in.

"You can't be real. You can't be the person, the being I talked to all those years ago. They were dreams. My imagination. A silly child wanting a play companion." She whispered the words, but they were all too easy to hear in the calm air.

The huge creature, and he was huge even in this modified form, lowered himself to sit in front of her. His legs crossed as wings moved slowly up and down.

His version of a cat's tail. Should've seen that before.

"Yes, no, real and enhanced." His voice reminded her of a purr. McKenna had mentioned how it made her want to run. Toni just wanted to feel it rumble around her.

"Which means what? And I swear to god if you tell me you're my fated mate, I'll cut off your wings."

His eyes widened and then a barking roar emerged while his wings shook up and down. Toni crossed her arms and stared at him. Waiting.

When his laughter faded and his wings stilled, he looked at her. "No. Though there are a few species with pheromone-driven mating needs that stay together for life. Drakyn are not one of them. We have no mates, at least not in the way you mean. It is always a choice, two that wish to be as one for a time."

"Then why have you been in my dreams all my life? And always like this," she waved a hand at him, taking in his entire form, "an adult and in this form?"

"This is the form I tend to be in most of the time. And I've been an adult longer than you have been alive."

That creeped her out a little bit, but if Kaylid didn't age, the odds were Drakyn didn't either. It would be another thing she would need to get over. "That explains the age, not why you've been in my dreams. Hell, you took me flying. Why?"

Rarz looked at her, but even with the swirl of colors she could tell he wasn't seeing her. Her temper had just about frayed when he responded.

"It would be easier to talk to you in person, mind to mind, not via representation of our subconscious. But call it a family gift. Be it through quantum string pulling or something else, your parents had enough Drakyn in their genetic makeup that when they had you, the amount of Drakyn genes enabled you to tap into our quantum space. At least while you slept. I found you there. It interested me. You fascinated me. I learned much about this world, your world, through our talks and interaction. It is one of the reasons I was chosen for this mission."

That surprised her, but also made her feel better. Declaring undying love might have resulted in death for at least one of them.

"So why was I pulled here? What do you want?"

Rarz tilted his head, wings pulled tight against his back. "I think you are overestimating what this is. Or at least what it means. This is a place most of our nestlings are drawn to. It lets them play with the other forms in their minds, learn how to function, and get guidance from those of us who are older and wiser. It has been many cycles since a non-Drakyn born has found their way here. I asked to take you under my wing. There isn't a great plan or even anything devious. It is a place to play and play with others."

Toni blinked taken aback.

It's a playground? A virtual game. That's it. I have to stop reading all those paranormal romances. I'm not thinking straight.

"So this was, is all in my mind?"

Rarz tilted his head. "More like you joined a shared mind reality. Here. Most people avoided you, mostly because I think they were a bit scared of you. But look." He pointed towards the far trees.

Scared of me? He could kill me by whipping his tail around. Why would they be scared of me?

She let her gaze follow to where he pointed. There in the trees she caught hints of movement. Narrowing her eyes, she almost let out a squeak of shock as it felt like she had zoomed in. What had only been vague shifts in shadow or light, now she could see small dragons running around everywhere. Toni was glad she was still sitting on her ass, as she might have fallen over from the sudden disorientation.

"What? Wait, how can I see them? I'm so far away." She couldn't take her eyes off the dragons. So many colors, hues, some that she didn't have words for other than boring green or yellow. They all had four legs but a few, mostly larger ones, had wings. All tinted into shades from the lavender light that she craved to put names to, to find ways to carry those colors back with her.

"This is a reality of the mind. You wanted to see it, so you did. This was never meant to scare you, only show you that you were part of a larger whole."

That did manage to get her attention and she looked back at him. "Why didn't you explain all of this to me when I originally came here?" She had started to say dreamed, but this wasn't a dream. Was it? Even now she couldn't say for sure.

"Would your younger self have understood or cared? As I remember it, you wanted to fly and run and look at the moons. This was a place for you to be that your everyday life of school and chores did not allow for."

Toni looked back at the dragons, not arguing his point. For all the world it looked like they were playing something similar to soccer. As she looked closer, she became aware of some presences above and in the trees. Huge and subtle, like they were there but not there, watching and hovering but not actually interacting with the children.

"Are those parents?" She asked the question, waving at the trees above the playing young dragons.

Nestlings is a good name for them. I get the feeling they are young, younger than my two.

"Parents, relatives, elders. Rarely do adults interfere in their explorations here, though occasionally they may create something to challenge or distract them. Mostly they are here to prevent anything from causing real damage."

She glanced at him; eyes narrowed. "You can get hurt here?"

"If you damage a wing, the physical damage will not carry over. But young ones have powerful fears sometimes, and some of ours have been through the slaughter of their families. Those images can become real here and do damage. The adults watch and step in. Then there are ones like you. The nestlings would not know how to interact with you, much less communicate, so the young adults like me are asked to come in." He waved at her. "After all, being able to study your form enabled me to help your world now."

That comment snapped her attention away from the children and firmly back on him.

That means something like Nightmare on Elm street is possible here, but the adults make sure it doesn't happen. And he was chosen or chose to come to interact with their token human.

"Did you know we would be changed? That they were going to change some of our people into Kaylid?"

Rarz took in a deep breath, his wings tight against his back. "They set off that wave towards your planet about fifty years ago. At any point they have about twenty waves going out, set to hit different worlds every four to seven *reyan*. So yes, we knew it was headed your direction, and our mathists, what you would call scientists, calculated the wave would impact Earth."

Rage coursed through her, a hot living thing, and she clenched her hands tight into fists to stop from attacking him. "Then why didn't you stop it? Why didn't you stop them?"

"How?" He didn't get mad or defensive, he just looked at her, his eyes now a muted pastel of colors.

That threw her off her rampage and she frowned, looking at him. "What do you mean how? Stop it, make us immune, something?"

"It was a cloud of nanobots over twenty of your miles wide and almost thirty deep and over five thousand miles long. It rode the cosmic winds, using micro-jumps to soar through space at rates greater than the speed of light. Every one of them was smaller than a grain of sand. We have no ships, we can't move planets, and even if we had created portals to grab them, we would never have grabbed even one percent of them. So instead we tried to contact your people. But you weren't ready for an alien to walk out of a portal, and again how could I help? We still don't know how to stop them. We have no ships. No allies that are willing or able to help." A note of pain entered his voice. "We have no way to stop them from killing our people other than fleeing. War is not our skill set." He took a ragged breath. "And even worse?"

She looked at him, sensing what was coming.

"We needed the wave to hit Earth for you to even have a chance at believing us." Grief laced his tone, and Toni closed her eyes.

He's right. Humans would have never believed or taken him seriously. Even if he had changed, we would never believe people all over the world would change.

Rarz stood and looked off in the distance, taking his attention from her for the first time. "Working with Ash made it so we could at least find people that might have a chance of talking to us. Your world is so huge and fragmented, we couldn't figure out how to communicate. We've tried with other worlds. The results have rarely been pretty. They never believe and then when it happens, we are to blame. They fall fast to the Elentrin and all we can do is grieve." His worlds struck like blows and she couldn't take it anymore, it hurt too much.

Toni turned her attention to the innocent nestlings romping so far yet so near to her. "Will my children find their way here?" This was a safe topic.

"Maybe. Jamie for certain. He has a mind to play the math game. There are several that have felt him brushing the edges of understanding that the quantum repository of knowledge exists. But his joining with the others may or may not change that. He has a brilliant mind for math."

She watched them play, saying nothing, but visions of the storming of Normandy beach, the jungles of Vietnam, the slaughter of indigenous people, danced through her mind. Oh, she hadn't been there for any of them. But news footage and all too accurate movies and television shows gave her visual images of the wars humans had been fighting since they learned how to wield fire as a weapon.

"Then maybe you found the right group. But I warn you. Having humans as your allies means you may pay a price you never anticipated."

"Will my people survive paying that price?" His question was serious, and she turned to look at him.

"Maybe. But the people they become on the other side may not be ones you recognize."

"We will be alive. And in the end that's all that matters."

They both fell silent and watched children play in a make-believe world under two moons and a lavender sky.

Chapter 4 - Waiting Game

Asteroids have slammed into multiple places across the globe: the United States, Brazil, Russia, France. There is no doubt they are another weapon of the Elentrin whose ships still hang like giant pieces of trash in orbit around our planet. The death tolls are still coming in, but the greatest devastation is centered on Australia. In addition to the asteroid that came down outside Sydney, there is also a tidal wave generated by the asteroids that fell into the ocean. That wall of water is headed directly for Australia and looks like it will come on land at the already beleaguered Sydney. Currently authorities are trying to evacuate the city, but that effort is being complicated by the previous strike. That asteroid disrupted power grids for Sydney, making communication difficult. Currently millions are trying to flee the incoming water and deal with the dust and debris from the previous hit. ~ TNN Invasion News

Toni woke from the dream confused, yet a sense of inevitability settled into her. She still had questions, still didn't understand everything about Rarz

FAMILY

being with her, or the pull he had on her. But for now, she would watch and maybe her own emotions would settle into something more recognizable. The rush to get up to the ship drove everything else to the back of Toni's mind, though she always knew where he was. It was like having a blind spot in your vision, you checked it constantly to make sure it was still there.

Though I don't know what I'd do if he disappeared now. I still need to know too much. And talk to Jamie about this math stuff. Why didn't I know?

The action on the ship, fighting through it, killing people, and then facing what the other captains ordered left her sick to her stomach and trying to find her balance. When McKenna sent her back to Earth, while she stayed on the ship, Toni didn't protest as much as she could have. Maybe should have. But the need to see her kids, to see Charley and Nam too, made it hard to throw too much of a fit. If they were all going to die, she'd rather be with her children. The best part was Rarz was staying up on the ship. Which meant she could avoid him. The thought that if he died up there, she'd never have her questions answered she firmly squelched.

The quick message from Kenna wrenched at her, the well of emotions between all of them almost drove her to her knees. It ramped up Toni's need to find her kids, to find Kenna's, to let them all know they'd never be alone.

"Mom!" Jessi and Jamie waved at her from across the tent. Then the two wove through the myriad adults like smart missiles, impacting her faster than she expected. The vise grip of their hugs eased some of the ache in her soul. "Did you hear what we did? We helped people."

Toni returned the hugs as she guided them over to the side of the tent and out of the way of the people streaming in and out. Cass and JD had been pulled to one side by someone who struck her as a staff flunky, but she focused on her children. "I heard. I'm so proud of the two of you." Lifting her head, she looked around the crowded area. "Where are Charley and Nam?"

They both closed their eyes for less than a second before they popped back open. "He's over at the cafeteria tent." Jessi said, her tone giving no room to doubt.

"Nam wanted something to eat. He went to get her a grilled cheese sandwich. They make them for us." Jamie offered just as sure and Toni fought an all too familiar wave of worry.

They are healthy, happy, and probably saner than we are. They will just grow up to be something I could never have imagined. They just need to know I support them.

"They?" She asked instead, focusing on the little things.

"The cooks or, well, the people cooking. I don't know if they are real cooks but the sandwiches are good." Jessi nodded emphatically as she talked.

"Sounds good." She started to ask if they could go get one, but she felt more than saw someone coming up to her. Toni turned and saw Geoff Sextan as he approached. She didn't say anything but the clutching on her kids tightened until they protested in her mind. Toni thought it was telling that they did it only where no one else could hear.

"Ms. Diaz." He nodded his head in a not quite bow, but something like a weird salute.

"Mr. Sextan." At that moment she couldn't remember his rank and really didn't care.

"We wanted to talk to you about what you saw on the ship and maybe ask you some questions. Verify that the other ships are gone."

Toni tilted her head at him. "Why?" She didn't intend for it to come out as aggressive as it did but refused to apologize after the word left her lips.

He blinked, taken aback. His eyes flicked down to Jessi and Jamie then back up to her. "We wanted to discuss what was seen on the ship and verify that the other ships really left."

Bullshit.

"No." This time a flash of anger went past his face and she lifted her hand. "I don't know what you really want, but your military people, Roark and Coran can tell you more than I can on exactly what went down. You have satellites and other equipment to verify there are no ships in orbit. If you want to know if McKenna and the Elentrin we've suborned will manage to land that ship? I have no idea. You can follow it with satellites and computers better than I can." His eyes narrowed as she spoke, and she felt a low growl coming from the kids. "Which means you want something else, and I don't care. I have no idea if McKenna, Perc, or even Rarz, not to mention Ash and Thelia will bring that ship down in one piece, much less walk away alive. I'll spend the time waiting with my kids and hers. Because if they succeed, you'll have a lifetime to dig through that ship and get all your answers. If they fail," she gave him a smile that held no humor, "then it doesn't matter at all, does it?"

Sextan blinked and the anger faded from his face. "I guess I hadn't thought about it that way. You make many good points. I apologize for intruding." He glanced back down at the kids. "I think they have some ice cream in the mess tent. If you get there soon there might be some left." Geoff looked back up at her and nodded again. "Ms. Diaz." With typical military efficiency he turned and walked away.

"Mom?" Toni moved her attention to Jamie, her solemn little boy. He looked up at her with eyes too old to belong to a seven-year-old. "Is Kenna going to die? And the dragon?"

She wanted to lie, to tell him it would all be all right, that in the morning all of this would seem like a bad dream. And that would do nothing except teach him to doubt her words.

"I don't know. I hope not. But they are doing something very dangerous right now trying to save everyone. All we can do is not distract them and keep our fingers crossed that they succeed."

Two sets of green eyes looked up at her, the narrowed brows giving away so much about what they thought. They hadn't learned to keep their faces blank to hide their emotions, yet.

I hope they never do. I hope I can always look at my children and know what they are thinking, feeling.

But that was a false hope and Toni let it fade even as Jamie nodded slowly.

"If the numbers I heard from some of the soldiers are true, they are going too fast. They're going to crash."

Jamie's calm words sent cold dread through her, but she exhaled slowly trying to stay calm.

At some point we need to talk about him and math, but for now I'll let it be.

"Then distracting them by pinging would not be good right now. Why don't we find Charley and Nam and that ice cream? I'm sure McKenna will be fine."

Both children cast her a sideways glance, but they didn't respond, instead they led her to the tent where Nam and Charley sat at a table, each munching on half of a cheese and ham sandwich.

"Toni!" Nam all but chirped at her and Toni sat down next to her, one arm hugging her to her side.

"Hey. I see you got sandwiches."

The little girl nodded but kept eating. A bubbly enthusiasm flowed out of her and Toni enjoyed the mood lift. Yet another thing to talk to Rarz about. McKenna had mentioned Nam's empathy, but no one had time to deal with it then.

"Have you heard from McKenna? I haven't wanted to ping her since she spoke to us in case..." Charley's voice trailed off and Jessi, who had sat next to him, leaned into him.

"No. And I'm not bugging her either. She'll let us know when they're safe. Perc is up there too. She has friends, people to help her. Even Rarz will try to make sure she comes back to us." Toni tried to project calm assurance, but since she had her own doubts it was hard to lie convincingly.

From the looks she received from the kids she could tell they knew she was trying to be positive. Nam smiled up at her. "The dragon is coming back. He needs to show us all the things."

Toni's mouth quirked. "All the things, huh? Well, I don't know about that, but I did hear there was ice cream here. You guys interested?"

Avarice for sweet dairy lit up their faces and Toni treasured the small amount of normalcy.

Children wanting ice cream. Not sure anything else is more normal.

"I'll get it," she offered as she released Nam and pushed herself to her feet. Even her cat liked the ice cream. Exhaustion beat at her, but the only thing that mattered right now were the three lights in her mental dashboard.

"I'll help."

She jerked slightly at the voice form her side and looked down to see her daughter. So tall already. They looked more like they were nine rather than seven, but it was a side effect of shifting and the nanobots trying to adjust to Charley.

She'll look like the pictures of my grandmother when she gets a bit older.

The emerald eyes were a family trait on her father's side. Always passed down no matter the color of the spouse's. They looked at her and brought with them memories from her childhood mixed with the fresh visit to the mindscape land.

Oh, there are so many things left to ask. Please make it back so I, so my kids, can get the answers.

Toni wrapped her arm around Jessi and smiled. "Good. So how much ice cream should we bring back?"

"Hmmm." Jessi titled her head seriously considering the question. "Depends. Are they bars, cones, or bowls?"

"Ooh, good question. I guess we'll have to find out." Toni replied. The ice cream being considered was in bars, so they settled on two each for everyone. Jessi winning over the corporal behind the counter with a smile. There weren't many kids here, so everyone knew these four and their translation duties. The two of them walked back, hands full of ice cream bars in boxes. Reaching the table, they parceled out the chocolate covered delicacies. You never turned down ice cream.

Or if you do, I'm going to be asking what is wrong.

Smiling, Toni sat down the chair, enjoying her own serving of chocolate and dairy delight, when the lights in her mind for Rarz, Perc, and Kenna all went dark.

"Mom," the words burst out of Charley's mouth, the ice cream bar tumbling from his fingers, forgotten as color leached from his face. All the kids went ridged and tears started to leak down Nam's face.

Oh please, by all the gods, please no.

Chapter 5 - Watching the Show

Everyone is watching the skies and the light show that has resulted in so much damage. The fiery impact in New Mexico is dominating everything. Was this done by humans? Aliens? Is it another attack, or it is a signal the war is finally over? And is it another weapon or was it a ship as some have speculated? While most of the world knows the ships that had orbited our planet seem to have moved away, is it a trap or did someone, some miracle save us? All we can do is wait. All air traffic over or near White Sands has been grounded so it may be a few hours until we know anything. ~TNN Invasion News

Toni frantically prodded at the dim lights in her mind, then asked in the mindspace, ~Wefor?~ Nothing but silence met her query. She felt her heart thudding so hard she feared the kids could hear it. Trying to focus, Toni looked at the mind links again. They were dim, not black.

Unconscious, they're unconscious.

The relief made her babble out words. "Unconscious. They aren't dead. Did they crash?" She looked around for anyone she could see, but the milling military personnel blocked her ability to see anyone.

~JD, Cass? Are you with anyone that can answer what happened with the ship?~

Cass's thoughts came bubbling back fast. ~Asking. We felt her go black. She's not dead right?~

~No, not dead. What happened?~

Silence stretched long and tight, ready to snap at any second. All the kids watched her, eyes wide, ice cream melting, forgotten in the fear for their family.

~Confirmed. The ship crashed. It wasn't a controlled landing, but they are telling us the speed was greatly reduced, so they managed to control it somewhat. People are being deployed out there now. We don't know anything else. But it's a big ship and they're saying it seems to be mostly intact from satellite pictures.~ The rumble of JD's tone took away the steel supports that had been holding her upright.

Toni sagged against the table and watched the light with half of her attention. The rest of her mind she brought back to the kids who all looked pale. They had heard JD, so they knew.

"See. They're back. Unconscious but alive. I'm sure they'll wake up soon." Trying to be positive was damn exhausting, especially when half the time she didn't think they believed her.

Charley looked down at his melting ice cream. "I'm not hungry anymore." He stood picking up the empty box and a full box and started walking towards the huge green trash cans, wobbling a bit as he moved.

Before she could get up to go after him, Jessi leapt up and was at his side, her arm wrapped around his waist. Nam had clamped onto her with one arm, so Toni let Charley be and held Nam, while Jamie grabbed her tight from the other side.

"They'll be okay. You have to believe that." Toni whispered it fiercely in her ear. The girl nodded burying her face into Toni's side.

She felt more than heard the words Jamie sent Nam's way, but she didn't force her way into the communication. Breaking their trust like that would be unforgivable. They sat there, alone in the swirling waves of people as they waited.

~Her light is on, their lights are coming on.~ Charley's shout in their mind jerked her attention to the switchboard in her mind.

~Kenna? Perc? Are you guys okay? Guys?~ She could hear everyone clamoring at the same time going crazy as the lights would brighten then fade.

~I'm here. We're both okay. Shush, please.~ McKenna's voice, sore and tired as it was sent a breath of fresh air though her and Nam sagged bonelessly against her. Charley and Jessi had come back to the table at some point and they both looked just as relieved.

~What can we do?~ JD asked but then they all backed off as McKenna focused on what she needed to.

The knowledge that McKenna and Perc were alive let Toni keep it together. They let the communication to her go quiet, figuring she needed to concentrate.

"Come on, kids. We need to get over to JD and Cass." They didn't even argue. Taking a minute to throw their ice cream away, they followed her closely—Nam holding her hand, Charley bringing up the rear. The camp was in chaos, people running around, shouting orders and questions. She thought she saw Burby and Sextan but didn't bother to get their attention.

~McKenna?~ JD said, his voice a low murmur in the mindspace.

~Yeah.~ She seemed distracted and Toni felt her heart clench as more worries sprouted up.

~You should have half the camp headed your way. From what I can see and overhear, help should be there in about five minutes. The tension is riding pretty high.~

~Okay.~ McKenna paused and Toni continued her determined path to the others. ~Ash didn't make it. We need to honor his body.~

All of them stopped as if someone had cut their strings. Even the kids who had never met the being, but she could feel how stricken they were when they realized this was another person who had died.

~How do you want to do it?~ JD asked, his calm assurance a lifeline. But Toni needed to get away from people. She looked. There against the wall was an alcove they could use. Quiet. Maybe no one would look at her and wonder at the tears on her face. She didn't know why she had cried; it was Ash's fault they were in this situation.

And his fault we had a chance to save our world.

~I want to be there, we need to be there.~ Toni blurted it out, but the way the kids crowded her she knew it was the right thing. They all needed to be there to say goodbye to the being that gave everything for their world.~

~Just you guys. We can get the others later, for now, this is our private moment.~ McKenna agreed after what felt like an eternity.

~Give us ten minutes to get everyone gathered.~ While JD spoke, Toni had the kids up and moving to a relatively quiet area of the crazy stadium.

They stood in the small area waiting for JD and Cass. Both in human form, they still moved through the crowd with people creating a way for them. Was it JD's bulk or just the determination in their faces? Either way she felt a bit better with him standing beside them.

"We ready?" she asked, looking at her motley crew. Charley still pale, Jamie and Jessi with their teeth gritted as if withstanding something, and Nam, holding onto her like a lifeline.

~Yes. Rarz, if you could open a portal please?~ JD stepped aside and they stood watching the silver swirl coalesce into something even more wonderful. They were screened from most people just walking by, and given all the drama going on, most people weren't paying attention to anything outside what they needed to do right that moment.

A few minutes and I'll be able to make sure she's really okay.

~Let's go. I want us on the other side before anyone realizes we're leaving.~ His comment prompted her to look around again. Just in case.

"He's right. Step through, kids." Toni kept her voice calm, though she itched to see McKenna, Perc, even Rarz.

"Does it hurt?" Jessi asked, her voice a bit shaky.

Toni looked down at her, confused. Then she realized they hadn't been through a portal. They were driven to the base. The kids had been in the hotel the entire time they were running through all the practice stuff. Then they were moved to the base by car, she assumed. This was probably the first time they'd even seen one.

"No. It doesn't hurt at all. It's kinda neat. Wait until you walk through, then we'll be on the other side of the country. Faster than an airplane." She included all the kids in this comment. Charley looked a bit relieved, but Jamie had that thinking look on his face, while Nam's hand didn't release.

"I just want to see McKenna. Can we go now?" Charley's voice had sharpness and need to it she recognized all too well.

"Yes, go guys. I'll be right behind you." She switched communication methods as she squeezed Nam's hand back. ~Rarz, is there an issue if I carry Nam as I go through?~ In all the practice they'd always gone through solo. Even the wounded.

~No. You are fine if she wishes to be carried.~ His response instant.

"You want me to carry you?" Toni asked Nam. The little girl's head went up and down so fast Toni had to fight back a laugh. She scooped her up and herded her other three charges through the portal.

~I can feel it. I can see how it is created. I wonder if I—~

Toni cut Jamie off. ~Not now. Later when all of this is more stable. For now we need to go say goodbye.~ She set Nam down and the girl sped off with Charley, heading to McKenna like a cat to tuna. She felt the energy from the portal collapse behind her, energy that she longed to play with. McKenna mentioned it called to her, for Toni it screamed. All but begging her to play with it. Mold it into new possibilities.

The relief matched the joy washing through the mind space as Charley and Nam impacted with McKenna. She watched long enough to make sure she was really there, but then Toni found her attention pulled to Rarz. He stood near a depression in the sand, the body of Ash lying in the middle of it, limp and forlorn. It hurt to look at him, a man who had given everything to stop the Elentrin, to die so close to success.

"Kenna, we better do this soon." JD's comment pulled her out of the haze of thoughts, a mixture of sorrow and aching for something she didn't understand. A purpose maybe? Surely, she could be more than just a mom or wife?

"Rarz, if you would do the honors?" McKenna's voice sounded thin, shaky, in the bright desert air.

Jessi and Jamie stood near Toni, though their eyes were also on Rarz as he seemed to straighten a bit and walk to the other side, away from them.

"You will all need to step back." The sound of his voice riveted her attention again, the visit to their virtual world springing back to full intensity.

He sounds different here than there. Why?

The rest of the world seemed to fade away as she felt, smelled, the change. Unable to tear her eyes away as the dragon from the warehouse morphed back into existence. This time, though, she wanted to run and climb on his back and ride him like she had as a child. Here the yellow sun made his scales gleam like spun gold and the red seemed darker and harder, more like armor than anything else.

Jamie's voice, sounding like he'd found a book he'd been looking for, filtered into her transfixed attention. "It's a real dragon, a real live dragon."

As if channeling her dreams, Nam cried out, "I wanna ride!"

Oh, I do too. I want to ride until I think I can touch the twin moons again.

Toni smiled as McKenna caught the little girl, reminding her of why they were there. But even the trips to the planet of lavender sky didn't prepare her for what happened next. With little fanfare, Rarz reared back and through a tiny swirling orb of silver between his huge front claws, breathed fire. Her breath caught in her throat as white and yellow flames exploded into existence, the wash of heat palpable even from fifty feet back where they were.

The summoned flames covered Ash's body like a blanket of light, turning him into ash in seconds, the flames licking at what had fed them for so short an amount of time. Toni watched the black flecks of ash drift up into the clear blue sky.

May he find the reward he earned and see his family again.

She didn't catch who started the song first, it just seemed to be everywhere, filling her, pulling on her emotions, joining her with the others. Knowledge that could only have come from an AI flooded into her mind and she began to sing.

Toni knew she couldn't sing, had never been able to keep much more than "Happy Birthday" on tune and mostly in key. But for this one song, the notes that poured out of her throat and joined with the others were perfect, on key, and melded into a harmony their planet had never heard. She put her heart into it, hoping someday her children would sing this haunting song for her.

Chapter 6 - Project Management

Reports of a large object striking the New Mexico desert have been confirmed. Is this another asteroid? The reports tallying destruction coming in from the US are small compared to other parts of the world. Sydney took a big hit, as did France. It remains to be seen what the death toll is from those. Russia seemed to escape the worst of it as the impact was in a relatively unpopulated area. There is too much smoke and fire to see via the remaining satellites the amount of damage from the other hits. The Earth is bracing for the next volley if indeed this is all a trick by the aliens. ~TNN Invasion News

As the ethereal tune wound down, the shouts of soldiers coming up behind them distracted her. She saw McKenna bent over, talking to Nam. Jessi and Jamie looked up at her longingly.

"Go. See her and I'll deal with this. They'll need my help anyhow." The kids took off, though she didn't know how much was to see McKenna and how much was for a chance to get closer to the dragon.

I can't blame them for either.

She turned and faced the oncoming soldiers, with weapons up and faces that made her want to laugh, she stepped in front of the tide.

"Is there a problem?"

I can take this for now. McKenna was just in a crashed ship. She needs recovery time. Time with her kids. She's done more than enough.

They all but slid to a halt in front of her, faces pale, eyes wide, and locked onto the dragon behind her. She knew he was still in that form; the energies would have changed if he had shifted into something else.

The leader, his hands gripping his rifle so tightly his knuckles were white, glanced at her. His gaze rested there for less than a second before it darted to Rarz then flickered back to her. He licked his lips, swallowed hard, and croaked out a question. "Did that dragon just breathe fire? Is that a dragon there?" His voice cracked on the word "dragon" and Toni fought not to smile.

"Yes, and he was in control of the flames. And yes, that is a dragon, but technically he's a Drakyn. An ally from another planet to help us fight the Elentrin." She paused and looked around. "Speaking of which, there should be one around here. Female with purple hair?"

"Oh, yes ma'am. We're extracting her from the ship now." He waved behind them and Toni caught a glimpse of purple on a stretcher.

"She didn't die?"

"No, though she is badly injured. We were warned to take precautions when dealing with her. Therefore, she is both restrained and we have at least two soldiers with filters near her at all times."

Am I happy or sad she's alive? Does it matter? That is one person who just became firmly someone else's problem.

"Then I would say you are well on the way to getting things taken care of. We'll be back over there in a bit. Perc and I..." she paused to point Perc out, though she narrowed her eyes, realizing he was hurt from the amount of blood coating him. As was McKenna.

Damn dragon distracted me; I should have seen that sooner.

"...are the experts on the systems and the ship. You'll be working with us more than anyone else. Let us finish burying our dead and we'll be over there."

"But they burned the body. There was a dragon?" His voice cracked as he said the word, eyes wide.

"Yes, a dragon. I'd expect more o them depending on how this all works out. Now go. I need to talk to my friends, and then we'll be ready to help you. Do any of you have wipes or something I can clean up blood with?"

The leader, a captain maybe, Toni still didn't have the ranks figured out, and didn't care enough to spend the time to worry about it, snapped out a command. A few seconds later another person ran up, shoving a container of what looked like baby wipes at her.

"Here you go ma'am." The young voice cracked, and Toni cringed, feeling old all of a sudden.

"Thank you. Go on boys, we'll catch up with you."

The captain kept looking back at her and then Rarz, but finally they drifted away. Though she had to smirk at the many looks backwards from everyone. Shaking her head, Toni moved towards Perc and McKenna, determined to assess the damage and clean up what needed cleaning.

"Arm now!" she snapped out the words to Perc who looked at her, eyes widening a bit, but he handed her his arm. While still in warrior form his forearm was bare of fur and still showed a red gash, though mostly closed. Getting a wipe from the container, she started to clean off the blood. "Explain. Why are you covered in blood and why is McKenna protecting her arm so very much?"

McKenna glanced at her arm and sighed. "Broke the arm. Wefor says in another few hours it should be fine as long as I don't stress it." She nodded at Perc. "He can explain the wound and his reasoning. I'm still trying to accept what it means." Nam and Charley were glued to her side, while Jessi and Jamie stared at the dragon, longing in their eyes, but the heat of the pit still too great to approach.

Toni glanced at Perc, but the muzzled face and whiskers didn't tell her anything. She cleaned up the blood, giving him time.

"Ash was dying and asked us to save Elao. So I did."

Her hands froze, and she glanced up at him. "You have an AI in your head now too?"

"Yep. She's quiet right now, trying to restructure, but we think we got enough of her components to enable survival." His voice flat, and he kept looking between Ash's remains and McKenna.

"Ah." Toni stuffed the used wipe in a pocket and pulled out another one and set to work on McKenna's face. "You have smoke and blood all over you."

I don't know if I could have done that. Much less the way he did. Is this a good or bad thing?

"Yeah. Got a little crazy there for a bit." McKenna turned her head, ignoring Toni wiping her face. "How many do you think survived?"

"More than would have if you hadn't brought the ship down." Toni put away the wipe and looked at her two friends. "You did good. I'm going to ask Rarz to take you and Perc back. He'll need food. I'll deal with the people here if you deal with the kids?"

McKenna's mouth curved in a tired grin. "Why do I think you might be getting the better part of that deal?"

"Because you have active braincells?" She shooed them towards the ship and people. "Give me a minute and I'll round up the kids and send them to you. Make sure you get that braced. Just because it'll heal doesn't mean you need to chance banging it around."

"Yes, mother." McKenna voice held love and affection. She and Perc moved slowly towards the milling people. "You four, too." Toni addressed the kids still lingering, staring at the dragon. She forestalled their complaints. "When this is all over, I'll see if you can ride the dragon." Two sets of green eyes started at her, intent. "Yes, I promise. Now go with McKenna and Perc. They're going to stay with you until I get back."

They spent another few seconds looking longingly at the dragon then spun and tore off across the sand to catch up with the others.

Toni glanced at the depression, still so hot it felt uncomfortable, and wished she knew what else to say. How to honor that man. But there was still so much to do, they didn't have time to explore what his loss would mean.

~Rarz? We need to talk and the others really need to go back to the base.~

The red head lifted and looked at her, then at the depression radiating an intense heat. He reared back on his hind legs again, and once more a tiny portal appeared, and he seemed to roar. Or breathe? Or something like that.

Toni flinched back instinctively, unable to avoid it. That first wave of heat had been insane and from the ashes left of his body it would incinerate her. But instead of heat, a wave of cold hit her. The cold so intense she stepped back, her body shivering. Then it faded.

~That should help.~ His comment barely registered as she moved forward slowly. Where seconds before the inferno of heat had existed, now almost icy cold existed. Surprised, she moved over to the depression and looked down into it. Where the depression of white sand, made of gypsum and calcium sulfate instead of quartz had been, soft giving, it had changed drastically. Now there was a fine powder of white in the area, reminding her of dry wall substance.

Odd, I would have thought glass or something. Shows you what I know.

Shaking her head, she looked up and focused on Rarz, who looked back at her with the same intensity.

~I still have many questions to ask. I need to know what you meant about Jamie and the math game. I need to understand why I ended up in that land. What did you mean about my family traits?~

~All Kaylid are descended from my people. You and your children are purer, meaning you have more of the Drakyn DNA woven through your cells than any Kaylid I have seen on this planet so far. I would suspect your green eyes are an aspect of this.~

That flashed her back to old stories, ones her dad would tell as Mom teased him about marrying a demigod. The laughter and joy in those memories had sustained her after their deaths in the first year of her marriage to Jeff.

~I see. Okay no, I don't. But there is much going on here. You mentioned Kenna and I could learn to control portals.~

~It is in your skill set. Already they call to you. Do you have issues remembering complicated sets of instructions or long lists of values?~

The odd question made her shrug and she looked back towards where McKenna and everyone else had headed. They were walking slowly towards the ship, the soldiers milling around. In the distance she could see more dust trails rising. Others would be here soon.

~No. I've always been able to. Not photographic memory but I could store it easily. I memorized the response book for the 911 operators in the first week.~

~You have number operators?~

Toni choked out a laugh glancing back at him. ~People who give advice in emergency situations. But the answer is no, I have no issues remembering things like that. Never have. Dad was super smart too, doing math and stuff in his head.~

Rarz ducked his head in an odd bob that she took to mean 'Well, there you have it.'

He didn't say anything else and she sighed. ~Can you give everyone a portal back to the staging area and then shift to human and help me deal with the rest of these people? McKenna needs a break. And I think Perc needs some time to adjust to Elao.~

~I would be honored.~

That struck her almost as a tease, but the dragon face was unreadable. With another shake of her head she turned and started towards the spaceship and stumbled to a halt. For the first time the size of the ship registered, and she sucked in a sharp breath. It had to be bigger than most aircraft carriers. They had talked about it on the ship, Wefor giving them the specifics, but from the inside it didn't mean much except as an abstract number. Now looking at it, the end of the ship so far away that it seemed like miles.

And they landed that?

The trail of destruction behind them did go on for miles, but they must have bled off enough speed, because while the ship was warm, if not hot in the desert sun, there wasn't an impact crater.

~Wefor?~

It took a moment, but the AI responded, softer and quieter than normal.

[Yes, Toni?]

~How fast were they going when they hit?~

[Exact numbers are not available, but Thelia managed to slow it greatly. Top estimate would be about 500 miles an hour. Due to the angle, she managed to let the earth help bleed off the excess speed.]

~Damn. Good thing then?~ She didn't know why it came out as a question.

[Yes. Without her assistance with the computers, it is likely the impact would have been much more direct, and most would have died.]

~Huh. Good to know. How' McKenna and Perc?~ She didn't bother to hide her worry nor care if any of the others overheard her.

[They are tired but will be whole soon. They need calories and rest more than anything else at this time. Elao is trying to make the merger easy but it is taking some effort.]

~Thanks.~ Toni sensed others listening to the question. An odd sense of relief flashed through the mindspace.

~Where would you like the portal to place you?~ Rarz's question threw her until she realized he had asked in general, not her specifically.

~Here please.~ JD spoke, and he must have managed to transmit an image to Rarz because a few moments later Rarz spoke in their minds. ~Thanks. You sure about staying and dealing with this, Toni?~

~Yep. You guys deal with the people back there and I'll deal with them here. Though I expect people are going to want to come out here also.~

~Probably. In fact, I can guarantee it. I already see people, multiple people making a beeline for us. I'll ping you when we have something concrete,~ JD offered, and she felt him disengage from the mindspace.

"You ready to go deal with panicked people who aren't going to be happy that half their prisoners just disappeared?"

Rarz tilted his huge head so one eye looked at her, an eye that she had to fight not to get lost in. The swirling colors were so hypnotic it was hard. ~Is that what we are? Prisoners?~

Toni shrugged, looking over at the soldiers who did look like they were having a full-out panic attack.

"Maybe. More likely guests that they don't trust and don't understand. You more than most."

~Ah. Your species prejudices. We have found them to be consistent through many sentient species, though we don't really understand them.~

"You think that might be because you can take any shape? If shape is like clothing to you, then no shape would ever seem any less valid than any other shape."

He stood there frozen, head pointed at the people in the near distance, though she doubted he actually saw them.

~That is an interesting observation.~

~Well speaking of shapes. Want to shift to something less intimidating?~

He turned to look at her again, and she couldn't help but notice teeth twice the length of her fingers. A cold sweat broke out on her body no matter how much she reminded herself he wouldn't hurt her. Probably.

~You find me intimidating?~

Toni's mouth dropped open. She closed it with a snap and forced herself to reply calmly. "I think you're a teddy bear. All the people over there with weapons probably won't take my word on that."

A snicker of laughter, Cass she recognized, caused her to snap the usually open link shut.

I don't need a peanut gallery right now. Though I now have more sympathy for McKenna.

Rarz didn't respond, but she felt the swirl of energy around him. Glancing back, she could see his form warping, and a minute later a man stood there dressed in the same kilt and tank as everyone else, when they had gone up on the ship.

"Where do your clothes go when you change forms?" The question slipped out before she could stop it. But dang it, it had been driving her crazy. "And why didn't you shift it over when you did the warehouse demo?"

"It stays in quantum storage until I need it. It did not occur to me that night. All those beings watching me made me more nervous than I had expected." He shook his shoulders a bit, an odd look on his face. " I do miss the wings in this form. I always feel off-balance."

Rarz brushed his hair back and looked at her, the swirl of his eyes more subtle with the shadowing of his brow. "I am ready to escort you back."

"Escort? Wow, make me feel fancy or something," Toni said as they headed back, but the frown on his face told her the joke had slipped by him. "Never mind. Yes, let's go deal."

With that they walked back into the panicked confusion of three groups of military personnel, all of them looking for the person in charge.

Which at the moment is me. Joy.

Chapter 7 - Restrictions

It has been two days since the ships circling Earth vanished. The US government has issued a statement that the aliens have fled, but they do have some under custody. Further information will be provided when it is obtained. While the sight of empty skies is a boon to most, many questions are being asked now that the immediate danger has passed. How could this have been prevented? Did people know ahead of time? Why weren't we more prepared? Who is to blame? The world is demanding answers as loved ones are buried and people start to deal with the aftermath, always with a wary eye on the skies. TNN Invasion News

Exhausted, all of them fell into bed at the end of each day. Toni spent all her time accessing computers and helping transition the information on them into media that others in both government and private research could access. Even Elao couldn't figure out why Toni couldn't get the computers to recognize other people, which meant everything fell on her. Occasionally she thought about Thelia and asking if she could come help, but that topic seemed to be surrounded in don't ask, don't tell vibes, so no one mentioned the woman.

The kids still worked via phones even though they were slowly getting more translators in and they still regarded it as a game, so she let them enjoy it, keeping tabs on them mentally while she worked. The next surprise came when she showed up at the ship one day and Burby and Rarz were waiting for her. Rarz didn't surprise her. He needed to be at one end of the portal, and he hadn't been at the house, but Burby did. He looked exhausted and older.

"Toni."

She nodded at him as she walked over. "Doug. What's up?"

He glanced at Rarz, who in his human form looked grave, a common expression lately. With a shake of his head Doug looked back at her. "I take it McKenna is elsewhere today?"

Alarms went off in her mind and Toni felt her worry spike. "Yes. Working with refugees and helping smooth out some issues with the non-human Kaylid. She can talk to them and Perc is helping, he's almost fluent. But for the most part, more and more stuff is getting done without us. Why?" They had been slowly being cut out of the inner loop, something that annoyed McKenna much more than Toni. Toni didn't care, she just wished she could get rid of more responsibility, but constraints weren't anything she could change.

Burby pulled out his phone, frowned then shook his head. "I knew that." He rubbed his temple and then looked at her. "So what can we do to lower the uproar going off like crazy?"

Toni blinked at him, completely lost. "Um? Out roar?"

"You haven't heard?" He looked at her, obviously surprised.

"Doug, I come here, I work. I go home, play with the kids and pass out. All my friends are in the house with me, and while I'm here it's all work-related. What am I supposed to be paying attention to?" Her patience frayed, and she fought to not let it leak out. Having four very bright energetic kids helped with that. Thank the stars for Carina. She quirked a smile full of wry humor at herself at the phrase that had slipped into their vocabulary. She blamed Elao, though maybe Ash affected them more than they had thought.

"True, I didn't know how much you paid attention to social media lately."

"Very little. After watching the meltdown with McKenna going live, we kinda all quit. Our families know how to get a hold of us, the rest of the world we don't care about." She looked at both of them and folded her arms across her chest. "Spill. What's going on?"

Doug groaned, rubbing his bare skull. "I figured you'd be asking for explanations, not me having to give the back story. So here it is." He cleared his throat and met her eyes. "Someone asked Rarz a question in the presence of reporters and he answered, not understanding the significance. Per him, as his people don't age the way we think of aging, it didn't occur to him Earthlings might be all excited about it. He pointed out that Kaylid will never age as their cells have perfect regeneration due to the bots' interference, or assistance, depending on how you look at it." Another glance at his phone. "So people and the media now know that all Shifters are immortal."

Only years of experience of never letting children see how their actions affected her let her keep her face blank. In all reality she wanted to groan. "We are not immortal per se. Most people know that, given the number of Shifters that were killed during the invasion. We just apparently don't age once we hit a suitable level." She looked at them and then shot a tight mental note to Rarz. ~Under no circumstances ever, do you mention McKenna has the ability to change people. That can never get out. We would be hunted if that happened.~

Rarz paled, his gold skin acquired a sickly yellow color. He nodded at her, that much of human interaction he had figured out. ~Understood. That will never be spoken of aloud.~

With that, Toni redirected her attention to Burby. "Okay, so it's out. There isn't anything we can do about it. What do you want?" Her exhaustion level meant her patience with most government bullshit had reached her limits.

"I really had hoped you would say it wasn't true. Nothing, I guess. Any other gotchas we should know about?"

Toni threw her hands in the air, glaring at him. "How in the hell should I know? I've been a Shifter for what, three-four months? Every time I turn around, I learn something new. Why aren't you interrogating the captured Elentrin? Thelia alone should be a gold mine of information."

Doug didn't respond to that, just suddenly looked uncomfortable. "Okay. Thanks. This should be the last week of what we need from here, so maybe your lives can get back to normal. I need to meet with all of you tomorrow. I'll set up a meeting time and place." With that he turned and trudged away, looking like the weight of the world lay on his shoulders. For a moment Toni almost called him back but pushed the urge away.

I'm not responsible for any of this. None of us are and we're all doing our best to make sure we help all we can.

She turned to look at Rarz who had hung back. Rather than talking to him, she opened the mindspace and spoke to everyone. ~The ball has dropped, and it got out that we don't age. Expect fallout. Apparently, the social media has already grabbed and run with it. So be aware. For the love of god no one mention the ability for us to change people. That's the last thing we need.~ A collective groan came from all the minds and she knew the kids were listening too. ~And the SecDef wants to meet with us tomorrow.~ She looked at Rarz as she kept speaking. ~I think we should drive in. Might be easier and make it look more normal. We know the portals are out too, but I don't think anyone has leaked how they are being produced. Or has anyone heard that?~

~Not yet, but then I haven't been paying attention to much of anything. Been too busy,~ McKenna replied, and the others agreed.

~I'll pay more attention. They've copied just about everything and have some other data source that I didn't provide. But yeah, I think I'm about done here.~ Cass said slowly. ~Though that might explain why I've had three people ask me how old I am. I didn't think anything of it at the time.~ There was the impression of a sigh and the shake of her head.

Neither Perc nor JD commented on that, but Toni figured men didn't get asked their age all that often.

Rarz lingered near her but she just shrugged and went into the ship. People were waiting for her and she got swallowed up by the technical needs of people wanting information and forgot most of the conversation until Rarz appeared to usher her home.

She didn't know when that had become habit, but his appearance signaled it was time to go and magically people found other places to be.

"Home, Jeeves?"

Rarz, he'd been mostly in human form the last few weeks, arched both eyebrows at her. He looked a bit funny with both dark brows high on his forehead.

"It's a joke. Don't worry about it."

"Your culture has many turns of phrase that do not make logical sense and as I understand humor, they also are not humorous."

Toni shrugged as she walked out with him. "I'll be the first to admit humans are weird. But we play on culture as jokes. Hard to explain."

He didn't respond as he created a portal and they stepped through into the back yard. They tried to keep it to a corner of the yard where it wasn't likely anyone would be. She knew he would have ferried the others back, but her days seemed to be longer since she was working on the west coast while the rest of them had mostly been moved to the East Coast.

Cass and JD had already started dinner by the time she walked in, but the mood was glum.

"Do I even want to know?"

"Reporters," McKenna all but spat the word. "Everywhere I turn. Glad you guys don't need my phone to contact me, because I gave in and shut it off."

Cass sighed. "I've have mine refusing all calls not from Helena." Cass talked to her sister at least every other day, so that made perfect sense.

Perc, who came in from setting the table, hip-bumped McKenna a little with a smile. "I gave up and forwarded everything to my lawyer friend, Laura Granger. Got a second phone and gave her and my parents the number. It was easier."

Toni blinked. She couldn't remember where her phone was. She looked at Carina who was in the living room playing on hers. "Are you getting bugged at all?"

"Nah. They don't know I'm part of this motley crew yet." She flashed McKenna a smile. "And I'm ignoring anything on social media. Too negative lately. Mostly playing games with my friends. We were talking about when school would start back up. I'm ready to graduate." A frown crossed her face. "Though I don't know that I'm ready to leave you. And I'm still serious about wanting to change."

McKenna went to bite her lip, then stopped. Toni snickered; it was a bad habit to have when in warrior form. "Let's wait a bit. I don't want you to regret it. And we have time. I'd rather see how all this social stuff shakes out first before we do anything irrevocable."

"What? Be responsible and think things through?" Carina laughed, her amusement bright and contagious. "That's fine. I have all the time in the world. After all, you already prevented the end of the world, right?"

Her upbeat mood helped get them to dinner in a slightly less dour atmosphere though it sank a bit when McKenna spoke. "I don't know for sure what

Burby wants to talk about, but I'm just going to avoid the immortality and please, no one mention even causally me being able to change someone." She cast a look at the kids and Carina. "And that goes for you guys too."

Jessi rolled her eyes, prompting Toni to glare at her until she ducked her head.

That child of mine. My mother must be rolling in laughter right now.

Charley looked at McKenna, his voice very serious. "We wouldn't talk to anyone. Besides, why would I want to talk to anyone outside the people here? I mean the translating is kinda fun and we're getting really good at it, but I'm not talking about anything important with them."

The adults collectively fought back grins and laughs as Charley categorized the work they were doing, soothing scared humans in their own language, that everything was going to be okay, as not important.

Ah for the worldview of children.

McKenna cleared her throat, the corners of her mouth still twitching. "Be that as it may, let's be careful? We can't do anything about the information that has gotten out, but we can prevent new stuff. Rarz, I don't think your appearance has been noticed yet, at least not by the media. It might be wise to keep it that way."

He nodded but didn't say anything, once more with that odd look on his face. Before Toni could ask what he was thinking, Perc's phone rang. Given what they were just talking about, everyone fell quiet.

"Hey, mom, everything okay?" There was silence on his side and Toni at least didn't try to overhear.

They'd all learned to try and provide as much privacy as possible to each other.

"Okay. Thanks for letting me know. I'll get someone out there to take care of it. You guys be careful, okay?" Another minute of silence. "Love you too. Bye." Perc set down the phone and signed. "Someone defaced my house. Apparently, some graffiti and broken windows. When the security company couldn't get a hold of me, they contacted my parents." He shrugged. "I'll deal with it. In the bigger scheme of things, not a big issue."

"What is it with us and our houses?" JD asked, mostly rhetorically.

"Hey, we didn't have anything to do with that. I swear." Charley blurted and Jessi and Jamie both looked a bit pale nodding their heads frantically.

McKenna and JD started snickering. "We know. Just people being silly because we can shift. But that does mean no more shifting in public for you guys, okay?"

Nam looked a bit confused while Jessi and Jamie had matching stubborn expressions; Charley, however, looked thoughtful.

"People don't like us 'cause we can change?"

Toni nodded. "That's part of it. And we're worried they might hurt you, just for that alone. So no giving anyone a reason to look at you and be angry."

Jessi and Jamie had hard-core pouts going on, and Toni tried to think about how to explain to them so they wouldn't shift outside just because the adults said not to.

"It's like being a foster kid. If I tell them I'm your foster son, I'm not as good as if I was yours. People think things and act different. Just like when they saw my mother, all beaten up and on drugs, they would think I was like that, too." He looked at the twins, a frown on his pale face. "We can't shift 'cause that will give people reasons to hate us. And we don't want that." Charley said this all, not looking at anyone, but Toni could feel him bright and powerful in her mind.

"I don't care if they hate me. They don't mean anything to me." Jessi's eyes were narrowed as she stared at Charley.

"And if they hurt McKenna because of us? Just like when they punished her for Jalmer being stubborn?" Jamie's voice was quiet but the other three all paled.

"Oh." Jessi swallowed hard. "No, I don't want that. I won't change. At home only."

Toni blinked and looked up to see pain on McKenna's face. The dinner fell silent after that and then everyone went their own way. The kids to bed, or more to play and talk in their shared room, and the adults to deal with their own issues. When McKenna and Perc when out to the back deck, Toni gave them space and spent the evening reading and trying not to think about tomorrow.

Chapter 8 - Money Buys Nothing

Now that everything has calmed down, and people are starting to believe the aliens are gone, the crash in the desert is rippling around the world. An alien craft here on Earth? It is the dream of all the UFO fanatics worldwide, but at what cost. No one denies we may learn much from this crash, but would it be worth the thousands dead, and the tens of thousands that were taken from their families? A growing opinion is we should refuse to learn from it, but others point out they may be back, and no one is willing to be at the mercy of any alien ever again. ~TNN Aftermath

The next day they opted to drive themselves to their meeting, though it did take two cars to fit everyone. Rarz rode with McKenna and Perc, while Cass and JD rode with Toni. Though they kept all the conversations light, most of them were stressed. JD had a message from Anne Holich to call her this evening on her private number and that had ramped the tension up even more. Toni was oddly glad Carina was the closest thing to family she still had beside a few distant cousins. Carina stayed close with her family but living in California and going to school while the rest lived in Texas meant lots of emails and created and emotional distance. She could understand why Carina wanted to be part of this group. Right now, she didn't know how she could live without them.

"So how is it going on your end? I finally have all the techs trained and they're leaving tomorrow to start getting the people in the ship undone. I heard they were coordinating with the Red Cross to ferry them back to China. No one seems to know who is in charge in China anymore," Cass commented.

Toni glanced up into the rear-view mirror and saw Cass leaning her head against JD's shoulder. She smiled at the image.

They're adorable. I'm glad they found each other. JD's a great guy.

She pushed any other thoughts and relationships and anything like that to the side. Thinking about relationships always ended badly for her. Driving what had become an all-too-familiar route, they didn't chat much, mostly commenting on how life seemed to be coming back to normal. Going through security seemed normal, no harder or gentler than usual, so she didn't think about the vague odd questions from yesterday.

They walked into the conference room and she stared at the people in it, then shook her head and headed to coffee station. With relief Toni made a cup of green tea. She'd already had her caffeine fill today and she wanted something in her hands. It made her feel less awkward.

~Mom?~ Jamie asked in her mind.

~Yes?~

~Can we go do something tomorrow? We're getting tired of the house.~ He didn't whine, they all seemed too old for that.

~Carina has fun stuff planned for you today. But I'll see what I can do. Either tomorrow or the day after?~

~Fun stuff? Like?~ Jessi chimed in, sounding a bit more awake.

~Like, you'll have to ask her and wait until she's ready.~

~We need to change her. Having to go find her to talk to her is too much.~ Jessi whined, and Toni fought back a laugh, her mind bringing the image of her lying in the blanket nest with her arm thrown over her face. A true drama queen.

~Imagine having to call people on phones to talk to them? Or horrors, go find them in person?~ Her voice dripped sarcasm and she heard the kids groan in unison at how lame adults where. ~I know, I'm so old. Okay, we're starting our meeting. I'll talk to you later.~

~Bye mom, bye Toni~ filled her mind as she turned to watch the Secretary of Defense.

Doug finished making his coffee and then sank into the chair at one end of the table. Christopher stood against the wall behind him. With a grunt of effort Burby set his briefcase on the table, and took a long sip of coffee, not looking at any of them. She really wanted to hug the man whenever she didn't want to strangle him because of his job. He just looked beyond exhausted but his avoidance told her they wouldn't like this conversation.

~So be it. I'm ready to be a nobody again.~

Glancing around the room, she realized they had all paired off. Cass next to JD, McKenna and Perc holding hands, then her. With Rarz sitting there, both awkward and relaxed at the same time. The social dynamics of this might drive her crazy. Doug cleared his throat pulling her attention back to him.

"The headaches you have all given me are insane. I'm still not sure if I should thank you or sentence you all to prison. Even the president doesn't know what to do with you and your spectacular return to Earth. You brought back people but even more problems. One of them too damn pretty for her own good."

Ah. Thelia is with them. Is it sad I don't know who to root for in that battle of egos? I can't say I like her, but it would be nice to see the government find someone they can't control.

Toni tuned back into the conversation, they were discussing social media and the direction public opinion was swinging. None of it stuff she could argue with, the little time she had spent on social media that morning made her very glad none of the kids had cell phones or tablets.

"I know," McKenna was saying. "But I'm not sure what to do about it. We're the most well-recognized, and going back to work right now with this backlash isn't wise. Perc had his house vandalized and our sergeant asked JD to call her tonight. Which means we might not even have jobs to go back to. Living might be a bit tight for a while."

Toni flinched at that, another reality she'd been avoiding. It would all depend on how many people knew Tonan Diaz was a Shifter. Much less a Shifter involved in all of this.

"Well, that at least I can help with." Toni jerked her head up and looked at Doug. "While the government recognizes that they will need to work on making sure the law of equal rights is upheld, it doesn't change how people react. We can't help all

FAMILY

Shifters or Kaylid, but you few we can help." From out of the folder he pulled out checks and handed them around the table, skipping only Rarz. "In recognition of your service to your country and the world. We were trying to get you the Medal of Freedom, but the tide of public opinion put a damper on that."

Toni looked at her check, then read it again. McKenna's choked voice broke the odd tension. "Two million?"

"Considering what continuing to fight this war would have cost us? Not to mention the information on the ship you brought to us. Personally, I think it should have been in the tens of millions, but—" Burby sighed and once again Toni had to repress the urge to tell him it would all be okay. "Congress has just as many idiots who follow social media as does the public. It isn't much, but there are also checks here for the kids for their translation work for five hundred thousand." He slid one to McKenna and two to Toni. "I wish I could do more for you. But I've already turned in my resignation. The end of next month is my last day on the job and I can't say I've ever been happier to quit something."

Toni looked at the money, more money that she had ever seen. ~All of us got two million? And the kids got five hundred k?~ Her thought barely above a whisper.

~Yea.~ All of them seem awed by the money except Perc. He glanced at it and shrugged.

Oh yeah. That was probably his sign-on bonus. Good for him, but for the rest of us? This might be the only way we make it.

"I had not known how to broach this idea, but perhaps this is as good a time as any." Rarz's words pulled her out of her thoughts, and she looked up to see everyone looking at him. Probably with the same emotions she had. Confusion and curiosity.

~Did any of you know about this?~ She asked, but there was a resounding no from everyone, so Toni stayed silent as McKenna prompted him for more information.

"The Elentrin are still out there attacking my people and we are a species that breeds very slowly. Many of the worlds they tried to take from us but failed have housing and land. These planets would support human life, being very similar to Earth in most ways. We need people who can fight, innovate, teach, people who will help us learn how to face the Elentrin and I fear some of the other species out there in the vastness of this universe. We have only explored this galaxy, there are untold more out there."

Toni reeled back, fear and rage driving words out of her mouth before she could think. "You want us to come with you and be your cannon fodder instead? Let my children die to fight your war?"

The look he gave her caught her, and she found her anger frozen. "No. I'm offering to provide homes for all Kaylid. I'm asking if some of them would be willing teach us and maybe fight with us. I'm offering passage to planets with empty homes that need life brought back to them. I'm offering you a chance to come to my worlds. I'm offering hope, for all those who aren't welcome here."

Toni zoned out at the discussion. Her mind locked on old memories she'd almost refused to believe anymore.

Is it possible? Is what he is offering what haunts me in my dreams?

Toni didn't say anything for the rest of the meeting. They headed back to the house after making a stop at the bank first. She didn't know about the others, but that level of money made her nervous. She'd figure out what to do with it in a few days, but for right now she didn't want it in her hands. She'd lose the blasted piece of paper.

They got back to the house and as one, everyone turned to look at Rarz. But before anyone could start asking all the questions that bubbled in them, JD raised his hand. "I think I need to call Anne and see what she has to say before we do anything. All of this is coming as a shock and I think we need more information before we can even ask intelligent questions." A half-sigh, half-nod from most people. "Rarz, think about what you need to tell us. Because you aren't just talking about us, right?"

"No, it would be hopefully millions of your Shifters." His calm logic rubbed Toni the wrong way. She wanted him mad or defensive or apologetic. The logic and calmness made her feel guilty. Besides, the logistics involved with getting millions of people off a planet made the struggles with people in the ships seem simple.

"I'm going to go talk to my kids. They earned the money so I'm going to tell them about it."

"Oh, good idea. I'm going to do that, too. JD, let us know what Anne has to say." McKenna looked at them then quirked a smile. "My life is nothing like what I thought it would be, but right now I'm going to go talk to my son."

Toni couldn't hear it, but a minute later Charley came up from downstairs, with the other kids trailing him.

"Hey Nam, Toni and Kenna need to talk to the others. You want to help me make cookies?" asked Cass.

Nam smiled up at her and nodded.

~Thank you, Cass,~ Toni sent. Cass responded with a smile and the two headed into the kitchen with Cass asking what type of cookies she thought they should make.

Jessi and Jamie looked at her, a bit wary, but waiting.

"We're going to take a walk. We won't be far." McKenna said as she headed towards the door, Charley walking with her.

JD headed for the stairs, but paused to speak to the room. "Rarz, you think about that and how we could even do that. Much less if we should. I'm going to go call Anne."

"And we three are going to go out back and talk." Toni fought a smirk at the look the twins exchanged but they just nodded. The three of them traipsed through the kitchen, Jamie tossing in his vote for peanut butter cookies.

As soon as the door was closed both kids looked at her, odd expressions on their faces.

"What?" asked Toni, surprised. They were maturing so fast. She tried to look on the bright side, the number of tantrums and other bratty behavior had pretty much disappeared with the addition of Charley.

"We know we can't be in trouble; we haven't done anything. And while people are upset, you don't feel like you're upset with each other. So we can't figure out why you want to talk to just us and not everyone." Jamie said slowly and it dawned on Toni that they were still talking to each other mentally.

"You might be more paranoid than anyone I've met. No, you two and Charley are not in trouble, but it's personal, so we figured you get to decide who knows."

"Oh," Jamie said, looking at Jessi, frowning. "Why wouldn't we want Charley and Nam to know?"

"You may. But that is something YOU get to decide. Not me." Toni paused, wondering if her seven-year-olds would get the difference. Was she being stupid giving them this courtesy?

Twin brilliant smiles erased her worries. "Thanks, Mom. We'll probably tell them, but thanks."

So mature, so adult. What else is changing faster than normal?

The thought distracted her until Jessi huffed. "Well?"

"The government paid you money for your translation work. I've opened up accounts in your names and put the money in there for each of you. I don't want you to touch it until after we get settled either at home or someplace else. That much is still being discussed. But you have a lot of money. Obviously, I would like you to save some for your future, but once things settle down you've earned spending some of that on fun stuff."

Their eyes lit up. "Can I get a bi-,"Jessi broke off halfway through her sentence and frowned looking at Jamie, who had an odd look on his face.

"Can I get some books? Like ones for a tablet or e-reader. Could I get one of those?"

"Yes." Toni didn't hesitate. She'd put on parental controls, and she knew Jamie would take care of it. "Jessi?"

Jessi kicked the deck not looking at her.

"What were you going to ask?"

Jessi shrugged, still not looking up but she answered. "I wanted a bike, but being a cat is more fun. And me riding the bike as a cat is silly. Really, I just want Charley and Nam and JD and Cass and Perc to all live with us. I don't want to go home and not have them there. I don't want to leave here, 'cause it means we leave them."

"Ah." Toni fell silent. How did she answer that? "I don't know what to tell you right now. But I'll think about what you said."

Jessi just shrugged. "Okay. But no. I don't need anything." The little girl, so much like the pictures of Toni when she was young looked up at her. "How much did they pay us?"

"You each got five hundred thousand dollars." Toni said the amount slowly and waited.

The kids shrugged. "Okay. Is that like a lot?"

She looked at them blankly and then laughed. "Yes. About what I would make in oh, seven years at my job."

"Oh," they said in unison. "Mom," Jamie said, his voice slow. "I think just leave it for now. That's a lot of money."

"I will, but you earned it, so you need to know. You'll need to pay taxes on it, but I'll take care of that." Which opened up a whole different can of worms, but she'd worry about that later. IF there was a later.

There has to be a later.

Their heads jerked up and looked at the house. "Charley's back. Can we go?"

"Yes, yes. Go." Toni rolled her eyes. Her place in their lives had been firmly supplanted by Charley and Nam. Should it hurt more?

Walking back into the house, she closed the door they had left open. JD was coming down the stairs as McKenna fell into a chair.

"I know they're kids, but I never thought telling someone they had been paid half a million, would be met with "Okay," McKenna muttered as she sat on the couch.

"Yeah, me too. Oh well, at least they aren't running around wanting to buy everything. That mean we're doing a good job?" Toni asked, sinking down next to McKenna.

"So. Talked to Anne." JD's voice told her everything she didn't want to know, and Toni braced for the next round of drama.

Chapter 9 - Parks

Sydney is gone. The famous Opera house, the beaches, the people. What was once a thriving city is a wreck of debris. The asteroid hit on the outskirts, creating local earthquakes, a cloud of ejaculate, but while the crater was impressive, outside about a ten-mile radius the damage was repairable. Until the tidal wave hit. The two-mile-high wave slammed into the city and while evacuation notifications had been made, there wasn't enough time to flee far enough inland to avoid the wall of water. At this time over 90% of the population of Sydney is presumed dead.
~TNN Aftermath

In the end it wasn't anything they hadn't expected. JD let them know both he and McKenna had been placed on administrative leave. Toni had already been notified she was officially terminated, but she had just refused to even deal with it. But she could see the impact this had on her two friends. All of them talked about everything except Rarz's offer. No one could face the idea of leaving their planet until they truly saw what was going on.

By the next morning stress had pushed Toni past her limits. With all of the drama for the last few days, if the government wanted her to come back, they'd have to beg. And even then, she didn't think she

FAMILY

would. She wanted to spend time with her kids. Remind herself of them before they grew up and didn't need her anymore. She'd planned a day in the park with the twins, something normal from their old life. Rarz hadn't brought up his offer again about a new world, but she knew all of them were thinking about it. But leave their home? Go to another world? It still seemed more scary than attractive.

"We want Rarz to come with us. We want to hang out with the dragon." Jessi looked up at her with her eyes as wide as she could make them. Playing up the sweet innocent look. The last thing she ever was.

"You do, huh? And what about Jamie?" Toni fought not to smile.

"Oh, he thinks so too. As do Nam and Charley. We think we should all hang with the dragon. We haven't seen him at all."

She tried hard to not let her body language change, but she still felt disappointed. "So all of you want to go out? What about McKenna and JD?"

Jessi shrugged, a distracted look on her face, which probably meant she was talking to the other kids. "We've seen them all week. We haven't seen you. You should take us kids out and the dragon. We could go to the park."

Toni sent a quick check to McKenna. ~You care if I take off with the kids for the day?~

~They talked you into it, huh?~ McKenna's amusement came through. ~Charley is here trying to convince me that Perc and I need to take a day to just relax. Not sure if he is trying to matchmake or something else. But nah, I'm good. I should contact Anne and Kirk in California anyhow. I feel so out of touch since we've been buried in ship stuff. I think I need to check in and figure out what's going on.~

~Then I shall fall on the sword of children for you and take them away.~

~Oh, please. You'll love it. Go have fun.~ McKenna's amusement came through clearly.

Maybe. She had missed the other kids too. But the dragon?

Drakyn. You need to quit thinking of him as a dragon. It's rude.

~Rarz? Would you be interested in going to the park with me and the kids?~ She felt stupid even asking. He'd probably say no. Why would anyone want to hang with four kids and an over-stressed mom?

~I think I would enjoy that experience. It has been overwhelming of late.~ His thoughts came through clear and calm.

Toni looked down at Jessi. "I guess you got your visit to the park with Rarz."

"Yay!" Jessi did a little impromptu dance that had Toni laughing.

"Go get changed into park clothes and I'll make a picnic lunch." The words had barely left her mouth before Jessi was scampering up the stairs shouting for Charley and Nam.

She can talk in their minds, why in the world is she shouting?

Toni abandoned the eternal question of children and their behavior in favor of trying to find stuff for a lunch. While some things were returning to normal, it was taking a bit, and fresh food still remained in short and tight supply. A bit of creative digging and she came up with dried apples and bananas, peanut butter sandwiches, cheese sticks, salami, and a bunch of crackers. Not perfect, but enough for them to have something to eat, especially with an early dinner.

She got everything tucked into a backpack along with a blanket. They were going so high class. She laughed to herself. This sort of normalcy was part of what she had missed so much.

~You guys ready?~

"I believe I am appropriately garbed?" Rarz's voice came from behind her and she had to tamp down her immediate reaction, though whether it was fear or something else, she didn't know anymore. Instead she turned slowly to see him in his human form, still large and imposing, but less awe-inspiring than in his dragon or warrior form. Someone had gotten him jeans and a T-shirt that stretched tight across his body. Something about how his jeans fit struck her as odd, but she didn't have time to dwell on it.

"Dragon man," Nam's whisper-shout preceded her launching across the kitchen to grab Toni's leg, even if her eyes never left Rarz.

The child was ready to climb on him as a dragon, but now, with him in human form, she is shy? Children I swear, if they drive me this crazy as kids, as teenagers I'm going to need drugs to deal.

"His name is Rarz," Toni spoke quietly but not trying to hide what she said. "Why don't you say hello?"

There must have been mind chatter she wasn't aware of because Nam stood up, pushing away from Toni's leg. Her lower lip stuck out a bit, as if pouting but cuter. The child had so much cuteness, it worried her. Luckily none the kids pushed too much. They were almost too good at times. Another aspect of what they were, probably.

"I'm Nam Bara." She stated it and shoved her hand out at him, a flicker of trepidation flashing across her face.

Toni sighed in relief when Rarz crouched and held out his hand shaking hers gravely. "I am pleased to meet you Nam Bara. I am Rarz Goldwing Liryline, but I am known as Rarz."

The smile that flashed across the girl's face made Toni want to coo at the cuteness, but she just nodded. "See, now you know each other. Ready to go to the park?"

"Yes!" The chorus of words came from the other room and Nam pushed away to join them.

Toni grabbed the backpack off the counter, then handed another bag with some water in it to Rarz. He nodded gravely as he took it and they headed out the door. The kids waited for them at the driveway, acting like they hadn't been out of the house in weeks, instead of at the base daily helping with translation needs. They headed down the street staying a few feet ahead of the adults, but not racing too far out. All of them were still too jumpy.

The normal noises caught her attention first. Traffic sounds in the distance, the sound of music from the nearby houses. Rarz walked, matching her pace, but she watched his head swivel as they walked towards the park. His gaze would linger on one thing, then another, but she could never figure out what caught his attention.

"Is this normal life for people?"

"What, going to the park and walking like this?" Toni didn't know for sure what he really was asking. "Or not being at war and going to work?" She continued waving her hand at the cars driving around, traffic having picked up even more over the last week when the news of all the ships being gone had gone public.

"I suppose that is the question I am asking. What is normal life for Earthlings?" His voice even in human form sounded different. Like James Earl Jones was whispering in your ear. She still hadn't decided if she loved or hated it. Either way it reminded her he wasn't human, every time.

They crossed the street while Toni considered her answer. "There isn't any one normal life. There are lots of variations on normal. But in a general way, yes. This is normal. Going to the park with the kids, people going to work, cars driving around. This is as close to normal as I've seen in weeks."

Following the kids, they headed to the play area where a few others were. Some people looked at them funny, frowning as if they should know them but Toni ignored them all, finding a place to lay out the blanket. She sat down as the kids raced towards the monkey bars.

Rarz followed her lead, sinking to the ground with that strange grace. Toni kept an eye on the kids, but she watched him in her peripheral vision. "What is life like for you?"

"For me or my people?"

"Both."

This time he fell quiet. Toni let the silence lay, she could wait.

~I could show you. It might be easier.~ The whisper in her mind seemed almost too intimate, private. But the lure of seeing worlds she'd never seen overcame any reluctance.

~Sure.~

Toni had no idea what to expect, but via the connection he had spoken to her with, a fog of color appeared. She closed her eyes to focus on it and it clarified, creating an image in her head. But rather than something static, like a picture or drawing, it moved and flowed with sound, tastes, even sensation. It felt like she stood there, in the middle of some fantasy land. Stunned at what she saw, she stared—entranced. Around her a small bustling town, with many in what she thought of as the warrior form, moving back and forth. Some had wings, some didn't. The clothes matched what she'd seen in the not-dreams but rather than frantic yelling and fleeing, the Drakyn stopped, chatted, moved around. The houses matched the elegance she'd seen before but seeing it in the full light of a red sun, it seemed both charming and all too real.

Everything was clean and neat, in patterns that tickled at her mind. It struck her like small village life but as she paid attention, she saw a few automated machines, noted the simple elegance in the lines of things they worked with. No smog that she could sense, and a level of quiet that confused her until she realized there were no car or engine sounds.

Young Drakyn were playing in a park while others seemed to be strolling somewhere dressed in more formal clothes only to walk into a portal and disappear. A small open market had several portals hanging in the air. And she could hear the buzz of some insect like a constant harmony under everything else.

~This is your world?~

~Yes. A normal day. We don't have the workdays with weekends like you do. Our structure is different enough I'm not sure how to explain. At least our cultural structure.~

She couldn't walk through it, but she turned around inspecting everything, feeling like she stood in a movie set created just for her. A shout from Jamie caused her eyes to snap open and focus on the kids, but they were climbing on the bars and having fun. Being able to make noise had raised everyone's spirits. Other kids were just as loud, and the watching parents all seemed resigned and amused.

"Maybe someday I can visit." They sat there quietly, and Toni enjoyed that he didn't need to talk as she thought about what she had seen. "Are all your planets like that?"

"Similar. As almost all Drakyn can create portals, we don't have any of your transportation issues outside the occasional wagon. Different planets tended to have different focuses given each planet's unique composition. But now, with three of our worlds taken over by the Elentrin and two more attacked, most people don't want to leave home. They are scared."

"How many planets have you colonized?" Just the idea of multiple worlds being colonized fascinated her.

"Last time I counted, ten. But four have been abandoned, and one is still under discussion. It is outside the normal Elentrin range and we managed to chase off the last raid there with minimal damage."

"Oh. The Elentrin killed that many?" Rarz just nodded, the look on his face too harsh to look at. She would have said more but Jessi and Nam came running over to her.

"Mom, can he change into a dragon here? We want to ride him."

Toni responded before Rarz could. "Not here. His existence hasn't been made public. I have no desire to be in the middle of yet another media storm." She saw the resistance on Jessi's face and pout on Nam's. "I said no. It's too dangerous, and we don't want anyone to get hurt because they think he's a monster."

Though I doubt anyone could hurt him, they could hurt the rest of us though.

Jessi's face fell as she thought about that. "Okay. Can I get something to eat?"

"I don't know if you can, but you may," Toni, mocked reprovingly. The grammar correction had Jessi sighing but she responded correctly.

"Mom, may I have something to eat?"

"Yes, you may." Toni started to dig out the food while Rarz handed each of the girls a bottle of water. The appearance of food called the boys over as if by magic. They plopped down on the blanket, snacking and enjoying the sun.

Toni had no doubts the kids were scheming to figure out how to get a dragon to play with, but for now they could scheme. The occasional look by an adult was starting to get to her and she couldn't figure out what was so interesting about them.

~Toni?~ McKenna's voice pulled her out of her contemplations.

~Yes?~ Just the tone of McKenna's words had her on edge and looking for enemies. When would reality get back to normal and stress in a friend's tone made her think someone was pregnant or way too drunk?

~You guys should probably come back now. Blair is here and says she needs to talk to us.~

~We just got here.~ The sun felt good, the kids were happy, and she rather enjoyed being outside and not in the dry sand of the desert. It dawned on her the sun had moved more than she thought. ~Wait.~ She glanced at her watch, surprised two hours had passed. Maybe between the walking, the vision, and talking, more time had passed than she thought.

~And I'm sorry, but what she's shared so far has worried me. So come home. All of you. Please?~

That alone was enough to get her up and starting to back up. "Okay guys. Sorry to cut it short. McKenna needs us." The magic words of 'McKenna needs us' stopped any imminent whining and within ten minutes they were all up and heading back to the house. At a much faster pace this time. Charley had a frown on his face, but didn't seem panicked, so Toni figured McKenna had reassured him.

So back home and see what drama has happened now.

Chapter 10 - Backlash

With the struggle to get back to normalcy, crimes that were committed earlier are now being reported. The number of calls to report dead bodies has risen in the last week. Many are understandable and tragic. People dying at home, too scared to call for assistance during the invasion. Looting of businesses, squatters living in homes, and a few murder-suicides. The most sensational of which is the death of long-time partners in the DC area. A police officer and her wife, a government employee. Information on that one points to a murder-suicide mostly likely as a side effect of the stress the whole world was under. ~ TNN News

They arrived back at the house, worried, but not freaked out. There were no extra cars in the driveway, so Toni figured Blair hadn't arrived yet. She'd met the woman that once, so wasn't sure why she was coming here. Maybe to talk to Rarz? But she had called McKenna. Too many questions and no answers.

The kids had managed to expend more energy than she expected, and they decided they wanted to read for a bit. The cats were more than willing to take a nap, but Charley wanted to do something, so reading had been the compromise. They streamed up to their room while Toni disposed of the picnic remnants. Rarz walked into the kitchen with her, seeming unsure of what to do. Before Toni could decide what she wanted to do with him, put him to work or send him away, McKenna walked in.

"Thanks for coming back. Sorry I interrupted your day." She looked at Rarz. "What did you think, Rarz? Enjoy your picnic?" McKenna leaned against the door jamb as she watched him, face inscrutable.

"The experience was enjoyable. Though other than letting nestlings run off energy I am not sure of the purpose." He stood in the middle of the kitchen looking too big and out of place in this area.

McKenna glanced at Toni and they shared an amused smile. "Sometimes that is the entire purpose, but often it's to enjoy being outside and just relax."

Rarz had a puzzled look on his face but didn't seem to have another question. Carina came in, flashing a smile when she saw them.

"Hey, you're back early. I was thinking. I need some supplies and they said the mall was opening today for limited hours. How about I take Jessi and Nam to get them a few clothes and what I need. That little girl is growing like a weed and what we have for her is getting too tight."

"Fine by me," Toni said reaching for her purse. "I still have about fifty cash. See if you can get Jessi a shirt or two. Slightly loose would be better. Might let me clothe her for an extra month. And you're right about them growing like weeds. I just have more shirts for Jamie as he's been wearing Jeff's old ones for play stuff and he has a long way to go before he'll grow out of those. I'll worry about school clothes when we go back."

McKenna had been frowning but nodded. "Same. Get Nam a dress maybe? She seems to like them a bit better than Jess. Give me a minute to grab my wallet. I'll give you cash and a card, but if the machines are working use the card. I need to see when they're going to be finished with us here. I'm ready to go home."

"Sure thing." Carina took what the women handed her. "Want me to swing by the grocery store and pick up anything?" That started a whole other conversation, but soon enough Carina and the two girls were in the car and headed out. It almost felt like normal.

Carina had been gone about two minutes when another car pulled up into the driveway, and Blair Lewis got out. Toni and McKenna were still standing in the open garage trying to decide how to pack up when they were allowed to go home.

Wonder if we could talk Rarz into just opening a portal. Surely that can't be harder than doing one from the planet to the ship. Then we can just walk through.

"How can we have gotten this much more crap in such a short time?" McKenna asked looking at the piles of stuff.

"Children have reproductive properties on things. Besides, there are three other people's stuff here as well, plus I'm pretty sure that hat is Rarz's." Toni replied before turning to smiled at Blair. "Hey. McKenna said you need to talk to us?"

Blair gave them a smile, but Toni thought it seemed forced and tense. "Yes." She looked around. "Are the others here?"

McKenna frowned and Toni felt the frisson of worry enter the mindscape. "Well Rarz is inside, or he was. Perc, JD, and Cass are at the ship. Perc and Cass were answering some questions for military engineers. I think, JD went for moral support or to hang with Cass."

Blair chewed on her lip a minute then shrugged. "Not like you can't tell them what I'm going to pass on. But I'd rather talk to you inside." She didn't look twitchy, just worried. The feeling of a storm heading her way intensified in Toni's mind.

"Want something to drink?" Toni offered out of habit as they entered the house. They didn't have anything besides water and coffee. Again, they needed to go shopping.

"Just water," Blair replied still looking distracted and scoping out the living room as if she expected to find someone in it.

"Take a seat. I'll be right back." Toni cast McKenna a fast smile then headed into the kitchen. Relieved she'd chosen water, so she didn't have to make excuses about everything they didn't have. Some childhood lessons you never seemed to lose.

Rarz stood there, looking out towards the back deck, his back to her. "Anything wrong?" she asked as she moved into the kitchen.

"No. Enjoying the peace and reflecting on my joy that the Elentrin did not destroy your world."

"Me too." She got the glasses of water. "Want to come listen to what Blair needs to tell us?"

"If you do not mind. It would be interesting."

"Nah. I have faith she'll tell us if it's classified or something." Toni walked in, Rarz following like her own personal dragon. That thought made her mouth twitch, but it faded as she looked at Blair. The woman had tight lines around her mouth and paced the living room. Toni shot a look at McKenna, but she just shrugged, frowning.

"I brought the drinks."

Blair spun, almost jumping, then relaxed as she saw Toni and Rarz, though this time Rarz didn't capture all her attention. Which created more storm alarms in Toni's mind.

The woman nodded at them distractedly. "Oh good, you're here," Blair's voice was absent as she paced another minute around the living room. Toni could almost feel her gather herself and settle down in the chair, looking at the three of them. Toni and McKenna sat on the couch, while Rarz sat in the big armchair JD favored.

"I know when we met a few weeks ago, Mr. Burby introduced me. But I don't think he explained why I was there. And with how everything went down on ships my special brand of insight wasn't needed." She felt silent and Toni frowned.

It was McKenna that prompted Blair. "So what do you do? Or would you have done?"

That seemed to pull Blair out of wherever her thoughts had led her and for the first time Toni thought she actually saw everyone there. "Argh. Sorry. My thoughts and the patterns that I'm seeing have me scattered. I'm a cultural anthropologist, and normally you think that anthropologists work on understanding other cultures. Well, I primarily study ours. They grabbed me because of Rarz, but he had enough knowledge of this world to not need me. Then they wanted me to interact with the Elentrin. We have three now. Scilita, Thelia and one of the crew from the ship you brought down. A male. I can't remember his name right now. I've been trying to understand their culture so we can figure out how to work with them or at least recognize insults."

"Huh, I didn't realize that was a job." Toni's comment sounded flippant, but she didn't mean it to.

"Oh, you have no idea. Cultural attachés are usually sociologists advising on how to work with different groups. The Chinese and Japanese usually required two or three so we don't make idiots of ourselves. Didn't always work, but it helped." Blair waved that away. "But while fascinating, and I expect to get multiple books out of that culture, that isn't what has me freaked."

Toni just waited, though already her short patience was being stretched. She wanted information now, not trying to pull it out of people.

Gods, the kids are going to kill me when they become teenagers and hide even more stuff.

Blair took a drink of water and Toni saw her hands were trembling as she set the glass down.

What is going on? We just survived an invasion from another race. What could get her this shook up? And why come to us? We're almost out of the limelight.

"Here's the thing. I've been monitoring social media just because it is a great bellwether for any cultural group. Obviously during the invasion, it was used to pass information and warn people. But right now, I'm seeing something spread and it's creating a pattern that I recognize."

"Blair, what are you talking about?" Toni blurted out, trying to figure out what she could mean. They'd already survived one social media firestorm. What was another one?

The woman ran her hands through her hair. Dropping her elbows on her knees she looked at the ground for a minute before lifting her head to stare a McKenna. "You don't understand. This isn't various things coming up from different places. Someone is guiding this, spinning it, creating a cult of their devising. This isn't random. It is planned, directed, and it's working." She all but hissed those last words.

"What do you mean? Planned? Directed? To what?" McKenna asked this, leaning forward and Toni mimicked it, confused as to what the woman meant.

Blair turned her head looking at them. "Really? You haven't been paying attention to what's going on?"

"When?" Toni asked exasperated. "We're either at the ship or passing out. The few times in between I'm spending it with my family. We've already given everything we can to everyone else."

Blair blinked and leaned back with a bitter laugh. "I guess that's both good and bad. I know this was mentioned to you, but I don't know if you realize how bad it's gotten in the last week. There's someone working very hard on placing the blame on the Elentrin invasions squarely on Shifters. Making it out as if Shifters, if Kaylid, caused this entire thing. They are spinning pictures they got showing us helping other aliens off the ships and making it so that we are seeing a serious uptick of resentment and hatred against the Shifters. Already it has caused riots, lynching, and at least fifty deaths just in the United States alone. Someone is making a concerted effort to start the holocaust all over again with Shifters as the focus and I'm terrified he is succeeding. He's playing on the fears, the valid fears, of people worldwide."

"You mean someone is trying to make us look like monsters?" Toni couldn't help her incredulous tone. It sounded like the plot to a bad novel. "Like we are the ones that caused the attack? The changes?"

Blair made a sound that might have been considered a laugh but it chilled Toni to the bone. "Trying? This person, or persons, aren't trying. They're succeeding. At the rate this is going, the Elentrin will be looked on more favorably than Shifters are. I don't know if it's just one person or several, but it's spreading like wildfire and some of the pictures they have are real. Which makes it worse. When you have evidence to support your claims, it makes refuting it much more difficult, especially when what they're saying is essentially true." Her hands had fisted so tightly they were going white at the edges.

"Can you show me what you mean?" McKenna's question helped focus Toni's spinning mind. What were the ramifications?

"I'm really surprised you haven't seen these, but then maybe not. Last time I checked they weren't allowing cell service at the crash site." Blair dug her phone out and flipped through to her social media account. "Here. This is a good example of one of the pictures going viral."

Toni leaned forward; her head so close to McKenna's she could smell the citrus-scented shampoo Perc used. On the screen was a picture of a decidedly non-human based Kaylid, the four arms were a dead giveaway, being helped from the portal towards a tent.

The image, while shocking just for the juxtaposition of alien and human, the blaring headline under it was what snagged her attention. "US Military Helping Aliens. They orchestrated the Invasion!"

"Oh, come on, people don't believe that, do they?" McKenna raised her head to look at Blair.

"If it was just that, they might not have. But look." She kept flipping through various images, showing the wreckage and the canisters being pulled out, a Shifter attacking a man, a short vid clip of a Shifter losing it and attacking people in public—shifting as he did so. The images kept coming each with more damning headlines. "They have people helping them that are on the ground where this is happening, and they are choosing the pictures wisely. Since no one else has any of them, there isn't another side of the story coming forward. Everyone I've talked to at the government says it's a phase and will cool once the shock of the invasion wears off." Blair shook her head, tight lines around her mouth.

"That might have been true, but now there are more and more traditional churches picking up the banner of shifting being evil and the reason all this happened. It's changing public opinion fast. People are dangerous when they are scared. Heck the Shifter abstinence wave is growing by leaps and bounds and anyone that wasn't public about it already is now going into hiding."

Toni leaned back and resisted looking at McKenna for an answer, but McKenna asked the next question anyhow.

"So why are you telling us? What do you hope to gain?" her voice was cool, but not cold.

"I'm not sure. Something wonderful, natural, but staged so it can be filmed?" Exasperation filled Blair's voice as she stood pacing again. "At this point I think I'm telling you so you can be aware of the rapidly shifting cultural climate, but also because you are one of the very few visible Shifters that might have any hope of swaying the public."

"It isn't like I can stage a fight against a monster in the middle of Time Square for them to believe we're the good guys. We're just people, nothing more or less." McKenna's protest created an amusing image of McKenna with a sword up against a horrifying demon.

Toni snorted her amusement and the two women turned to look at her. "Was just thinking she could fight Rarz here. Would be entertaining."

"Are you kidding. He damn well blew FIRE! He'd just melt me." McKenna gave her an incredulous look then rolled her eyes as she took in the smirk Toni gave her.

"I did not blow fire. And I think that presenting me as an enemy would be counterproductive for your planet."

Toni turned to look at him, the question of how he did it on the tip of her tongue when Jessi all but screamed in her mind.

~Mom! Carina's hurt. They're hurting her. Nam is screaming and they won't stop.~ The level of fear and terror in her daughter's voice had Toni on her feet and claws coming out of the tips of her fingers with no conscious thought of her own.

~What is happening? Where are you?~ Her words poured out of her and she vaguely registered Rarz and McKenna standing next to her. All she got was a jumbled of words and emotions. Emotions that burned and stung and coated her mind like sticky burning tar. Panic welled and she heard and felt Charley and Jamie clamoring just as loud, their emotions adding to the chaos assaulting her mind.

Panic and need to get to her daughter overrode everything else. ~WHERE ARE YOU!~ The words, the thoughts came out like a command and suddenly she saw a store, clothes laying around, Carina on the ground wrapped around a tiger cub screaming a wailing cry. Boots kicked at her, the braids flying, but she curled hard around the tiny cub, blood coming from various cuts and bruises forming from the assault.

"They're at Target, about three miles from here," Toni snapped out and turned towards Rarz, stilling seeing through her daughters' eyes. "Take me there, NOW!"

"Of course," Rarz said without hesitation. She felt a gentle brush of thought, then it traveled down that link to her daughter, her terrified daughter. "I have her location. Opening the tunnel now."

To the side of them the silver swirl, which had never looked so good, started to appear. Blair stood off to the side, face pale, eyes wild, but she didn't ask questions, just got out of their way. Later Toni would need to thank her for that.

She waited, tense, even as she kept seeing boots kicking Carina, the crying cub, people yelling and shouting, trying to grab the people attacking Carina. Attacking her friend.

~Go,~ his voice whispered in her mind, but she was already moving through the portal, racing towards the terror she felt from Jessi. As she stepped out the connection snapped, and she saw everything in a single glance that seared across her soul and her mind.

They were near the girl's clothes, Carina lying on the floor wrapped tightly around Nam, who had quit crying, but lay curled into a tight ball of orange and black fur, her clothes tattered. Jessi was under a rack of clothes, tears streaming down her face, tracking across a red welt that looked like a boot print. Three men were kicking Carina shouting words like 'Monster,' 'Abomination,' 'Your fault,' and 'You should all die.' People were gathered around, a few trying to stop them, but the men had obviously knocked a few people down and she could see security on their radios talking and waiving their hands, but not interfering.

The details hung in her mind's eyes for a long crystal second, every detail clear and sharp. Then Jessi yelled out, "Momma!"

Everything snapped back into real time and she took two fast strides towards a man who had just lifted his leg to kick Carina again. Her hand went around his neck, claws piercing his flesh, and she heaved. She threw him into a rack of shirts in the boy's department on the other side of the aisle.

"Get away from Carina!" Her voice came out as a low growl and people scrambled back. Behind her she heard gasps as McKenna and Rarz came out. Toni could feel their presence solidify behind her as she growled at the other two men. Her teeth lengthening as she snarled. "Get away!"

One of them sneered at her while the other paled and backed away. "You're one of them. A damn alien. It's because of people like you I lost my parents. This is all the fault of your kind. You should all just fucking die." He made like he was going to swing at her, but a huge hand grabbed his arm before he could complete the swing, or she could gut him.

"I think not." Rarz lifted as he spoke picking up the man easily. The man went pale, as Rarz, still fully human, picked up his entire body the way you might pick up a toddler. "This is not acceptable behavior according to your society."

The man wiggled up, couldn't get his arm free. Toni dismissed him from her mind as she knelt next to Carina. "Jessi, go through the portal." Jessi hung back, looking at her, and Toni took a few precious seconds to look up and lock gazes with her daughter. "I love you. You did the right thing. Now get home. Charley and Jamie are there, as well as a woman named Blair. You know her. Stay there until we or the others get back."

Tears still wet on her face, the left side swollen and red, Jessi nodded and streaked through. That removed one factor. Around them people were protesting, and she could hear sirens outside, but none of that mattered as she looked at Carina.

"McKenna, come here and get Nam and get home. I need to get Carina to a hospital."

"How badly hurt is she?" McKenna asked even as she came around and pushed the rack of cloths out of the way.

Toni didn't answer, didn't want to say, but McKenna wasn't stupid. "Damn. I," she broke off the words and continued into in the mindscape. ~I can change her. Will that help?~

It was an option. A real one. But first, crouching down next to her she touched her gently and Carina flinched, arms going even tighter around Nam.

"Carina? It's Toni. We're here. Let McKenna take Nam. We'll make sure she's safe." She kept her voice low and gentle, focusing on the girl who had been family for the last four years.

Carina looked up at her, relaxed her grip on the little girl, and then her whole body went slack.

Chapter 11 - Fear

Fear is the new word of the day. Fear the aliens might come back. Fear of Shifters. Fear of governments. Fear of loss. With the ripple effects from China still being in shambles since the invaders left, wariness has become a way of life. While the normal everyday things seem almost back to the status quo, some people are looking down the road. With no computer chips, what good will the science in the ship do? With China facing an easy ten million deaths, how will that affect food and other purchases, things the US relies on. And even more people are looking at their neighbors and seeing the monsters that brought all of this down on the rest of us. ~TNN Aftermath

"Fuck," the curse word came out as a growl. "McKenna get Nam out of there now. I need to get Carina to a hospital."

McKenna had already grabbed the tiger cub, who wrapped around her, whimpering in the most pitiful way. She stood holding the girl and looked at Rarz. "You willing to do a bunch of rapid portals?"

"I will do anything that is needed," he replied, his voice centered, but his shoulders twitched as if flexing wings.

~Then I'll talk as I move.~ McKenna matched her words to her thoughts as she went back through the portal. The next few comments came out in the shared mindspace broadcasting to everyone. ~Cass, JD, Perc, we need you now. Get to a place and Rarz is going to drop a portal for you. I need you at the house. Rarz once they are here, I need you do whatever Toni tells you. Odds are you'll need to grab me. Be ready. I'm through.~

~We're at a safe place. Find us.~ Cass came through and Toni could hear her and Rarz talking. It wasn't straightforward, as he had to be on one side of the portal.

"Toni?" He asked behind her, but she was too busy trying to assess the damage to Carina.

Where are the damn paramedics?

"What?" Her comment snapped out, but she didn't have time or energy to care about being rude.

"I will return shortly."

"Fine." She dismissed him and felt the portal close with him on the other side. She lifted her head and speared one of the security guards with a glare. Young, over-weight, and obviously scared to death, he held his radio in a death grip, face pale as he looked around, frantic. "You!" Her voice sharp. The young man looked at her, eyes wide.

"Yeess?" The word stuttered out as people were starting to recover from the sudden appearance of the three of them.

"Where the hell are the paramedics? I have a badly injured woman here. I need them now."

"Okay, I um, I..." he babbled and lifted the radio. "Are they here yet?" His voice high and sharp.

The idiot she'd thrown to the ground was whining and complaining behind her as she heard the rush of feet.

Finally, what the hell is wrong with their response times?

She looked up, but instead of EMTs or even someone with a decent first aid kit, three police officers rushed in, guns drawn. Snorting she returned to Carina.

~We're back at the house. Cass and JD are staying with the kids. They'll keep them safe. We'll be to you in a minute or two.~

~Kay,~ her response distracted as she finished the assessment on Carina and felt panic bubbling up in her chest. The hard kicks had broken at least three ribs, and from her labored breathing Toni feared at least one or more had punctured her lungs. A huge knot on the back of her head indicated brain injury, while her stomach was ridged and hard to the touch. Only the fact that her legs twitched and she'd been able to release Nam gave Toni hope her back hadn't been badly damaged.

"What is going on here?" someone behind her demanded. Toni ignored them and laid Carina out carefully. The blood bubbling up from her mouth had her throat tight, but she breathed, and her heart was still beating, so anything else she did would make it worse. With no open wounds there wasn't anything Toni could do.

A hand grabbed her left shoulder, pulling her away from Carina. Muscle memory from lessons she'd never learned reacted. She clamped down on the hand with her right hand, rose and spun, driving her elbow into the person's stomach. As her elbow hit, the blue uniform registered but she really didn't care. At some point her claws had receded, so when she decked him it was with just her fist, but she hit him with more power than her body should have held.

His jaw broke in an audible crack that had people gasping. The man buckled and went down in a boneless heap even as the other two cops started yelling at her, their guns drawn.

Rage, fear, frustration all fought for priority in her mind. Grabbing onto her patience, learned after years of being a parent, she looked at them. "Don't touch me. I'm not armed and obviously tending a wounded woman. Get the paramedics here now." Each word came out ice cold.

"Down on your knees, hands in the air. Do it now!" Once of them screamed, even as the other went for their radio calling for two buses.

Toni ignored all of them trying hard not to shift and left the rage and fear out. She dropped to her knees and focused on the girl who was all but a sister to her children. She leaned down and felt her pulse at the base of her neck and moaned. It was getting erratic and her breathing was more labored.

"I told you to get your hands in the air. Get away from that woman." One of the cops still shouted even as people were screaming and cowering. Toni didn't know what she was about to do, but the portal opened behind the cops and McKenna, Perc walked out looking like normal humans. Then Rarz followed them in warrior form, which distracted everyone. Rarz had put on his wings and the effect rocked you back on your heels. Something about him screamed majesty. An effect he hadn't used much around them the last few days. But it pulled all eyes off her.

"I think everyone needs to calm down. Officers, we understand you're doing your job, but no one needs to be shot today." Perc's reasonable tone and huge size had everyone pausing, at least when you could look away from Rarz.

Everyone stood frozen for long heartbeats, when the sound of wheels and running disrupted the tableau.

"What is going on here?" An older man, with short black hair, traces of sliver on the edges, and yellow brown skin came racing in followed by a pair of paramedics with a gurney.

"Finally! Over here. Now!" Toni gestured them to Carina. The cops were all waving their hands and yelling, but Toni tuned them all out and moved out of the way of people. The only chance Carina had.

The man and woman did their own assessment and Toni hated how their faces tightened. With quick efficient moves they slipped Carina onto a back board and got her up on the gurney.

They got the information from Toni. While Carina was too old to need a legal guardian, Toni was listed as her emergency contact and medical power of attorney. Knowing her blood type and being able to provide details of what happened helped.

"Got it. We need to get her into the ER stat," the man said, even as they strapped Carina in. The other paramedic putting in an IV.

"Where are you taking her?"

"ER at Mercy Medical. You coming with us?"

"No. I'll be there shortly though. Might beat you there."

They cast her a look but didn't say anything as they pushed the bed out of the store, their speed telling Toni how serious it was. She followed them with her gaze, then let it go and moved her focus back to the cops and her family.

Another set of paramedics were coming through the door and one of the cops directed them to the cop on the floor. Toni reached for the wave of guilt she expected at hurting someone, hurting a cop. And nothing was there.

Knowing she'd probably be arrested and refusing to feel guilty, she headed over to where it looked like McKenna and the others had calmed things down. Or at least all the guns were holstered, and no one looked ready to shoot anyone.

"That's her. She's the one that decked Jules. Broke his jaw. We heard it break," one of the younger cops, the one who been shouting at her said, though at least it sounded more like a statement than an accusation. That had to be progress.

The older man, a sergeant from his insignia, waved at the paramedics and sent them over to the now moaning police officer. He kept glancing at Rarz, who stood there like a bodyguard—imposing and silent. But he managed to face her and talk to her.

"Can you explain what happened here? And why you hit my officer?"

"He grabbed me. I was tending my -" she hesitated then lied without much compunction, "cousin. Who'd been attacked by multiple men. One of whom I threw off her. When he grabbed me, I reacted. I already had reason to believe people were attacking without provocation." She shrugged. "At that point I didn't care if you shot me, I didn't trust anyone."

He sighed and looked over at the security guard who stood there, still pale, but calmer. "Does that match what you saw?"

"Yes, sir. Though no one expected her to walk out of a shiny swirl in the air. But what those men were doing weren't right, but… " he shrugged in helplessness and Toni wanted to sneer. He outweighed Carina by at least fifty pounds, and he looked like he would have been about four inches taller than her as with heels on she'd barely hit five feet eight inches.

"And the man she attacked?"

"I stopped him from assaulting a woman protecting a child." Toni ground out.

"Protecting an animal," muttered one of the cops.

Toni bristled and felt the jaguar come to the surface again, wanting to lash out, but she didn't have time.

"Look, my cousin is being taken to Mercy. I need to get there now. Am I'm being charged?" she demanded. Toni was done asking for anything. Right now, the only thing that mattered was Carina.

The sergeant looked at all the people involved, the fuming officers, the man being carted away by the EMTs, the people ranting and raving, and then the dragon that had everyone cringing. "Please leave contact information. We may need to talk to you about this."

"Fine." Toni wasted far too long giving her contact info to the surly cop. He grudgingly admitted he didn't need anything more but warned her not to leave the area. She almost, almost, snarked back asking about leaving the planet but kept her mouth shut and turned to Rarz. "Can you take me to Carina now?" Portals were faster, so a portal would get her there before the ambulance and then Toni would figure out how to help the woman who'd always been there for her. A friend, a confidant.

"I'm going too." McKenna said, and Toni just nodded. She didn't care if the whole group came now, but she needed to get in there.

"Rarz, please?" She would beg if it helped, but for now she just asked, ignoring the rest of the world.

"I would take you there gladly, but I do not know where she is." Even in the dragon warrior form he seemed kind. He said these words as if it hurt to tell her this.

"But you've gone to other places?" She felt her control fraying; she should have gone with her. "You found Cass and JD," a note of panic in her voice.

"Yes. I knew them, could talk to them. I do not know Carina, nor is she part of your mind group."

"But the spaceships!" Frantic stress ate at her and she fought her desire to grab him and shake him.

"Were objects above a planet I could sense and almost see. They were independent and distinguished from everything else." His voice calm though his wings twitched in time with her pounding heart.

"Damnit." She fumbled for her phone. Where was Mercy General? And where were they? It took her a moment to figure it out, then it snapped into place. "Take us back to the house. It's closer to Mercy. NOW!" Toni didn't know if she could be any more terrified if her own kids had been in that ambulance. This was Carina. She'd been there since the kids were two. And she had left her alone with strangers. Hurt and maybe dying. Alone. All because of stupid rules and because she had assumed.

Assuming makes an ass of you and me.

The old phrase ran through her head. It didn't help.

Rarz didn't even argue, he just opened the portal. Toni was running through as it finished forming, stumbling into the house. Righting herself she dived for her keys and purse before heading towards the door at a dead run. JD and Cass standing back, worry writ large on their faces.

"Mom? Where's Carina? Mom?" Jessi's wail almost stopped her, but she could talk and drive.

~They had to take her to the hospital. I'm going there now. No, you can't come. I'll let you know what's happening. I promise.~ The words were said while she slid into the driver's seat and started up the car. Before she could pull out, McKenna and Perc slid in too.

"We aren't letting you go alone." McKenna's voice was fierce, and Toni just nodded as she slammed the car into reverse.

She caught sight of Rarz in her rear-view mirror. He stood in the doorway watching them, a look on his draconian face she couldn't interpret.

~Mom?~ Jamie this time. ~Tell her we love her.~ Worry and grief coated his thoughts.

~I will. She knows.~ That much Toni knew for sure.

The drive there passed in a blur of pushing the laws to the limits and not caring how many she broke. She pulled into the parking lot for the ER. Resenting the time to get her seatbelt off and the car shut off before she took off running towards the sliding doors.

Too long. It took too long to get here. Where is she?

Toni headed to the front desk ignoring everyone and everything else. The nurse in charge there, a large black man looked up at her. He didn't have a chance to say anything before Toni blurted out her question.

"Carina Watkins was brought in, assault victim. I'm her emergency contact. Where is she?"

He pulled back a bit from her, eyes widening as he flicked to behind her. Toni knew it was McKenna and Perc and that meant she didn't need to worry about anything. The man glanced down and looked at his list. "The doctors are with her now. They were asking for you. Consult room 1." He pointed to a small room off to the side. I'll let the doctors know you're here."

The three of them barely fit into the small room. None of them even bothered with the available chairs. McKenna and Perc leaned against the wall letting Toni pace. She needed to move and every second that went by made it worse.

A soft tap at the door and she spun, looking at it as it opened. An older woman, hair going steel grey, skin the color of toast, and eyes that were the same gold brown as McKenna's pelt stepped in, shutting the door behind her. The room which had felt so close and tight before seemed huge, and the space between her and the doctor impossible to cross.

"You are Toni Diaz? Ms. Watkins had your name in her wallet, and you talked to the paramedics on the scene?" Her voice had a soft lilt to it that didn't disguise the sharp intellect or the news that Toni knew was coming.

"Yes," her voice cracked as she said the world and she clenched her fists, feeling sharp claws digging into skin.

"My name is Doctor Saluda. I am sorry to tell you this. Her heart and lungs were punctured multiple times. One rib shattered completely and sent shards into multiple organs. She coded on the way here and the efforts to revive her made the damage worse. I am sorry." Toni heard genuine grief in the words, but it didn't matter. She wanted to scream, to beg. But she'd been here before. This wasn't the place to rage.

Ma-" her throat grabbed the word, ate it and she had to fight to swallow over the arid landscape of her heart. "I'd like to see her." It wasn't a request and apparently the doctor knew it.

"If you'd follow me?" Nothing else was spoken as the woman led them through a busy emergency department to a back room. The efforts they had gone through to try and save her were obvious from the blood and medical detritus on the floor. Toni didn't care. She moved over to the still figure. Carina lay there, her skin with a grey undertone she'd never had in life.

"I am so sorry. This is all my fault. I should have left you with the kids in California. You should have never been here with us. I should have never been here. Damn them, damn them all." The words for all the weight they carried came out as a tender whisper.

Toni brushed the braid off her forehead. "I'll let your mom know you died a hero. She should know you were the bravest and kindest person I've ever known." Everything locked down inside her, Toni leaned over and kissed the still warm forehead.

She longed to take deep cleansing breaths, but the hospital stank of fear, illness, and blood. With a shallow breath Toni turned to the doctor. "I'll provide the information. Can you hold her until I set up the arrangements?"

FAMILY

"Of course." The doctor handed her a small card. "This is the contact for our morgue. They'll help with anything you need. Again, my sympathies."

Toni nodded absently took the card and headed out, away from the chaos and points of failure. McKenna reached out and gently took the keys from her hands.

"I'll drive."

Toni didn't even bother to fight, just sat down in the passenger seat and shut down. This she refused to tell the kids via Speech. She would damn well be hugging them when she told them.

The silence in the car didn't feel heavy or fragile, it felt supportive. Her family would be there for her and they would help. In the end that was all that mattered.

Walking into the house everyone there turned to look at her. She didn't have to say a word.

"NO!" Jessi and Jamie collapsed in tears and Toni pulled them to her cradling her children as death impacted them in a way their father's never could have. Before long she was in a pile of kids and they cried over the loss of a woman they loved.

I'll make it right, Carina. I swear. I'll not let your sacrifice be in vain. They will regret taking you from us.

Chapter 12 - Goodbyes

The newest twist of viral imagery after the invasion has appeared. A lizard-like being, with wings that call forth mythological dragons was taped at the scene of another Shifter-centered attack. Even the people around are obviously scared of this being. Here you can see him cowing cops at the scene. Reports are that the woman who threw one of our citizens across the store won't be facing charges. Are officials being lax on Shifters now? The last thing we need is special treatment to a group that already has so many advantages. ~ Harvey Klein Talk Show

"Toni?" The quavering voice had Toni turning and opening her arms wide.

"Mama Watkins," she murmured even as she pulled the older woman into a tight hug. With long braids like her grand-daughter's, Marissa Watkins held Toni tight.

After a lifetime of grief, she pulled back and looked Ton straight in the eye. "My daughter is a bit upset at you. But I know you loved Carina like you loved your own children. She will come around, eventually. My Lorina holds a grudge like some people hold secrets. But come, tell me how my granddaughter died."

"With honor and protecting a child," Toni assured her then guided the older woman to a couch and began to explain the entire story. She explained about the dragons, the ship, and how instrumental Carina had been in making sure they could focus on trying to do what they could. "And I should never have let her go. I didn't realize the atmosphere had become deadly. I swear."

"Now you stop it. You didn't attack her. You didn't even put her in danger. She took two little girls shopping. That should never be a crime. But thank you for bringing her home and letting her friends fly out here." Marissa's voice held compassion and Toni hugged her again. In her lifetime the elder Watkins had buried a husband, a son, two, now three grandchildren, and one brother. She knew about loss.

"Thank the government. They owe us a bit, so they arranged all the flights and paid for her cremation." Toni sniffed, wiping her eyes from the tears welling there.

"Politicians doing something worth offering thanks for?" Marissa cast her a skeptical glance.

Toni choked back a laugh. "Maybe not the elected ones. These were the ones we had worked with. They made sure it was done."

"Then pass my thanks on to them. Now, let's go say goodbye to my granddaughter. The hero."

"That she was," Toni whispered as they stood and joined the others. All of them had come, dressed in nice clothes. Even Rarz had a suit made that met funeral protocol. Christopher was there as a representative of the others. He and Burby had made sure all the charges against Toni had been dropped and manslaughter charged against the three men. After that she blocked out all the discussions focusing only on this funeral and her kids. Calling Marissa and

Lorina had been the hardest thing she'd ever done, but she wouldn't let anyone else make the call. Carina had been her responsibility.

It had been decided Christopher would come with them, and he hovered, trying to keep tabs on everything. The news had blown the story up. Some channels painting Toni as a vicious monster, others as a protective mother. Either way, they wanted comments and pictures, and Toni had started to feel hunted. Something that drove the cat side of her slightly crazy.

They had hoped moving the funeral to Texas, mainly for Carina's family, would help to deter people from causing a fuss. It hadn't worked.

Leaving Mama Watkins talking to Carina's friends that had come out for the funeral, Toni went to check on Rarz. Partially to make sure he was okay, but mostly to avoid Lorina. She knew Carina's mom wanted to start a fight, wanted to lash out at the only people she could. Toni really didn't want that to happen, but she understood Lorina's rage and grief. All too well.

"Rarz, any problems? You okay?" She asked as she peeked out the door. The Methodist Church had a nice foyer with large glass windows in the door, making it easy to help screen people. Everyone coming had put their name on the list, so it wasn't hard to check that they were invited. One of Carina's cousins oversaw that. A tiny girl, she had a backbone of steel. Rarz and Perc switched out to give her the muscle backup, though Toni had no doubt she could handle herself.

Rarz stood at the door, his huge human form still not enough to convince all of them to go away. Toni came up to him and the few reporters trying to brave getting past him.

"You okay out here?"

"I do not understand this behavior. Why intrude on grief, it is a special and holy time. Many of mine have never known anyone to die. Even among the Kaylid, death outside of violence is rare and unusual. At least with the freed ones." His voice dropped and she thought he was close to saying something else when one of the more aggressive reporters lunched forward.

"You say 'rare' is that because they are immortal? Are you a Shifter? One of the new aliens among us? The monsters living under our skin?"

Toni could feel his energy rising and the dragon threatening to come out.

"No. Don't." She whirled, her eyes meeting Christopher who had already headed their direction. He was very good at knowing when things were going sideways.

"Christopher, take this over. He can't, we can't risk that. We can't risk him." Her voice low urgent. Something about the energy leaking out of Rarz registered because the reporter had stepped back, but the camera kept filming.

Christopher nodded at her. "I've got this. We done?" Carina's cousin glanced at her list and nodded.

"Yes, just about everyone is here. The ones that aren't probably aren't coming."

"Good. Go mourn her. Both of you. She deserves that much." He nodded and shut the door in the faces of the reporters standing in front of it.

Toni flinched back. It was more than Caroline had gotten. They had left her in the street. Her eyes closed and she didn't know if she'd ever forget that.

"Don't." His voice stopped her as she turned away, head bowed. "She knew the job. She was damn good at that job. And she would never blame you for doing what you did, what you had to do. You honored her the best way you could. You called and you remembered. That's all any of us can ask for in the end."

Toni nodded and pulled Rarz away. "Just sit here, out of the way, and watch our rituals. I know it doesn't mean much to you, but for us it is the last thing we have of those we lose."

His look towards her made her pause, but she shook her head and hurried away, needing to give Carina's family her attention. Today they mattered more than anyone else.

Toni left Rarz in a seat near Cass; she at least could keep him occupied for hours asking questions. Taking a deep breath, Toni headed for Lorina. Avoiding it would only make it worse. And anything Lorina said couldn't match what she already had told herself. McKenna and the kids were in a corner, so they would probably miss most of what was about to explode.

I hope.

"Lorina? I am so sorry," with every bit of sympathy and grief laden her voice , Toni spoke to Carina's mother. Toni would have done almost anything to make this easier for this family friend. The mother of the girl she'd loved like a sister.

Lorina spun, her thick braids jangled as she whipped around to face Toni squarely. Of Latino and

Africa descent, Lorina Watkins was a striking woman. She may have been about five foot five, but her personality would make most people look small. Long thick dark hair in hundreds of tiny brains, laced with skulls and other charms Toni recognized from her childhood. But what caught her now were the two dark pools of grief where there should have been eyes. Toni recognized that look. She'd seen it in the mirror often enough in the months following Jeff's death.

"You!" The woman spat the word. But Toni just nodded at her, understanding the anger and rage. "This is your fault. You and those damn Shifters. She was normal, human. If you hadn't dragged her into this world she would have never been at risk. How dare you show your face here? This is your fault. You got my daughter killed."

The worst part was her charges were substantially true. Areas with few Shifters suffered almost no casualties, something the press was playing up like crazy.

Toni sighed, her eyes closing as she remembered the last time she saw Carina alive. "Lorina, you have every right to be angry at me. But you can't be any more furious at me than I am. I trusted her. With my children, and she lived up to every ounce of trust I had in her. She was killed protecting a little girl. Because some bigot hated her because the child shifted. Because of her courage and strength my daughter and the daughter of my friend were kept safe. She was a member of my family and her absence is like a void in our hearts." Toni took a deep breath, surprised to realize she was trembling. "I know what it's like to lose those you love. She was family and she was loved so very much." Her voice broke on the last words. She never took her eyes from Lorina's, willing her to let Toni past the grief, the anger, the devastation.

Lorina looked away first as Mama Watkins put an arm around her waist. "I hear you. I just can't let go. She was going to call me today. Catch me up on what was going on. She was so proud of everything you and your friends were doing. She told me she wanted to be like you. But with all the anger, the hate swirling around, I just thanked the Lord every night she wasn't."

Toni managed not to flinch at that.

"But I still lost her to people that hate. Now it isn't skin color, it is fur. When will people learn to love like the good book tells us to? When will I get my baby back?" Lorina's voice was thick with tears and pain. Toni reached out to hug her, but Lorina shied away.

"Not yet. I can't. Maybe someday I can forgive. The Lord says I should, but I'm thinking He'll understand if I hold on to my anger a bit longer."

"I think so. I know I do. If you need anything. Call. I'll be headed back to California, tell me what you want me to send to you."

"Later. Not now. I can't. But whatever her friends want, let them have." Lorina turned and started to shuffle away, grief adding decades to her face and body. Then she halted. "Tonan?"

"Yes?"

"Send me her Bible. The one I gave her on her Confirmation Day."

"I will." The words came out thick and heavy. Toni had lost her faith so long ago, she didn't remember believing. At least not in a god. But Carina had, her family had, and Toni would never disrespect their faith by her words or actions.

The ceremony was a simple memorial ceremony. Carina's family and friends gathered to remember her, and they all tried to ignore the reporters all but surrounding the building. Everyone, except maybe Rarz, cried when the preacher talked about the sacrifice Carina had made, and the proof of her life sat in that room. The friends she had made, the difference she made in their world. Their choice now was to honor it or ruin what she had done.

Christopher came over and leaned down to whisper in McKenna's ear. She sighed and said in their shared space, ~We need to go. They're worried about more fallout from some other political stuff.~

~Why can't we portal? That was fun.~ Jamie's question held more than just the desire to portal, and Toni shot a look at her son.

~Because it would raise too many questions. We don't really want the public knowing about the portals quite yet, or that Rarz can create them.~

Jamie half-pouted but Nam pulled all their attention. "I wanna talk to Carina's momma."

"Oh, are you sure, honey? Lorina is hurting an awful lot right now. She misses her daughter."

Nam nodded her head gravely, at the second funeral in as many weeks. "Yes."

Toni looked up at McKenna worried, she didn't want the little girl to be hurt.

"Okay, Nam. You want me to take you over?" McKenna asked.

Nam looked over at Lorina, clustered next to her family and shook her head in a slow motion. "No. But watch me?" Her voice shook a bit.

"Okay. We'll watch you. If you need anything let us know," McKenna reassured her, running a hand down her hair.

Jamie start to follow her, but Toni pulled him back to her. "Let her be. She can talk to us at any moment. She's only going to be a little bit away. You can see her." The boy all but vibrated with the need to follow her, but Toni kept a hand clamped to his shoulder. She lowered her voice and bent down a bit, making the words for his ears, though any of the Shifters would be able to hear her. "Trust her. She is strong. Have faith she'll ask for help if she needs it."

Toni didn't know about the others, but she didn't try to listen in as Nam approached the small cluster of Watkins. She looked so tiny and fragile compared to these strong women, with personalities that all but glowed from them.

Lorina stiffened but sat down on a nearby pew and listened. They spoke for what seemed eternity, given Toni didn't think she could breathe while she watched. Nam lifted her hand and touched Lorina's face and the woman started to cry. But something about how she cried, seemed lighter and healthier than before. Lorina pulled the little girl into a hug, then Mama Watkins did, with the rest of the family touching her head with gentleness as Nam headed back.

"Someday she will be a powerful healer," Rarz said, his voice low but it felt like a prophecy as it rolled through her mind.

"What did you say?" Jamie blurted out the second Nam got near enough that he wasn't shouting.

Nam shook her head and pressed into McKenna. "Just what Carina said as she protected me. She needed to hear it. It helped her heart."

At least out loud Nam refused to say anything else to anyone of them, though Jessi looked stricken and looked back at the gathered clan multiple times as they left.

Chapter 13 - More Questions

A woman was killed the other day in a local Target. Witness accounts are conflicting, but everyone agrees there was a small tiger involved, a swirl of silver that people stepped out of, and another man was hurt as a woman grabbed him and threw him across the store with apparent ease. No one is sure why the woman was attacked, but the presence of the animal implies there may have been fear for their lives involved in the attack. ~ Local Baltimore News

The eyes of everyone on them, both friends and family and the reporters, were making all of them twitchy, especially McKenna and JD. She could see their hands reaching for weapons they didn't have.

Toni worked her way over to Christopher. He hung at the back, almost ignorable, except for what he represented. That they needed protection. "Christopher, we should just port home. The reporters aren't going to let us go easily. Rarz can create a portal for us and we can be gone in a few minutes." Her voice a bit desperate.

"No." His response was immediate and flat.

"It would be easier. We'd just be gone, and they wouldn't figure out how or to where?"

Dammit, I sound like I'm begging. Suck it up. You know how to handle funerals. Though last time I think being in shock made it easier.

Christopher turned to give her a sardonic look. "After that little stunt using the portal at Target? While I don't blame you, not everyone is fooled by the swirly silver description. Some people will figure out exactly what it is. Add in how many people saw stuff when we were pulling people off the ships and at the crash sites? That is a story waiting to break, but right now it's just still too unbelievable. Let's not associate you with portals any more than necessary. Everyone would prefer that Rarz is not linked to the creation of them. Right now, he is the only ace in the hole we have. No one wants to risk that."

Toni took a deep breath, held it, and then let it out slowly. "Point. Sorry."

"Toni, don't apologize. Everyone has lost so much lately. We're all edgy and suffering from PTSD in one way or another." He gave her a crooked smile, but there was little humor in it. "The therapists should see a boom in business for the next decade or two."

She choked on a bitter laugh. "Point. Either way. I think we're ready to go."

The socializing had wound down and some people had already left, though the cluster of the Watkins women remained. But she had nothing left to say to them.

With Christopher running everything, they managed to get out of the church without too many reporters noticing them. Christopher had arranged for Suburban's to be waiting for them, even with booster seats for the kids. Toni closed her eyes, after they had all clambered in, glad for a chance to relax.

The four kids were in the back, with Toni, McKenna, and Perc in one. Cass, JD, and Rarz were in the other.

She let the rocking of the vehicle and the gentle murmur of conversation, both physical and mental, soothe away some of her nerves. It didn't last long before a muttered curse from Christopher had her eyes jerking open and she focused on their surroundings.

"What's wrong?" McKenna asked while Toni tried to see through the tinted windows for whatever had stressed out the normally implacable agent.

"We aren't at a military airport, but a small private one and there are reporters waiting for us. We need to park a certain distance away and we're going to have to run that gauntlet."

~Should we shift?~ JD asked from the other car. McKenna passed on the question.

Christopher pondered it as he finished parking. "No. Given the current atmosphere, it would only fan the flames. My suggestion? Walk straight towards the plane. I've texted the pilot and they'll have the stairs down and waiting for us. Just don't respond to anything and while it might be intimidating, I doubt they will throw more than words. Keep the kids in the middle. Get out on the passenger side. I parked in such a way the other car is providing cover."

Shit, it's starting to feel like I'm living in a war zone again. I'm so tired of this. I want to go home, have my life, go to work, and just be normal.

Toni fought back the wave of self-pity. It helped nothing and if anything, made it worse.

"Okay kids, out. Stay in the middle," she ordered as the kids scrambled out. They looked a bit wild-eyed, since already she could hear the reporters clamoring and starting to come around the vehicles.

"Go straight," Christopher said, moving to the vee the two car noses made. "The other car is backing up now."

The words were spoken, and the other vehicle moved back as if on command and he strode forward, Rarz behind him as the point in a diamond. McKenna, Cass, then the kids in the middle with JD and Perc on either side, leaving Toni at the back, with the other agent leaping out of the car coming to back Toni up. He didn't pull a gun but she knew he was armed, and didn't know if that made her feel better or if it would set off a brushfire of public wrath.

She was so tired of public wrath. It hurt so much right now and the reaction of others just added salt to an open wound.

The second they emerged from between the two vehicles the reporters descended on them like a swarm of bees. Buzzing, and snapping, the shouted questions and camera flashes disorienting her.

"Did you know she would die when you let the paramedics take her?"

"Did you try to kill the man you attacked?"

"How do you feel about the fact your monsters caused a good woman to die?" That question, shouted almost right at her, had her spinning and Toni could feel her claws under the surface of her skin.

"Don't," the agent behind her said as he kept pressing her forward.

Toni fought back her emotions and tried to shut out the shouted comments.

"Do you know how many people died because of the asteroids? Why didn't you stop them?"

"What did you think would happen when you taught people to become monsters?"

"How can you live, knowing you've destroyed a man's life? He'll have a record because you stopped him from killing a monster."

Again anger rippled through her. Toni wanted to lash out, to show them what pain and having your life destroyed felt like. She should know.

~Toni.~ It was McKenna's voice. Toni looked forward, but McKenna hadn't turned around, still being hustled to the plane. ~Ignore them. We know the truth. What they say doesn't matter.~

But it did matter. The idea that Carina was being dragged through the mud and right now with the efforts to rebuild so much, no one would take a journalist to task for twisting the truth. That burned and stung like acid on an open wound but at the same time, McKenna was right. It didn't matter. No one could change what happened and Carina would be in their hearts and minds for a very long time, if immortality was a thing.

The steps up the plane beckoned, and Toni fled up them, hearing the last agent signaling they could close the door. He was local and would stay there.

"Everyone, buckle up. We have clearance and want to get out of here fast," Christopher spoke in his brisk authoritative way, and Toni was so exhausted from the emotions of the day that she didn't even bother to react. She made sure Jessi and Jamie were buckled in, while McKenna did the same for Nam and at least arched a brow a Charley, who had already buckled his.

Toni fretted the whole way home. Carina's death in some ways threw her off balance more than Jeff's had. She knew Jeff had a dangerous job as a police officer, and that was a risk. But Carina? She wanted to scream, wail, maybe kill someone. The danger was over. They had defeated the aliens, and she had gone to the fucking store.

Toni fought to wrestle her emotions down. The arrangements, dealing with the police, and consoling the kids had kept her busy and let her avoid her emotions for the last week. Now everything seemed to collapse on top of her.

~Mom?~ Toni opened her eyes and turned her head to look across the aisle at Jessi who looked back at her. The plane's engine began to rumble as they accelerated down the runway.

~Yeah?~ She managed to keep the mental tone neutral, maybe.

~I,~ Jessi broke off as Jamie elbowed her, his face peering around his sister to look at Toni. ~We love you.~

The random declaration of love had her fighting back tears. They'd been out of the lovey-dovey toddler phase for a while and had been in the I-don't-need-mom stage, being able to shift into animals had just made it worse. So this felt all the more precious for it being spontaneous.

~I love you both very much. Promise me to always be careful. Losing you, any of you, would kill me.~ Part of her expected the normal kid reaction of exasperation and embarrassment. But they both looked at her, green eyes serious.

~Yes, Mom. All of us. We've talked about it. We can't fight, we aren't big enough. We'll be good. But

Jamie and I want to learn portals. If we can do that, we could always be safe.~

~Huh?~ Her super intelligent response, linked with the look that must have been on her face had Jessi giggling. The sudden acceleration pushed her back into the seat giving her a minute to come up with a more coherent response. ~What do you mean by create portals? We aren't Drakyn.~ She didn't mention how much it called to her; she hadn't told anyone that.

~Jamie can feel them. All he's done is talk about them since we went through. Nam says you can too, but she and Charley don't feel portals, at least not like Jaime. He's been writing more math in his notebook.~ This time she dodged the elbow her brother threw her way. ~It's full of letters and squiggles and doesn't look like math, but he swears it is. But if we learn this, we would always be safe. Can we mom? Please?~

The mixture of begging and a whine made her smile. That at least was normal.

~Let me think about it. It isn't a no,~ she said quickly, before anymore wheedling could occur. ~But I need to talk to Rarz. There are things you don't know. Things I don't know if I'm ready to tell you.~

Jessi frowned at her and Jamie pinged with a curious sound.

~Just stay kids a bit longer, please?~ She begged, and was rewarded with a look of exasperation on Jessi's face, but they sat back and she could tell Jessi dove into conversation with the other kids.

Toni sat there as the plane leveled out, a thought pinging through her mind. ~Wefor?~ She was pretty sure she could talk to the AI without the others listening in, well Rarz might be able to, but she really didn't care if he did.

[Yes, Toni.]

~How old are my children? They are seven in Earth years. They should be worrying about toys and birthdays and squabbling over who is loved more. They respond and act like adults.~ She didn't bother to keep the stress out of her voice.

A feeling like a sigh brushed across her. [The shifting and bonding at an early age, added with the training that they were pulled into has aged them past what limited data suggested. Few children are infected, so the data had more holes in it than expected.]

The AI fell silent. ~Which means what? Wefor, what aren't you telling me?~

[From the development and logical processing of their language, reaction, and abstract concept comprehension they have exhibited, they are in their mid-teens. The scores for children between 12-14 are most accurate. Charley is a bit more advanced at 14-15, while Nam is still young, having been exposed for a much shorter time, but already she is pushing the 8-10 range in mental processes.]

The information didn't surprise her. Part of her wished it did. At the rate they were going by the time they were twelve they would be adults in everything except body and the odds were if they wanted to, they could get their bodies to mature faster. That thought gave her a sudden spurt of fear.

~They aren't going through puberty early, are they? That's traumatic enough, they don't need to do it now.~

Again a pause, which from the AI made her very nervous. [Not at this time. Their bodies are only aging at a slightly faster rate, though they are processing nutrients more effectively. While puberty could be rushed, the nanobots are programmed to avoid triggering any hormonal changes that are not beneficial. Currently their bodies are not ready for that surge. Another two to three years and the situation might change.]

While it didn't make her happy, she felt like she'd dodged the immediate bullet. She'd take what she could get.

~Okay, next question. Are they right? Can they learn to create portals? ~

The AI didn't respond for a few eternal seconds. [There is no reason they can't. But there is not enough information in the databases for me to answer that. Elao or the Drakyn may be a better choice for you on this topic.]

~Okay.~ But Toni didn't want to ask them. Not right now. They had another two hours or so in the air, and a nap sounded good. Anything to pretend for a while that their life was normal. And maybe visit a place with two moons in a lavender colored sky.

Chapter 14 - Consequences

Locals are up in arms as a resident of Baltimore has been charged manslaughter, and two others with accidental manslaughter, while the woman who attacked them faces no charges. The name of the dead woman is noted as Carina Watkins, and while she wasn't a Shifter, she was often seen in the presence of McKenna Largo. People are outraged that such blatant political weight is being brought to protect people that are why so many have died. ~Local Baltimore News

The landing and drive home held nothing unusual, outside of the strange remoteness from Rarz. But while Toni noted it, all of them were too tired, too full of grief to follow up on it. He hung outside talking to Christopher while everyone else headed in.

Toni had managed to change her clothes and had come back downstairs to figure out what they needed to do now. The urgency of the last few weeks had disappeared, and it felt odd to have free time; it felt wrong. The kids had changed, grabbed snacks and were outside, probably plotting world domination. At this point nothing they came up with would surprise her. She stopped.

~Wefor?~

[Yes, Toni?]

~If the kids start summoning or creating portals. Please let an adult know.~

[Ah, yes. That might be prudent. Monitoring for that will commence.]

She didn't even feel guilty, parental safety measures and all that. She found the others in the living room, looking as lost as she was. Rarz wasn't there, but she could vaguely hear him still outside talking to Christopher. McKenna looked up as she walked in.

"You doing okay?"

Toni shrugged. "Not insane, so I'll accept it as tolerable."

McKenna pulled her into a one-armed hug and Toni leaned there for a minute, enjoying it. Another bad part about the weirdness was the kids, much fewer child hugs. It sucked.

A phone rang and broke the silent, almost sad atmosphere. Everyone looked around as most of them didn't have their phones set to accept many calls. JD finally found his phone on the table by the door and frowned.

With everyone watching him, he answered it on speaker.

"Hey Anne. I've got you on speaker. Pretty much all the adults are here, but the kids are outside."

"Thanks." She sounded tired and something else. Something that had all of them leaning forward a little bit. "I just got the news today. Alisa and Sarah Buroky were killed two days ago in a mugging gone wrong. Their apartment was trashed and everything of value taken."

Toni frowned, the names didn't mean anything to her, but she looked up and saw JD had gone pale, circles almost appearing under his eyes as she watched.

"Any leads?" His voice came out as a harsh croak and Cass grabbed his hand, worry clear on her face.

"No. No leads, no clues, no witnesses. Even their surveillance system had been completely wiped and their phones were taken also."

"Anne, I'm sorry. I swear I never thought-"

"Stop it!" Her voice came out like a whip crack even if distorted through the speaker. "You didn't do this any more than you caused the aliens to attack. People are fucking idiots and all of this is just proving it more than usual." Both JD and McKenna flinched back, and Toni kept looking back and forth between them. Perc wrapped his arm around McKenna as they listened. "You have both been released from your contracts with the appropriate severance pay. All Shifters have been released and the department is adopting a very strict, don't ask, don't tell policy. The social media campaign to make Shifters the Nazis of the new age is working. I still don't know what you asked Alisa to do, but if she was silenced because of it, it is important. But..." Anne trailed off and the heavy sigh that followed made Toni hurt. "It might not matter. JD your home was completely trashed during the invasion or right after. McKenna I've kept up patrols by your house. Other than some graffiti you seem to be safe. For some reason that address was never entered into your HR records." A hint of smugness brought her to life for a minute, but then it faded.

"You both still have friends on the force, but the sheer amount of pressure to change how you think is damn overwhelming and with all the chaos going on, no one has time to think logically. You two are too recognizable and I don't know how to help that. But know what's going on out there. You can't think you'll be able to come back to your old lives. Those lives don't exist anymore." There was the sound of liquid pouring into a glass. "I don't know that I or Kirk can do much, or even anything, for you. But if you come back to Rossville, let us know. And guys?" There was a strange pause and everyone leaned forward slightly. "Thank you. I have a damn good idea of what you did for us, for the world. And that never happens without paying a price. So, thank you." Before anyone could say anything, Anne disconnected with a beep and the phone went quiet.

JD reached out a hand that shook slightly and picked up his phone, slipping it into his pocket. Cass took his hand as he settled back down.

Everyone just looked at each other, unsure of what to say or do. Toni knew she had no idea and was very glad that other than a few parents, almost no one knew she changed. Suddenly the rapid growth in her children might be a good thing. With the right ID they could pass as third graders, go to a new school and be in the same class as Charley. No one would connect kids that were years older with her.

Before she could go any further down that path the door opened and Rarz walked in. His presence seemed to break the odd tableau of silence. His look, though, had Toni standing up, not springing but standing and moving over to him.

"Is everything okay? You have a funny look on your face?"

"The emotion I am feeling is confusion. Does my expression reflect that?"

Toni looked at his face, the drawn brows, slight frown, and muted colors swirling in his eyes.

I guess I shouldn't tell him he looks constipated?

"Close enough."

"Ah. I must think on what Christopher relayed to me. The way your world does things is convoluted and makes little to no sense."

"Oh?" Cass perked up, looking at him and Toni could tell everyone would be interested in anything that distracted them from the little drama of their lives.

"Yes, tell us. Kinda nice to know everyone is as confused as we are." McKenna had a wry tone to her voice, but she waved to the chair next to where Toni had been sitting. Rarz moved through the area slowly, as if he was trying to make sure his tail didn't hit anything, even if he was in human form.

Settling his bulk into the chair, he closed his eyes. "Excuse me, I am trying to order my thoughts. The human approach to things makes little sense."

Toni wanted to laugh at that and could see McKenna and JD's lips twitching a little bit.

"The ship we landed."

Toni choked at that.

Landed? If that's what he calls landed, I'd hate to see crashed.

"It is a significant windfall of technology and science advancement, correct?" He looked around, as if to verify. Cass bobbed her head making Toni wonder how many papers she could write with what had been loaded into her brain. "Then why are they making all the information and the site itself a 'restricted military area' and preventing access to all but those people they have verified as allowed. Why are they not asking other nations, other scientists to come and learn what the Elentrin had in their databases? Why are they preventing the information from spreading? The Elentrin will come back. Should they not be doing everything possible to make sure when they return you have a way to defend your planet?"

There was a collective sigh and McKenna leaned back. "In one word: power. If they control the information, they have power. It's a power play to make the other countries come to them. They'll share eventually and build ships, but right now it's all about power and controlling the information."

"That makes no sense and wastes time you may not have." He didn't sound mad, just confused.

"Humans are not logical and never have been. Expecting it will just make it worse for you," Perc said, his tone wry. "But at the same time you'll be surprised as how fast they can move with the proper motivation, and trust me, right now humans are very, very, motivated."

Rarz nodded slowly. "If you say. But they are asking me to not use portals anymore, something I did not agree to. Portals are normal for me. I can not imagine not using them and they have no control over my actions." A flash of a smile on his face. "Though I do not think they understood my answer."

Toni grinned. "Something like, 'I understand your concern' but not that you're going to do it."

"Very similar, yes," Rarz said, nodding at her. "Though I think Christopher understood that I did not agree." He flexed his shoulders as if trying to stretch his wings.

FAMILY

They all fell silent until McKenna stood and started to pace. Toni wanted to smile as her friend did that. It was her signal she needed to think.

"Basically the government has cut us loose. Doug did say the house was paid up through the year, so we don't need to worry about it for a few more months. But they can't afford to be associated with us. They need to keep Rarz controlled and are locking down the biggest scientific treasure haul ever. The question is, what do we do now? Do we do anything? Or do we just do what everyone is telling us to do? Keep our heads down, pretend we aren't who we are?"

The questions fell like bodies into the silence. Full of weight and risk that they didn't know how to address.

"There is also the offer I made. Moving to one of the planets we have buildings on is still an option. Or even my home planet. I would be honored to show the Largo clan our worlds."

That took the breath away even more deeply than what McKenna had said and the area vibrated with possibilities.

A sound from downstairs pulled Toni's attention away and she shook her head. "Right now, I don't know. Moving to another world is a huge decision, one that would take months of planning. But those kids are going to need food and I need to spend more time with them. For now I'm going to make dinner for everyone and try to pretend this isn't a form of a prison camp, one formed by other people. I'm starting to think they aren't protecting us as much as trying to make sure we don't get hurt on their watch and they get blamed for it. I need to think and decide what I want to do, and what's best for my kids. They are my priority. My family comes first."

Toni turned away in the sudden silence, wanting to focus on something that could be accomplished. Dinner she could handle. More life-altering decisions made her want to run away.

She didn't turn back at the murmured conversation behind her, nor did she even try to listen in. Losing herself in the mundane and feeling the loss of Carina sharply across her soul, she tried to be a normal mom with a house full of people.

For days after the funeral, Rarz looked concerned and spent much of his time with people in DC, though never in his warrior form. He didn't say much about it, and they didn't ask. But the concerns Blair had brought to them came into sharp relief for all of them. They rarely left the house alone and all of them were even more wary as their faces were known. Toni once again felt like a prisoner and just wanted to go home.

Someday everything will go back to normal, right?

Chapter 15 - Home?

China has reopened its borders for the first time since the attack. The US is sending an aid mission to assess the damage. While it is not known who among China's leadership survived, there are rumors of a new purge going on. Anyone with prior positive comments about Shifters or the aliens has not been seen since. The current leader, a man referred to as Jin Lau Zhou, is a newcomer on the political scene. The last violent upheaval to China resulted in the communist rule. Everyone is watching to see where China goes now, and the existence of aliens that resemble some of their most revered mythical creatures remains to be seen. ~TNN Aftermath

In the days that followed the funeral and the surprise attack by reporters, Toni focused more on the children, all four of them, than anyone else. The children were quiet and depressed, missing the woman that had been such a fixture in their lives. Nam was affected the least of all of them, but even she seemed to pick up on the sorrow. But in a very real way she was the one that provided the greatest amount of comfort. Nam cuddled with all of them, and when in tiger form, only in the privacy of the house, she draped across whichever child had the bleakest look and soon enough they were petting her orange fur.

Toni couldn't shake the grief, anger, and guilt as easily. Every time she turned around looking for Carina a new wave of emotions would hit her and make her long for the ease of being drunk, or screaming, or something. Instead, she tamped it down and tried to keep busy, which wasn't easy.

She felt the worried glances the others sent her way, but she didn't care. She was done with all of this. Being a political pawn had been annoying from the start, now it ate at her. The idea of a new world called to her, but for now she wanted her bed, her home. With the government not needing their assistance, her world had narrowed even further. After the incident involving Carina, none of them were willing to leave the house alone, not even to go to the park which increased her discontent with everything.

Standing in her bedroom after a shower, Toni glared at her clothes. She'd worn everything they'd packed in that rush to get out of there at least ten times. She had come to dread getting dressed. She'd never been a clothes horse, but she'd enjoyed variety. At this point she'd worn everything too many times to count and she hated every item of clothing at this point. Add in the fact that it had started to cool down which meant the shorts she had grabbed from California were not as warm as she would have preferred. Besides, Maryland got colder sooner than California did. There were stains on half her shirts, and most of what she owned still hung on her. The need to go shopping and get new clothes that fit called to her also, but she didn't want to be in public, around strangers. She was still putting on weight, but since none of them were gorging, it was taking a while. The only ones that shifted regularly were the kids. You never knew what form they would be in at any given point. Half the time they even slept in animal forms, in a cuddled pile of adorableness.

Everything ate at her and while she knew the others were talking over options, she avoided it. The idea of another world wasn't anything she was ready to talk about, despite dreams and long buried desires. Exposing that part of herself felt too raw, too vulnerable. She hurt enough right now.

In an effort to keep herself busy, plus the fact that the two couples were enough to make her crazy with their cuteness, she'd taken over most of the cooking. It gave her something to do and juggling enough food for five adults, four kids, and Rarz required her attention and frequent grocery delivery.

On a normal night, food prep and cooking were something she did with grace. That night everything went wrong in the kitchen. The rice boiled over, the oven was set to broil instead of bake, the vegetables had rotted, and she dropped the bowl of chili on the way to the table. Everyone pitched in to help mitigate the disaster, but the cascade of stupid, small, petty disasters broke her ability to stay quiet and deal. "When can we go home?" she asked in the middle of the meal. All conversation froze as everyone looked at her. "What? We're trapped here as their token, controlled Shifters. They don't need us anymore; they don't want us. Hell, I won't go back even if they beg. Too many people know we're here and I'm ready to go home. They have even reduced Rarz to phone calls, scared of him being seen with them. I don't want to be here anymore." Toni struggled to not whine, to keep it as logical statements, but her voice trembled.

I want to go home. Is that so much to ask?

"We have the money. So I guess anytime. Though we probably can't expect the government to pay our way back and airfare is still expensive right now." McKenna said, a thoughtful tone to her voice.

"Is there a reason Rarz can't port us back? He never agreed to quit porting, regardless of what they think." Toni didn't know how or why Rarz seemed to have moved in, but he had. Slowly mimicking their habits. He'd taken Cass's room when she had moved in with JD. How he fit in, she wasn't sure, but he had become a part of them in the last week without her ever making the conscious decision to include him. But since the day Carina died, he'd just been there. Part of their odd little group. A part she'd come to depend on.

"If you can show me the location, I can take you there." His voice soft but again that undertone of power. "Though are you sure that is where you want to go?"

"Well, I have no desire to stay here. We did what we set out to do. The immediate threat is over. I can't fight what the world thinks of me. I'm tired of the clothes I'm wearing. I'm tired of so many people. I'm tired of strange beds. I'm just tired. I want to go home." Toni was horrified to realize she was close to tears and slammed her eyes shut and focused on breathing. She felt a hand take hers and squeeze. She didn't have to look to know who held her hand. Cass was always the one with her heart on her sleeve and the more precious for it.

When she felt like she wouldn't break down into tears Toni opened her eyes and looked at everyone.

The others looked like they agreed with her general sentiments, if not the almost tears.

"Toni's right. It's time to go home. Rarz, if they still need us occasionally are you willing to port us back here? Though from the last conversation with Burby that would surprise me." McKenna asked, but she didn't look as happy about the idea as Toni expected.

"Of course. But you did not answer my question. Are you sure your home is where you want to go?"

At this point all of them looked at him, a bit confused. After glancing at each other McKenna broke the odd pall. "Where else would we go?"

Rarz smiled, showing off teeth that weren't quite human. "My world? Other worlds? Remember we have entire worlds that need to be more populated. Or others with no population at all that could be colonized. I have informed your leaders that the negative reactions being fostered in your media has dissuaded many of my people from having any desire to come here. The latest rise in violence is very concerning. But there are many who would welcome new colonists or even just visitors. But we need people on these worlds before all the infrastructure created falls into pieces."

Toni felt her mental world view realign. Even his previous comments hadn't really registered as more than a joke. But Rarz didn't joke, not like that.

"Wait. While you've talked about it, you can't mean just walk out the door and move into another world. Just settle like that. It would take time and planning. We can't just say okay and go to another planet like the way you would visit another city."

Visit the planet with two moons? See the purple sky for myself?

She didn't know why it had never occurred to her. Why she hadn't asked to go there. To let the kids see it.

"Why not? You came here with as little planning?" He sounded so calm and reasonable, it terrified her. It couldn't be that easy.

"We could see many dragons?" Nam asked leaning against Jamie a bit, her eyes wide.

"Yes. In all the colors of your rainbows. They would delight in nestlings. So many of ours have been killed."

An aura of hope and wonder sprung up around the table, but before anyone could say anything Toni interjected.

"Not yet. We need to go home and see if we even have lives anymore. JD might be able to salvage something from his damaged house. None of us have jobs, but we still have responsibilities, things we need to do. The money the government gave us will last for a while. But for right now I want to go home. Sleep in my own bed and see what life can be. See how bad it is before we run away from our world." She didn't voice her fears or concerns or how very much the idea tempted her. If she had been single, no kids, her answer might have been different, but right now she needed familiar places.

"Toni has a point. I need to see if my house is standing," Perc said, his voice thoughtful. "Talk to my friends and parents. I don't know if I could just walk away from them."

"Helena and the kids are clamoring to see me," Cass spoke and reached out to touch JD. "Well, us.

Yes, I think we need to go home first," she finished looking at them. "Then decide. If nothing else, maybe a mini vacation in a few weeks. Exotic travel? Strange new places?"

Toni would have sworn Rarz looked disappointed, but he only shrugged and went back to eating. Everyone pitched in to do dishes after dinner, then drifted to their own things when done. Toni stood in the kitchen, looking out at the backyard of a place that wasn't hers. Driven by fear, constant change, and the ache for purple skies, the rest of her patience snapped. ~Kids pack up. Grab your clothes, we're sleeping in our beds tonight.~

~You sure?~ McKenna asked. Toni could hear the worry in her voice, but she needed to get away, to have some space, to figure out what to do. She'd been so pulled with the tide of events, now she needed to think, away from everyone.

~Yes, I need out of here before I lose it. Everywhere I look I see Carina. I don't know if home will be any better, but it can't be any worse and I need to go through all her stuff too. Send stuff to her parents~

~Understood. We'll pack tomorrow. You go. Let me know if you need anything.~

Toni turned and just like she'd known he would be, Rarz stood there looking at her. "Can you open a portal to my home? Please?"

For a heartbeat she thought he might refuse, but his head tilted looking at her. "Find it. Picture it in your mind. Feel it."

She did. Home. The house she and Jeff bought. Where her kids had lived. Where they had all lived. She knew every wall and wanted to be there.

The familiar swirl of portal energy tugged at her senses and she opened her eyes, not remembering when she'd closed them, to see the portal standing there next to her.

"We should go through first to make sure it is the right place. I will keep it open." Toni took one minute to grab her purse, everything else she would have at home.

She nodded at him and he stepped through. One breath later she followed. The portal tugged and pulled, and she almost reached for it. She craved to play with the energies that flirted at the corners of her mind, but a whiff of warm air caught her attention and she stepped out into the California sun. The golden light, somehow warmer than in Baltimore caressed everything. The familiar smells, the sight of the Sierras, the warm breeze wrapped around her, pulling her into her home.

Toni tilted her head up, eyes closed, feeling the caress of sun on her face and a tiny part of her soul un-knotted.

Home. I'm home.

She opened her eyes and doubt slithered in.

But for how long. Or is it really home anymore?

Chapter 16 - Grass is Greener

Rumblings in the highest levels of the government are talking about committees to address the status of Shifters in our society. China has already stated that from henceforth Shifters have a "less than zero status" and will be ejected from their country if found. This turnabout doesn't surprise many. China has always been moderately xenophobic as most Oriental cultures have been historically. Given the devastation the invasion had on both their leadership and their infrastructure, it is almost expected. If you are a Shifter you should avoid the orient for the foreseeable future. Though given current social view of Shifters, traveling as an "out" Shifter is asking for trouble.
~TNN World News

Toni didn't know how long she stood there before she shook herself and turned to look at the swirling oval. ~Jessi, Jamie, come on. The house is here.~

They didn't say anything, but she could feel the ripple of resentment as they trudged out of the portal. Even though Jamie looked back at the opening, his eyes narrowed, neither of them seemed excited at all.

Toni resisted the urge to scream. ~Rarz, close the portal. We'll be fine,~ she replied mentally as she looked at her house. The front lawn needed mowing desperately, which meant the back yard was worse. Somehow the entire house just looked sadder than when she'd left.

~Are you sure? I could come with you.~ He offered, and she felt an odd note of hope in his tone. She pushed it aside, entertaining the alien was not her job.

~Nope. We're good. This is just family stuff.~ She replied distracted by the weeds growing up in her driveway and a cracked windowpane in the front window. At least her garbage cans had been in the garage where her car should be.

~Ah. Very well then. You may call if you need.~

~Will do,~ she responded. She wasn't paying much attention to Rarz or his responses, too filled with relief and worry about being home. A mixed sense of dread and excitement filled her as she unlocked the house. The kids lingering behind her, their very silence evidence of pouting.

As she pushed the door open, a whiff of warm stale air escaped along with the smell of rotting food.

"Crap," she muttered. "Must have lost power while we were gone. Things went bad." She sighed but walked in, heading for the back door to open it and air the house out. The twins followed her, making every step seem like they were fighting against gravity.

"I don't want to stay here. Can we go back to the others? I want Charley," Jessi whined. Toni didn't have to turn around to know Jamie was nodding with his sister, the same pouting look on this face.

"No. This is our home and first thing we are doing to do is get it cleaned up. So go. Put your bags in your bedroom. Then get trash cans and trash bags. You get to help me clean out all the rotting food."

"But Mom—" Jessi broke off when Toni turned and gave her daughter an uncompromising look.

"This is not up for debate. You will do as I said, and I do not want to hear another word about it." Her voice hard and cold. They both sagged and trudged into their bedrooms.

You'd think I'd said they could never see them again. Not like I don't know they are chattering away in their minds right now. I just want to spend some time as just us. As just my family.

Even with the kids sulking and moving as slowly as they could, in three hours she had the expired and rotted food in the garbage cans and sitting on the curb, a load of laundry going, and clean unworn clothes on all of them. Jessi wore a newish shirt and seemed a bit happier with clothes she hadn't worn for the last month. They'd only taken about a week of clothes with them, so wearing something 'new' felt wonderful. Jamie had grabbed a book he had not packed and apparently not read.

While their resentment still lingered, at least they seemed a bit happier with familiar things around them.

"What do you say to Chinese delivery and a movie tonight? Then sleep in our own beds? We've got a busy day tomorrow." She offered, knowing they had a weakness for the nearby delivery place.

The two exchanged looks, shoulders sagged, as they replied," Sure, Mom."

I am not torturing them! I just want time, alone time, with my kids.

Fighting back anger, frustration, and to her surprise tears, Toni ordered their favorites and pulled up the streaming service. "Want to see what's new that you want to see?" She handed them the remote and went to change into comfy cuddle clothes. When she came back out, they had decided, something animated from Pixar. Either way, there were no dragons or aliens in it, so she approved of their choice. It wouldn't cause memories or questions, she hoped.

They curled up, watched the movie, ate Chinese food, and for an hour Toni felt like her world had almost gone back to normal. This felt familiar, safe, though she missed the feeling of Carina. Often she'd be gone on the weekends, so for now she could pretend.

"That was fun. Tomorrow we need to go through Carina's stuff and start shipping things and packing up the rest. Is there anything you want to keep?" She hated making them go through the process this fast, but her loved ones had already waited too long.

"Maybe. But tomorrow we get to go back to Charley and Nam, right? We stay tonight here and go back tomorrow?" The tension in Jessi's face created a ripple of worry through Toni.

"No. We have stuff to do here. You can talk to them, but you don't need to see them every day. In a few days maybe."

Jessi's lower lip began to quiver, and Toni watched in surprise. Unsure if her stoic, stubborn daughter was about to cry or throw a tantrum. Jamie reached out and touched her arm. Nothing else. The quivering stopped and Jessi just turned and walked into her room, closing the door quietly.

Jamie didn't say a word, just followed and did the same thing. Of everything, it was the silent door closing that freaked Toni out the most. She cleaned up the dishes, needing to occupy her thoughts. She checked on the kids, but if they were awake, they were faking sleep really well. It struck her as odd to see them in a bed by themselves.

Toni chased sleep, feeling like she was making a huge mistake but she couldn't figure out where she'd gone wrong.

The next morning the twins were up waiting for her, again overly silent in a way that reminded her too much of their animal natures. In an odd way she almost wished they would throw a tantrum, that at least she knew how to deal with. There wasn't much to cook with, but with dried milk and pancake mix she managed to get them something to eat. They would have to go shopping today if they didn't want to live on canned foods.

With a bit of chivying, threats, and muttered curses, they went to work on Carina's room. She pretended not to see the twin's tears after the first time she tried to hug them and they pulled away, and they didn't comment on hers. She found the Bible, and Carina's confirmation jewelry. She created that box with a few other objects she knew the Watkins would want. The kids each took something small, Jessi a plush monster Carina had kept on her desk and Jamie took her book of photos from the Hubble space telescope.

None of them talked much, though the sulking and slow movements drove her crazy. Toni knew they were talking to the other kids, but she enjoyed the relative silence as they packed up the proof

Carina had existed. Her friends had texted things they wanted, and she had boxes for everything. Her packrat preparation tendencies had made her break down all the boxes from when they had moved in. By noon they were done. A stack of roughly a dozen boxes sat waiting to be mailed and all of them were hungry. The grumbling stomachs reinforced that.

"I'm going to go see if the car starts. Then we're going to drop these off, get lunch and go shopping." She gave them a stern mom look, which felt odd. Lately, with the other two kids around, they were almost never poorly behaved. Today had been the worst in months if not years.

"Can Nam and Charley come now?" Jamie asked, and it took all her control to not yell.

"No. This is our time. They're with McKenna and the others. I just wanted to enjoy some us time. Okay?" She fought to not let her frustration and jealousy leak through.

Seriously, how the hell I am jealous about how much they'd rather be with others?

They sagged again but nodded. To her relief, the car started, but the red fuel light made gas her first stop. With the kids buckled into their booster seats, the ones in Baltimore had been new, she pulled out, headed into Rossville. She drove slowly, wanting a chance to look around, to see what might have changed. Traffic was light compared to what it might have been a month ago, but busier than she'd seen it during the invasion. It felt good to see the familiar landmarks, stores that she knew, and the smells of the area. Though as she filled up the car, she admitted she hadn't missed the higher gas prices.

"Okay kids, what're you hungry for?"

FAMILY

There was shifting in the seats and she saw them looking at each other for a minute, then Jessi declared, "Pizza." A choice that surprised Toni not at all. Though she wasn't up to a kid pizza place. After filling up and a quick stop at the post office where they did help her bring in all the packages, she headed for lunch. She took them to Rico's, a small mom and pop shop where she usually got takeout. As far as she was concerned it was the best pizza in the area.

As she drove through Rossville to the strip mall, she watched and felt a coat of despair paint across her soul. At least two billboards advertised 'anti-Shifter' stances, one religious, one a gym. As they pulled into the parking lot, she took time to look around. It seemed safe and sane, but that didn't mean much. Oh well, Raley's was two stores down, so they could just go there for grocery shopping. She just wanted enough for a day or two. And some staples.

After letting the twins out, who had unbuckled as soon as she stopped, they headed over to Rico's. One of the other stores, a nail parlor, had a 'No Shifters' allowed sign in the window. The next had a sign that made her cringe – 'Dead due to Shifter aliens'.

To her relief, Rico's was open and they were ushered to a table. The kids, predictably, wanted pepperoni, and she could live with that. They put in for a large, feeling hungry and the weight loss making her clothes still hang on her.

The news was playing on mute, but she caught glances of the captioning, and nothing it talked about made her feel better. More riots, people being attacked for being Shifters, and too many cops looking the other way. While America hadn't been hit as hard as other countries, just about everyone had lost someone they loved, one way or another.

The pizza arrived, and the kids dove in, but were still abnormally quiet. She knew they were chattering away with the others, cutting her out of their world.

Do I even want to know what they talk about all the time? And this is supposed to be family time, why aren't they spending it with me?

Parental guilt swept in as everything they had dealt with over the last few months flashed through her mind. With a groan of defeat, she pinged McKenna. ~I'm being an idiot, aren't I?~ She sent to McKenna privately, though who knows what that meant with Rarz.

McKenna didn't even ask what she meant. ~No. You're being a mom. You're stressed and worried. Home feels safer than a strange place. The kids, well, they are something I don't think anyone knows how to handle. And yes, my two are just as mopey as yours I bet.~

~I'll give in by tomorrow you know.~

The sound and taste of bubblegum filled the mindspace. ~Trust me, they have both asked at least ten times already if they can go 'visit' and they haven't been happy with my answers. By tomorrow I might be begging you. But take tonight. Be a family.~

The last words left Toni with a sense of disquiet. That was what she wanted right?

"You guys ready to go get some groceries?"

"Okay." Their lackluster response had her fighting frustration again. She dropped cash on the table, and they headed out. Even though no one said anything, she felt exposed and vulnerable. Was it the last few weeks of always having a weapon nearby, or something else?

Shopping wasn't quite the chore she had been dreading. The kids seemed eager to get it done and home, which made her suspicious as all get out. But she accepted their help and headed home with ice cream for them and a bottle of wine for her.

Chapter 17 - Complications

The stock markets are scheduled to reopen next week for the first time since the end of the conflict. No one is sure where it will head, and the commissioners have said they will be watching carefully and close it if there are any big fluctuations. The Tokyo and London exchanges are set to open two days later. Everyone is expecting science and tech stocks to soar, but since no one knows for sure what information has been acquired from the downed ships it is still an open question as to what the new plans will be for the future. Are we going to the stars or just protecting ourselves? ~TNN Talking Head

Pulling into the driveway her mental hackles went on full alert. There were two cars parked on the street by her house. As she parked, the car doors opened and people started to get out. She almost slammed the car into reverse when she recognized all of them. They were parents of the other kids that had been captured that day at the zoo. The day she still had nightmares about.

"Here's the keys. You two go on in. Each of you take one bag. And not the one with the eggs." She instructed as they waved to the parents. Curiosity flashed across the kids' faces but they didn't argue with her, grabbing bags as she walked over to the adults.

"You're back. We'd hoped so when we saw the garbage cans out." Sarah Johan blurted, while her husband Walter climbed out of the driver's side of their car. A pretty woman, with blond hair and brown eyes, but stress had added more than a few lines to her face. Walter's hair seemed lighter somehow, more gray? They all communicated after the kidnapping, her and the other parents, even those whose kids had not been on the bus. Charley's had never bothered, and the Bara's had been copied on the emails but never responded or shown for the occasional lunch or coffee. It had given her a bit of social outlet that week of hell when JD was at work. After the kids got back, the emails had kept up. Not often, once or twice a week, mostly parental bitches and the sporadic panic attack.

"You've been stalking me?" Toni said half joking, half not. She'd barely been home more than a day and people were already here. It pointed to people paying attention to her, and that wasn't a good thing.

"Yes, no, maybe?" Sorrel the father of Eliah said. His son had not been on the bus, but he understood terror. His skin was so dark it almost looked blue. A refugee from Nairobi, he'd been more aware of this sort of terroristic behavior. Where even then he'd been positive and reassured, now he looked tired and worried too. "We knew you left, but no one seemed to know where. You weren't responding to emails, so I made it a point to drive by on my way to work to see if there was any sign of life here."

Toni glanced over at her kids who, while they were headed to the door, were doing it a glacial pace as they watched the adults. She knew damn well they were relaying everything to the others, maybe even the adults. As if in answer to her thoughts McKenna piped in her mind.

~Toni? Everything okay?~

~You know, I'm supposed to be their mother not the other way around. Yeah, I'm fine. I'll yell if I think it's anything major.~

~We can be there in seconds.~ McKenna didn't say anything else but the wave of love and worry flashed across the connection.

~I know. And thanks. But this doesn't feel dangerous, just worrisome.~ Toni pushed her attention back to the three stressed adults looking at her.

"Yeah. I got pulled out of town." Toni paused and then shook her head. Paranoia was catching. "Come on in. I don't have much but I can make some lemonade." That much she'd managed to buy since even in animal form they liked the lemonade.

"Thanks." The three adults said as one. They helped with the rest of the groceries as she went into the house. Stress bled off a bit as they stepped in and shut doors behind them.

"Go take a seat, I'll be out in a minute. You two," she directed at the kids. "Play outside or in your rooms. Your call. And the answer is no before you even ask."

Jessi pouted but Jamie dragged out the book he'd been packing around and headed to his room. Jessi followed and Toni had no doubt she was ranting about the mean cruel mom.

A few minutes later, with four glasses of lemonade she joined her unexpected guests in the living room, handing out the drinks.

"Not that I'm upset to see you, it's just unexpected. Sorry I've been out of reach for a while but what's prompted all this?"

They exchanged looks she couldn't interpret, and that didn't provide any balm to her stress.

"You haven't been around people much have you lately? People that know you're a Shifter?" Sarah asked. Her hand wrapped around her husband's, and their knuckles were both so tight they showed white.

"Well, yeah. I mean I've been with my friends. And we are all Shifters. But if you mean out in public. Only in really controlled situations. What am I missing?"

Sarah started to shake and Walter pulled her tight and wrapped his arm around her. "Jalmer shifts, as do I, and most of our neighbors know. They've started burning effigies of animals in our yard. Our house has been egged with eggs and other worse things at least three times since the invasion ended. Sarah was told her position had been eliminated three days ago." His voice cracked. "They haven't started school back yet, but already meetings are being held to have shifting at school be punished by expulsion."

Toni looked at him, eyes wide, and worry sank even deeper claws into her.

Sorrel nodded. "Plus, they are talking about restricting children that shift to special classes. More and more people are flat out refusing to deal with anyone that is a known Shifter. Fear is rampant and people are lashing out." His excellent English had the slightest lilt that spoke of another language, but his gaze was steady and desperate.

"And the others?" Toni meant the other parents and knew they understood.

"They are just as scared, at least the ones that are talking to us. The Bara's daughter hasn't been seen in weeks and they won't talk about her. Morvoz decided to move. Said they were going back to Russia. They had family where no one would know they could shift." Sorrel shrugged. "That isn't an option for me."

Toni looked at them one at a time, searching and didn't like what she saw. Fear, desperation, and a fatality that terrified her. Memories of her father talking about things they'd escaped from in Peru flashed through her mind. The tide was turning so fast and they were making Shifters the guilty in this whole scenario, when they were the victims.

I hadn't wanted Blair to be right. But if this keeps up, will they even try to reunite the people taken? Will they want to go back when many of them have lost their entire families for the honor of being captured?

"Okay. What do you want me to do?" She could hear the kids in their rooms, barely, more because Jessi was never still and her feet kicked against the wall.

This time they didn't look at each other, they looked at the ground, their hands shaking. Sorrel was the one that looked up first. "You're friends with McKenna Largo, the cop, the one on TV. The one that warned us, showed us how to change. The one that saved the kids. Your kids."

She didn't know if his words were statements or questions. Maybe he didn't know. "Yes. She was who I've been with. Who I've... we've been helping."

FAMILY

What the hell do I say? That I'm one of the ones that boarded an alien ship and helped it crash?

"Is there a way? Something we can do? Can we become not Shifters?" Sarah asked and her husband growled and looked away. "What? I don't know what to do? How to help. My husband and son are being called monsters and I'm terrified my son may break under the strain. Non-Shifter kids won't play with him anymore. He cries all the time. I will do anything to protect my family." The last words were said with a ferocity that Toni understood.

Toni looked over at Sorrel who shrugged. "I left my country for a chance at a better life. I would move the world for my son."

Rarz's offer floated through her mind. Could this be the answer?

Do we run? Is it running away when you flee persecution? Isn't that how this country was founded? But to just walk away from everything?

Toni looked at Sorrel and fear and hope in equal parts washed through her. She needed something stronger and got up and came back with whiskey and glasses. She poured a generous splash in each and took a hefty swallow. She didn't care if they drank or not. Sarah reached out and sipped it, nose wrinkling but she looked steadier as they sat there.

"There is something. I had shoved it away as not feasible. But do you really think it is that bad?" She poked at it knowing it was a sore spot, something she'd avoided with their situation, but now she needed to face it fully.

Sarah just kept her hands wrapped around the whiskey, with Walter holding her close. Sorrel was the one that responded.

"I have seen this sort of thing before. Talking to other refugees. It has all the hallmarks of the starting of genocide. Fear is rampant and if this keeps up, they will try to kill us all. Maybe not in every country, but too many people see us as someone to blame. And there isn't anyone else."

Well, there are the damn Elentrin.

Her thought was sour as she took another gulp. But they hadn't been seen in public and there was the very real fact that it was hard to hate beautiful people. A weird thing about the human psyche. And Thelia could manipulate anyone to do anything.

"Would you leave everything behind? Friends, family, your life? You willing to start over from scratch?"

Sorrel just shrugged, his movement easy. Instead Toni focused on Sarah and Walter.

Sarah ducked her head as Walter lifted his head and met her stare. "Toni. If something doesn't change, I'll lose those things anyhow. Either to death or terror. If we stay, with it going as it is now, we will have nothing left to lose. It will have been taken from us."

"Sarah?" Toni asked, needing answers.

"I think if I'm willing to die to save my husband and my son, walking away from my home that is fast becoming my prison seems like an easy thing to do."

The words echoing what she had thought not so long ago caused shivers to run icy legs up her spine.

"Give me some time. I might have an option but be aware, I don't know what the cost will be."

"Will we be alive, unpersecuted, and have a chance at a life?" Sorrel asked, his face serious.

"I think so," Toni said trying not to lie. "But I can't swear."

"Then it is more than we have now." Sorrel's voice had faith in it, a faith that scared Toni half to death.

Can I live up to that faith, or is what Rarz offers worse than what we are running from?

Chapter 18 - Path Less Traveled

The much maligned policy of "Don't Ask, Don't Tell" of the 80s and 90s is back in full force. Reports of people getting new identifications and moving if they were known as Shifters is growing. No one wants to be seen as one of them. The brush that is painting tar over anyone presenting Shifters in a positive light is sticky and almost unavoidable. A new wave is sweeping the world, not just the US. Being a known Shifter, while not a death sentence, might make you worse than a sexual predator. No one wants you around. Not jobs, businesses, schools, or even those that you thought were friends. A brave new world, indeed. ~TNN Talking Head

Toni sent the parents on their way and sat in the living room staring at nothing. Her phone lay in her hands open to social media. She'd been researching and what she saw backed up everything they had said. What would she do to protect her children? What would it be like to grow up in a world that hated you? It would make the Jim Crow era seem kind. This wasn't regional from what she had seen, but global. Already lynchings were happening. Everywhere except a few areas where Shifters seemed to be the majority, the tide had turned sharply. There were even vague rumors of holding them civilly liable for the damage done across the world.

The asteroids had devastated areas. In many ways the US had gotten off lightly but China was in ruins. Images of remaining Shifters were shown lying dead on the streets, with no one even willing to deal with the bodies. How could it have changed so fast?

She glanced back down at her current viral image. A televangelist had been killed by a crazed hyena Shifter. His widow was talking about how Shifters were all animals and should be shot in the streets like rabid animals. The media and world lapped it up, already talking about new restrictions. Hell, from what she saw the US was being more measured than other countries. Australia literally had lost more than half of their population and the remaining half was too busy trying to survive. No one knew the long-term damage the tidal wave that hit that country had caused. The water went inland over thirty miles, leaving salt, dying fishing, and other things behind when it finally receded.

Crying wouldn't change anything. Toni looked around her home and the things in it. The memories. She hadn't been able to even go into Carina's area of the house. Did she have anything here? Anything to fight for?

Family.

The word vibrated and she closed her eyes thinking about family.

I'm a fucking idiot. Family is all that matters. Jessi and Jamie are my family. So was Carina. And so are Kenna, Perc, JD, Cass. They are my family. So what if I lose everything else? If I have them, I'll have the support I need to start again. They will never leave me. So why the hell am I sitting here in this house that is just things with my kids unhappy and my family missing all of us?

She wanted to laugh and cry and scream. Some days she really had tunnel vision.

~Interested in having us back for dinner?~

~Yes,~ the word was instant and from multiple people. ~We've missed you.~ She felt it then, what they had been trying to not push on her. Their love, their need of her in their lives, and mostly that they would always be there for her.

I am such a fucking moron. I need to learn to lean on people. Some of them will support you.

Lessons learned at Jeff's death had scarred her worse than she realized. Time to let the past go in more ways than one. ~Yeah. I'm a bit stubborn sometimes. I need to talk to Rarz, well, to all of you. Can he come get us?~

~I shall be there in a few minutes.~

~We'll be outside in about ten. Let us pack up first.~

Toni rose, feeling lighter already. "Guys, wanna go have dinner with Charley and Nam?"

"YES!" The shouted words and scrambling bodies as they rushed over to where she stood in the door.

The smile crossed her face and her heart. "Get packed. New clothes and put away the stuff I washed. Don't get too much. We can come back if we need to get more."

They didn't even respond, just grabbed their bags and stuffed things in it. Toni followed their example and went to get her own bag ready. She stood there in her room for a long time and realized there was maybe one big box of random items, memories, things, she would want to take. The rest? She gave a sad laugh and walked out. The rest had never mattered after all.

Together they left the house, locking up behind them. Rarz stood there, a silver portal behind him. She was glad she lived in a quiet area, but at the same time she didn't care. Portals, dragons, aliens? Anymore it just said home to her. The kids all but sprinted to the portal, running through it without a moment of hesitation. Toni aimed for a bit more decorum.

"Thank you, Rarz. We need to talk about your offer. Is it still on the table?"

Rarz tilted his head looking at her. "It is a serious and still viable offer if that is what you mean."

She laughed a bit. "Yes. Thank you." Toni patted his arm and walked through the portal and into the back yard of the house. The energies still pulled at her, but for now she ignored them though the possibilities of it being something she could do someday seemed less like a dream than it once had.

McKenna met her at the back door, an easy smile on her face. "How silly is it? You weren't even gone sixteen hours and it felt like there was a hole here."

Toni walked into her arms, enjoying the hug. "I know exactly what you mean. I'm not sure why I thought I needed to be with my family. That is where I am now."

McKenna squeezed her tighter before stepping back. "You're family, Toni. One way or another you are one of us. And nothing is going to change that."

The hugs she got from Cass and JD cemented that. Perc just gave her a smile that warmed her to her soul. She would have been happy to settle back into the easy comfort of this group of people but the reason she'd come back didn't change anything.

"We need to talk and the star of the show is going to be Rarz." They all gave her looks but no one said anything as they settled into the living room. She explained everything she'd been told and what she'd seen on the news. As she talked, Cass and Perc both pulled out phones and started to look, their faces growing dark.

After everything had been explained, Toni turned to Rarz. "So what do you or your people actually want? I mean some people may be able to build houses or settle worlds. But most, I think, are just going to be people like me. I'm not opposed to learning, but we grew up on tales of how our country was settled. I don't know if most of us would be able to do that level of deprivation or even have the skill sets to survive. I don't want to take them from one dangerous situation into another. Hell, I don't even know how we'd get the word out, without creating an even bigger problem."

McKenna, her eyes narrowed in concentration, spoke—each word slow and careful as if walking about a bomb. "I have a few ideas about that, but we may need some people to be the forerunners. They would be the ones that go there first, before we start creating a method to tell people. And remember, we have people all over the world we'll need to get the word to and get them from where they are to where they need to go." She looked at Rarz. "Toni is right, you need to tell us what you want or need from us."

Rarz looked around at them, his brows furrowed. "There may be a misunderstanding. While there are some worlds we know of that are untouched and would support life, your life. Most of our planets were ones we colonized with our methods, but the Elentrin came and killed many of our people. We abandoned our cities, leaving them there empty. But if you will work with us and help us fight if they come back, we want to build worlds with you."

Perc leaned forward his eyes sharp. "We? Your people? We've only seen you. Can you really speak so certainly about your people wanting this?"

Rarz tilted his head. "They have listened. They have seen. While some of the actions of Earthlings have distressed and concerned some, the consensus is that you are excellent partners. Many are anxious to meet you, but have not wanted to overwhelm you. Your world is going through significant social upheavals right now and the concern is that their presence may make it worse."

They all looked at him, but what he said clicked for Toni. "Wait. They see and hear everything you do? Like we share our interactions?"

"Of course. Why would I be here if I could not share what options I have and what I see?"

"Umm, how many are seeing and hearing this?" Cass asked slowly. The rest of them were understanding what it meant, kinda like being on video all the time.

"It is available to all, but only a few thousand actively monitor my actions. The rest take notes and then go to work on their own paths."

"Thousands?" Toni fought back a wave of nausea. She needed to be more sympathetic to McKenna next time. "What do they think?"

Rarz closed his eyes his head tilted a bit, and Toni choked back a gasp. "They are talking to you, giving you advice? How do you deal with it? If more than three or four of us talk at once I can't process it." McKenna nodded her agreement.

His eyes opened and the colors swirled at them, darker than normal. "It is not that bad. While I am sharing everything, only a few people can talk back to me and only because they are my superiors. It is not like I have all my sibs' nestlings chattering at me non-stop. The mindspace you use is similar but while everyone can hear and see, only a few can talk to me in it. Mostly warriors use it to store our logs so our people can see what happened. It is one of the tests for being a warrior, along with the mass transfer and storage."

Everyone relaxed a bit. Basically he was a live media stream people could see and hear, but only admins could talk to him. That made much more sense, though it still felt a bit creepy.

"So how would it work? I mean you're talking about creating a society from the ground up, with people bringing only what they can carry?" JD asked, looking thoughtful.

"Why would they need to limit it? I believe cars would be impractical as we have no gas. But there exist houses, electricity, empty buildings for businesses, parks, we want to build worlds, but all but three of ours have been abandoned and one is our home. The Elentrin are closer than they know to finding it. We don't want people to fight for us but we would dearly love people to fight with us."

Toni had so many questions. Their society seemed so much more open and honest; did they truly understand how petty, selfish, small-minded humans could be? That many of those that would choose to come would not be willing to work hard and build a world.

And what life do we have here? I don't think any of us can solve everything. But we have to try right?

Everyone sat quiet until Toni broke the lull. "Are we really talking about creating a path for Shifters to move to other worlds? What about their families, or where only one person shifted?"

That caught everyone, but then McKenna spoke. "We know we're immortal and that any children we have won't have the nanobots, but I can turn just about anyone. What," her voice caught, and she choked a little. "What if those that come are offered the choice. To be made into Shifters. Into Kaylid?"

Everyone froze looking at her. "Could we do that?"

[While biting people would be inefficient. With the knowledge Cass has, it should be easy enough to make super-concentrated shots that would insure infection and conversion. McKenna would have to donate the nanobots for that and control them.] Wefor spoke in their minds and all of them sat, a stunned look on their faces.

"Huh. Well that's an interesting option. You realize this means they could have children, children that could be changed if they wanted, when they became adults." Perc spoke into the weighty silence and McKenna took a sharp breath glancing at him.

[Wefor is correct. But with both of us working together it should be possible to create a self-replicating supply of infectious bots, though the incubation time would need to be longer to account for the lower amount invading the body.] Elao's voice was different from Wefor's but just as disturbing.

McKenna looked around at everyone. "Are we sure about this? You realize we are talking about setting up a migration off our planet to another world. To leave everything behind and create a life somewhere else?"

Toni looked at her friends, her family, then she looked at Rarz. His human form was so calm and secure. But in her mind she felt him, and he all but vibrated with excitement. An odd sense of joy bubbled through her and a smile spread across her face.

"I guess we are. My children are going to grow up on another planet. Holy shit."

Chapter 19 - Plans Realized

With all the changes, the various countries that are focused on rebuilding, the damage done across the world, there are serious questions about relying on global economy. More than one business has found itself in a bottleneck because the supplier doesn't exist or can't fulfill orders. This shake-up may both create more trade opportunities and the option for multiple local suppliers where before international companies dominated. ~ TNN News

Raymond sat in his office, his cool professional persona firmly in place. It didn't take much effort. Everything had worked out better than he could have hoped. With the tragic death of Willard at the tooth and claws of a Shifter, hyped up on more PCP than you could imagine, the pendulum had truly swung in his favor. Right now, he worked on writing another bit of legislation that would seem innocuous to most but would lay the groundwork to start removing self-determination from Shifters. Oh, there was no test that could identify them quickly—yet—but when it was developed, this little gem would ensure they faced mandatory civil service for a decade, and would make it so they could not get certain high-risk jobs—driving trucks, ships, anything where if they shifted they could possibly cause an accident. Linking it to the laws covering epilepsy and treating it as a medical condition really was a stroke of genius.

"Sir?" His intercom interrupted him. Shelia Combs, his efficient secretary, would only ping him if there was an issue.

"Yes?"

"Senator Warrick is on the line for you. He wants to talk about the new committee being formed, Shifter Assessment."

Raymond hesitated. He didn't want to talk to anyone right now. His own plans needed to get going as they would need very solid foundations. However, Warrick would prove to be instrumental down the road, and Raymond was thinking very long-term from now on. At least two committees were being formed to address the 'Shifter problem' and he'd worked very hard behind the scenes to load it with people sympathetic to his way of thinking. Senator Warrick was coming along nicely in seeing how destructive Shifters were to the fabric of their country, even to their world. That meant he couldn't afford to allow a hint of doubt to enter the man's mind or not be there for him at every turn.

"Send him through. Thank you, Shelia."

There was a beep and he hit speaker. He despised wasted effort, such as holding the phone to his ear. It was much more efficient to continue working while talking, especially when half the time the speaker just needed someone to agree with them.

"Robert. How you are this afternoon?" Raymond ensured his voice came through as warm and welcoming. Never let them know what you really thought. Everything was a performance.

"Ray, it's a great day. You should see some of the reports about the information coming out of that ship. Well worth the price we paid for it. The future gains will be incredible and all for the loss of a few thousand animals? We couldn't ask for a better trade."

In the privacy of his office Raymond let himself smirk. It had taken a while to convince Warrick that the cost other countries paid for this ship didn't matter, and since the US had mostly lost Shifters, it was a win overall. Besides, the ship resided on their soil and possession was the important part. They controlled everything and the management over the ship and the databases was the only thing that mattered. In many ways the knowledge would be secondary from the power inherent in restricting the resource.

"It is definitely a win for our country." Raymond kept his comments non-committal; you never knew when you needed to change your position. Easier to let others think they knew where you stood on everything.

"But that isn't why I called. I wanted to see if you had any information about this Assessment process. I know the procedures for identifying these animals are still flawed but do we have anything that we can use to drive it?"

Raymond smirked and hit a few keys on his keyboard. "Interesting you should ask. While we know there is a virus involved and it can be detected under a micron microscope, there isn't a current way to do a fast test. Think like the drug tests they can do with swabs."

"Ah. That was what I was thinking. So for now, maybe we can only do mandatory tests on people convicted of crimes? Instead of prison service, long term military or social service? Since they are damn hard to kill, they might make the perfect shock troops if any other country decides to get uppity with us."

Another smile, his tools were coming around nicely to the proper way of thinking.

"That would work, though we would need to add trackers so they can't run. Perhaps consequences to their families if they break their paroles or service, whatever it ends up being called. And if they get killed, well we can posthumously clear their record as a balm for their families. After all, they do vote. We don't want to make it seem like we are punishing them for something their loved ones couldn't control." Raymond managed not to sneer at the phrase loved ones. It took effort. Imagine being that tied to anyone that you would sacrifice your life for them. The greatest gift had been the death of most of his family when he was fifteen and he hadn't even had anything to do with it.

"Good point. We do need to keep the populace happy. Okay, for now I'll recommend testing anyone convicted of any crime. As we know, these animals will turn violent if given an opportunity. Having them in structured environments is best for everyone. I'll point out that we aren't trying to create leper colonies—which has come up already—but instead, environments where they are safe from harming others and can use their skills to help everyone. More of an assisted living community."

"Excellent, Robert. That would help people understand the need to protect everyone." Raymond

FAMILY

praised the man and in the next words he could hear the preening in the man's voice.

"Glad you agree. I just wanted to run it past you. I've got to go. I'll see if I can swing the people on the committee to my way of thinking. Talk to you later, Ray."

People are so easy to manage. I just wish he wouldn't call me Ray, but you deal with the small-minded as needed.

The phone disconnected and Raymond made notes on the conversation and added the links to the various medical references about how the virus could be detected. They would have to work on making it easier to find, cheaper and faster. While complicated DNA screening could be done on capital cases, doing those sorts of tests for every conviction would be prohibitive.

Next, he pulled up the economic forecasts. It was scheduled to go out in the next day or so and he was interested to see what the so-called experts were saying. He wasn't surprised to see they were saying the economy was due to face a huge uptick with the deaths in various parts of the world and the coming drive to build spaceships. The loss of workforce and the devastation of China and Australia were creating lots of job opportunities across the world. The shake-up coming in Washington because most elected officials were being voted out due to lack of confidence gave even more opportunities. He didn't know how it could be better.

With a full calendar, between meetings, research, and lunches with the right people, he enjoyed the quiet time he had this afternoon. From three on, no meetings. Perfect and rare for a Tuesday afternoon but it would allow him to focus on some long-term planning. Namely, figuring out how in another twenty years to pass the reins back to himself. With the immortality he should have from the virus, and the need to never let anyone know he could shift, he had the best of both worlds.

Ways to age himself were being investigated, and he had some special equipment he would order, slowly over months. But with everyone having ID and ways to run checks, he needed to start creating multiple identities to become down the road. The hard part would be getting a job again as a new person. But that could also be overcome.

After all, I'll know all the people to know and can mention my 'protégé' needing a job. And since I'll be incredible at it, it won't matter.

Especially if he publicly retired, looking old, out of shape, a young man with different hair would cause no comments on their looking alike, other than maybe a bastard kid. But no one gave a damn about that any more than they did if you were Catholic.

His star had risen lately with his subtle words and pointed comments. There was even talk of promoting him to a deputy assistant, one of the higher levels you could get to without being elected or military. It would put him in the perfect place to keep a tab on the pulse of Washington. And with the wave of new elected officials to ingratiate himself with, he figured he'd be ready to run for senator in two more election cycles. No one trusted a young man in office, and he'd need the age and older look to win.

In fifty years, who knows, maybe I'll be president. With Willard dead, he can't expose me. His wife knows nothing. The idiots trying to investigate me are gone. I'm not happy about the cop and NFL lug, but they don't know who I am. And from what I can see since the change in popular opinion, they've been keeping a very low profile.

Raymond knew they were staying in a house in Baltimore, but the funding on that would end in a few months, and they would find they were way too well known to get new jobs. Especially the cops. No one wanted to deal with them on the force, at least not anymore. Sports was screaming just as much about getting rid of all the Shifters. Everything was perfect.

A chance conversation with his niece, one of the family obligations he made sure to do pro forma if nothing else, had given him the clues he needed to figure out how to set up long term identity changes. Who knew fiction about vampires could be so interesting? All he needed to do was about every thirty years find a child that had died and acquire the social security number. Then start creating a life for the person over the years. When you had decades to plan, a little thing like this would be simple.

Now to create my legacy and see how to rule this country for the next hundred years.

Chapter 20 - More Visitors

The latest rumor that has appeared on social media about Shifters is gaining traction fast. The word is, Shifters are immortal. Now they can be killed as we've all seen, but because of how their cells shift and restructure they don't age. Think about this, they will never grow old. If one of them gets elected to the supreme court, they would never die, never retire. That possibility terrifies me. I don't know that the human race can handle so many people that will never die and give the rest of us a chance. ~TNN Science Adviser.

They all sat there looking at each other, then Cass began to giggle, and it spread across the room, until all of them were helpless with laughter. It helped to laugh so hard they were crying. Rarz kept looking around the room, his eyes wide, swirling with colors faster and faster. For some reason it added to the humor and Toni found herself choking she was laughing so hard.

It took a good fifteen minutes for them to calm down, with repeated assurances to the kids and Rarz they were okay. Toni felt lighter, more centered than she had in a long time. When they were mostly under control Toni took a deep breath and looked at McKenna.

"So I know I have a few people I need to go back and talk to but you mentioned you might have an idea about how to find people? Get the word out? And how do we do this? We can't bring people across the world here. Or go to everyone. There will be vetting and thoughts."

Something flashed across McKenna's face that removed the last of the humor. "I even have ideas about that. From a novel of all things. But first we need to see if it's more than just a few families that want this. I want to say the minimal viable population is a thousand plus. We'll realistically need tens of thousands. And families that will work and try to build a new world." She sighed a bit. "This isn't a small or easy undertaking. It could take years and things might change." McKenna shrugged. "First I'd like to see if we can get a few hundred to go with us. To go explore?"

Everyone nodded but Cass frowned. "Rarz, these planets, can they grow food that will sustain us? Can our plants grow there? Humans have issues with allergies."

[While humans might, Kaylid do not. The nanobots will remove any issues such as sensitivity to food products. You do not even need to fully transform for that defect to be repaired.] Wefor replied and Toni swore her tone had a bit of primness to it.

"They what?" Cass spluttered.

[The information was clearly stated. Any Kaylid has no food or environmental allergies.]

"Gods. If that got out. It could change everything." Cass paused and looked grim. "Or put targets on our backs. With all the allergies now, to find out we are immune to them and could share that immunity?" She shook her head suddenly fierce. "That can't get out. Someday, in the future, if we establish our own worlds and open trade with Earth maybe that's a medical advancement we can trade. But not now. Not with only our AIs and McKenna having any idea how to do that."

Wefor started to say something and Cass shut her off sharp and harsh. "No, don't tell us. Right now even knowing that adds to the danger. Later, years later, when we have a world, a society that's ready to meet other worlds, then we can talk about what is possible to do with these nanobots but not until then. The knowledge is much too dangerous."

The AI subsided and Toni shivered. Worried. So much was changing and might change even more. But the idea of walking under lavender skies called to her and she reminded herself of the fear in Sarah's eyes.

"Okay, but that still doesn't mean the food and plants on the other planets will support us, or even have the nutrients needed. We won't change children, so they'll need food until they're old enough." Cass pulled them back to the question at hand. "And most people will need the familiar plants and foods to help with this sort of transition."

"That is easy enough to find out and test. You are a botanist? A plant scientist?" Rarz asked.

"Botany biologist. But yes, that's what I am basically," Cass agreed.

"May another of my people come here?"

They all paused and looked at him. "Another Drakyn?" McKenna said, as if trying to clarify what he meant.

"Yes. I could ask my *Oppay* to come with some of our foods to see if it is tolerable to your bodies. It is our belief the AIs you currently host should be able to determine if there are any possible issues."

"*Oppay*?" Toni asked, sounding out the odd word.

"It is my understanding it is similar to the concept of mother, though not exact. We do egg hatchings, not births, so it is slightly different."

"Oh," Toni muttered the word, feeling stupid, though Cass's face lit up.

"I guess." McKenna looked around. "though outside in the back would be a better option than in here."

"Of course," Rarz responded, standing in smooth movement. I shall open it for her now." He walked out of the living room and Toni didn't even try to resist following him out.

Part of her just wanted to see another Drakyn, a female this time. But she also harbored a secret hope that maybe a whiff of his world would come through the portal. To let her know if it was as real as it seemed.

He was on the grass by the time she hit the back deck, and she felt everyone pile out with her. All of them were on the deck, watching. Rarz stood, head at a tilt, and Toni would have sworn he was arguing with someone mentally but no matter how hard she listened, she couldn't even feel a shadow of it. Her patience had frayed down to a nub before he stepped back, and the beginning of a portal started to appear.

Even as many times as she'd seen it and felt it, the creation of a portal still came across as magical and the desire to learn how to control her own portals pulsed in time with the swirling silver. It grew a bit bigger, though not even half as large as some she had seen him make. The ones for transporting canisters in bulk had been about twenty feet high.

A being stepped out of the portal and Toni just stared in surprised shock. For some reason she'd expected them to look similar. Even with the training sims, she'd assumed they were trying to make them look helpless. That all Drakyn followed his body type, like most people from Norway had blondish hair and pale eyes or someone from Hawaii had the typical Samoan build. Rarz was built like a tank in his human form. In his warrior form it was even more apparent. Thick shoulders and arms and even his height didn't damage his ability to move with extreme grace. JD and he shared builds, all muscle and power, but JD seemed jerky and slow comparatively. Perc was a bit slimmer as he had been a running back, needing the grace and speed, he also had the graceful movements. Even Rarz's head in his Drakyn form seemed stocky and blunt, not so this newcomer.

The Drakyn that stood on the grass and looked up at Earth's blue sky with fluffy white clouds had light yellow and green coloring, she looked like spring. A longer more graceful neck and eyes that seemed to sparkle when they swirled with pastels without the darker hints that Rarz had. Her body was whipcord thin but as she turned, it was with the grace of a snake, all smooth without joints. You could see her scales, but they looked elegant and Toni felt plain and boring next to her. While Toni assumed 'she' was the right pronoun, there were no curves or breasts like you subconsciously expected.

~Of course. They lay eggs. I don't know if they nurse.~ Cass said in the mindspace, her voice hushed as they watched.

~No. Milk has never been a mainstay. Though we do not meet your definition of mammals, neither are we reptiles.~ A new voice joined the mindspace, for some reason Toni heard water and the rustle of leaves combining to make it. Clear and soft, it was a voice that screamed amused mother, and made her relax.

Cass eeped and the mindspace filled with a wash of cinnamon fire. Toni didn't even have to look back to know that Cass's pale skin had flushed red.

~I am sorry, *Oppay*. We have not time for them to learn how to create non-public Speech groups. And as they are the only ones that can communicate this way, privacy was assumed.~

~Ah. Then I must offer my apologizes for intruding. However, if you would accept them, I am delighted to meet you.~

~Clan McKenna Largo, it is my honor to introduce you to Alinis Leaftouched Liry. *Oppay*, the adult members of Clan McKenna Largo.~

Toni glanced back at McKenna only to see the same surprised look on her face as what she felt. Since when had they become a clan? Much less Clan McKenna Largo.

Alinis didn't have wings or a tail, well at least not in this form. Her robes were in the same style Rarz had originally appeared in, but rather than his plain brown and tan, hers were in all the shades of yellow, from the palest color at her collar, darkening to almost brown at the hem. And it looked both comfortable and cool. At one side a large basket rode, with an object poking out of it.

~I am excited to be here. And I brought sustenance for you to try and see if it is compatible with your biology. Though I still contend the nanobots would have rectified any lacking in your systems.~

The way she said it made Toni think there was a long argument about it, but more like what was prettier sunrise or sunset, not anything that made a difference.

After a quick discussion they stayed out on the deck, setting the table with small plates, napkins, and forks. It seemed somehow surreal, given they were talking about fleeing their planet not fifteen minutes ago, to be sitting down to eat food from another world.

"My English not be as good if I speak. But will work to be heard," Alinis said in halting English. Most of them frowned at her.

"Why is your speaking so fluent in our minds, but not out loud?" McKenna asked as Cass seemed to go between the food stuffs being pulled out of the basket and Alinis.

"The Speech is not words exactly; it is thoughts and concepts that are translated in such a way that you understand them. At least for communication. The mind interprets almost seamlessly, and language isn't really an issue." Rarz explained as he settled down, a look of eagerness on his face as he looked at the food.

"How does that work for math and science that require very specific values?" Cass had riveted her eyes on the people again, her fingers tapping as if taking invisible notes.

"As long as you provided a concrete value and understand it, it is easy to communicate. But it is one of the reasons my people adopted this form. Writing and speaking out loud makes some subjects easier to communicate to gain that understanding. But the math game is usually held in a quantum space where the gamers all have their math worked out so far, that only by comprehension can you follow it." He shrugged. "After a certain level of math, it is something we do as easily as breathe. For us math is life, though the gamers take that to a new level."

Something that had been mentioned about Jamie and math flashed through her head, but Toni put it aside. That was for a later, once they figured out how and/or where they might live a year from now.

Alinis nodded. "You find symbols to communicate specific concepts."

"Ah, well we do that already, $e=mc^2$ for example. So that makes sense." Cass leaned back, but her fingers still tapped out their invisible notes.

I wonder if she really has notebooks in her head she fills out as she goes, a form of mnemonic memory?

JD had paid attention to everything she laid out. "So you're sure we can eat all this? And supply our bots with the caloric requirements needed to shift?"

Her head tilted to one side then back up. "It supplied enough mass over years for Rarz to turn wyrm." She said his name with a longer z, it felt more musical that way.

"Tell us?" Toni said, but kept a mental eye on the kids. She wasn't even exposing them to anyone else, much less anything that could be poisonous. They'd already seen the nanobots weren't perfect. Poisons could kill you, so could drugs.

Alinis pointed out various things, they ended up in four distinct groups: proteins, fruits, insects and honey.

"I'll freely admit that in my human form I have issues with the insects, so can we leave that for last? When I'm in my animal form it seems much less important."

"Curious. But you try?"

And they did. The honey tasted richer, buttery almost and Toni thought she could eat it by the spoonful. There were three types of fruit. Alinis named them but Toni couldn't track them all. But they all tasted fine, if a bit odd from what her mind expected. The insects were more flavorful than she expected, but they all agreed cheese or hot sauce would help. Hands down, all the cats loved the *lasm*, a delicate pink meat that flaked across her tongue. Dried or raw she wanted to gorge on it. That she put to the side for the kids, and the honey. They would love it.

"I think I feel better about the food. Our plants might not grow, but if you have found these grow on other worlds?" Cass asked looking back and forth between the two Drakyn.

"Our bees seem similar to what seen on your shows. They thrive all places. *Lasm* only in our ocean. But variations on all worlds." Alinis assured them.

"It might be rough at first, but with canned goods and the right supplies it should be fine. But are we going to be pioneers tilling the land?" Perc asked looking at them. "No offense, but most humans haven't had those skills in close to a century outside a few groups. Especially not without technology."

Alinis turned to look at Rarz then back to the humans. Toni couldn't read her scaled face, and wondered what she'd look like as a human, but she though it felt like confusion.

"I not sure I understand. Why would you not have machines?"

Everyone stopped and looked at her, and Toni knew she was confused. McKenna took the lead and spoke.

"Well, you don't have weapons, or need vehicles with your portal thing. We kinda figured you were an agrarian society. No tech, just simple basics."

Alinis and Rarz exchanged looks and their shoulders shook. Toni knew if their wings had been there they would have been bouncing up and down.

"We made an assumption, didn't we?" McKenna asked looking back and forth between the two aliens.

"Toni, do you remember when I showed you my world?" Rarz asked, a weird vibration to his voice she thought might mean restrained humor.

She blinked at him, confused for a minute, then the memory rushed back. After the bombshells from Blair and the drama with Carina she had completely forgotten. The memories flooded back into her mind and she smiled, remembering how nice it had seemed. "Yeah, I do."

"Wait? When did you get to see his world?" Cass's voice might have had a tinge of jealousy to it. Toni couldn't blame her.

"Not like that, not going there. He showed me memories." Excitement spurted up as she focused on him. "Rarz, can you do that again, for all of us? Share?"

"Or course, though *Oppay* would be better at it. Her gift in that area is much stronger than mine." He turned his gaze on his mother. "Would you be willing to share with these people? I have trusted them with my life and they have earned that trust multiple times over."

The gaze she gave Rarz was so textbook mom, Toni smothered a laugh.

I guess it's nice to know there are some universal constants.

"Yes. It would be pleasure mine. You must let me into your Speech for it work." Her voice lilted with the strange cadence. Toni kept trying to figure out what language it sounded like, but none of them she could think of matched the flavor of Alinis's voice. In contrast, Rarz sounded like a news announcer with almost no accent at all. What was there came across more as a deep bass voice.

"Umm? How do we do that?" McKenna asked. Toni shared her confusion, Rarz had just been there as if he'd always been a part of them. The other people were all brought in via the nanobots.

"Ah," Alinis murmured. A moment later a knock reverberated through the mindspace and a light, not round like they rest, but a triangle appeared on her mental dashboard. Before Toni could do more than peer at it, it lit up.

~Ah much better. It is easier and faster to communicate like this.~ Alinis voice filled the room like incense you wanted to sink into.

~Weren't you doing that before?~ McKenna asked much to Toni's relief, because that had been her thought.

~No. Before I was sending thoughts to all of you at the same time, while I could read your responses to me. This allows me to actively interact with you. Share emotions and images, not just Speech.~

All of them fell silent processing the information and Toni knew once they thought about it, it made sense. It oddly made her feel better, but still didn't address why they hadn't had to let Rarz in. She needed to ask him that one day.

"Makes sense when you talk about it like that. So now what?" McKenna sounded calm and curious, but Toni noted her hand in Perc's, both so tight together a flea couldn't crawl between their fingers.

~Now, let me show you Home.~

Chapter 21 - Other Worlds

Normality is starting to slip back into place in the US at least. While Tennessee and Utah will never recover, most of the US has seen a resumption of daily activities. Food deliveries are back to normal, if with slightly higher prices. Most government offices have been reopened and the Social Security Administration is posting extended hours to help deal with the death claims. Note that all cremations have been logged and any people not verified as cremated need to be reported to the FBI Missing Person section. ~TNN News

Somehow, even after Rarz did it, Toni expected something abrupt, sharp. But the world simply changed to a new focus. She heard the others gasp as the violet sky and the moons grew distinct. But Alinis took them someplace different from where Rarz had. While she thought he had shown her a small to medium-sized city Alinis started with what had to be a kitchen.

~It is easier to start with the small, then show you the big. But in many ways if what you are suggesting comes to fruition, this is of more interest to most.~

It felt like she stood there all alone, no one else with her as Toni turned and took in the room they were being shown. A large square box stood along one wall with a handle. She might have thought it a fridge, but it only stood out from the wall less than twelve inches. A recognizable sink, and cupboards full of dishes, were all things that while slightly odd, even avant-garde, were obvious. The clear panel with cells and insects climbing all over it, wasn't.

~What is this?~ She asked as she moved forward, noting pipes inserted in the wall with jars under them.

~Those are our *tisnes*, what you call bees. They are not the same, but a similar insect species. Most houses keep a hive in the kitchen to provide honey during the year.~

The idea fascinated Toni. Your own honey? She moved forward and noted the insects had eight legs and the hives, rather than hexagons, were octagons, but the blue and black bodies and wings did remind her of bees. The subtle buzz and scent of the honey felt so real.

~Where is your fridge?~ McKenna asked.

Toni turned, curious and looked around the room. The only option was the square box. But that made no sense.

~I believe you refer to as a cold box? It would be over there, in the wall.~

Toni moved back and reached out a hand. To her surprise and delight she was able to pull open the door and reveal a box. The front of it glowed and she lifted her hand to touch it and it went right through, into the interior. Inside it was so cold that most of the items stayed at just above freezing. She didn't see any plastics, mostly glass and ceramic, or fruits and meats. But she didn't see a motor or hear one.

~How do you keep it cold? Surely it must take a great deal of energy?~ She cringed at trying to figure out how to create electricity plants and run them. The enormity of what they entertained scared her.

~Energy? No. It doesn't take any at all.~ Alinis sounded confused, but the science-oriented Cass jumped right on it.

~Then how do you maintain the temperature?~

~The household association supplies all the houses in every neighborhood with heat and cold. Most of us donate a quarter of the day to manage the paths to keep the homes supplied. The system is polished enough that we don't need to monitor it at night.~

Toni turned and looked around; the explanation made no sense to her. Manage paths? What did that mean.

~*Oppay* is not explaining this correctly. As you have seen, all Drakyn can create what you call portals, we call them paths. When you build a neighborhood or even a city, people are either hired or a schedule is worked out create micro paths to our sun and space. The sun provides heat to everyone by creating a tiny pool of plasma that our piping structures tap into to heat water, food, whatever is needed. The amount of heat needed is minuscule compared to the power of the sun. We do the reverse with the cold of space, sending cooled water and air past that path and it is enough to keep all the houses well-supplied. It is something most adults can hold for a quarter day without any effort, yet they are always aware of it, able to sever the connection in a millisecond if needed.~

~Holy shit, that's how you cremated Ash. You pulled in plasma from the sun?~ Cass's voice was almost a screech, but Rarz replied with his normal calmness.

~Yes. So the two most basic issues of cooling and heating can easily be done with a few Drakyn. Or if you are capable of learning to control the paths, then you would be able to do it yourself.~

Toni spun around the room in awe. What had moments before seemed quaint and simple, now seemed smart and elegant. Free heat. Free cooling. A few hours a day. And they could show them how to do this. Hope jumped up as once again the idea proved not as impossible as she thought.

Alinis let her wander through the rest of the house. The sleeping chamber was a pile of pillows and blankets that would probably be more comfortable than most modern beds.

The bathroom, or as Alinis referred to it, the bathing room had a large tub in the ground. And by large, Toni figured it was about the size of a three-person jacuzzi. A large spout about six feet off the ground dumped water into it, and the entire ceiling looked like it was a mesh grate.

~Can we see that work?~ Cass asked, and Toni could almost hear her fingers typing as she took mental notes.

~The bathing chamber? Sure.~ Alinis seemed amused at their interest, but a minute later water sheeted from the ceiling. It looked like you would be standing under a rainstorm. ~The water intensity can be increased or reduced based on preference. All water is then processed and filtered going back into gardens or other needs. The bath itself has heating tubes around it to keep it at the heat desired. Most Drakyn enjoy soaking in the heat in most forms.~

The idea of soaking in a tub that didn't get cold sounded like heaven to Toni. She looked around trying to find the toilet. There, in a secluded alcove though it was at least twice the size of most bathroom stalls sat something that made no sense at all. A large shallow dish, with what looked like a grate at the base of it, sat in the middle of the room with three spokes over it like a tripod. Staring at it, she could see how you sat. And there looked like a waterspout at one point. But what about the rest of it?

Toni just blinked her eyes and shook her head leaving it as something to worry about later. They continued through the house. Their version of a living room looked more like a lounge with a fireplace and low chaise lounges. She didn't see any TVs but that didn't bug her. Most people lived off their phones. If they could create or replicate a cellular system? It shouldn't be that hard with enough time to plan. All in all, it was a building that humans could live in.

~How are all these built? The walls don't have visible seams and the swooping arches can't be easy to construct.~ Perc sounded thoughtful and his question caused Toni to look up. While most of the rooms had arches instead of square rooms, there were no doors.

~That, and where are the doors?~ Toni asked and she felt everyone notice that.

~All archways have privacy settings. Here, I will activate the one for the bathing chamber.~ A low blue light appeared in the archway and it darkened until you couldn't see through to the other side. ~All light and sound can be blocked, and the color can be changed to what is pleasing to each household.~ The light cycled through a variety.

~What tech is this?~ Cass almost sounded like she was on helium her voice was so tight with excitement.

~This?~ Alinis sounded confused. ~It is basic sound and lightwave control. Making sound and light into a visible being. Nothing that fancy. The solar collectors on the house power all of this and the lights in every room. We don't use electricity the way you do, but creating solar chargers for most of your technology should not be that difficult.~

~You have force fields?~ Somehow Cass's voice managed to squeak in the mindspace.

~I do not understand.~ Alinis sounded very confused.

Rarz spoke. ~Not like your stories have. But we do have solid light and sound barriers, though they will give with any significant force. A light touch they can withstand, the pressure of a hand they cannot.~

Toni began to see how advanced they were. Simple, yes. But when you didn't need machines for transport a lot of other things became easier. Imagine a world with no smog or exhaust?

~Our world smells awful to you, doesn't it?~

There was an uncomfortable pause, then Rarz spoke. ~Your world does contain more particulates than expected and that provides and discomfiting taste and odor.~

The mindspace filled with chuckles and giggles. ~Saying yes would not have offended us. Good to know.~ McKenna said into the laughter. ~Not needing cars could make a difference and is probably good. But if you want us to build spaceships, we'll still need factories. But that isn't anything I can really address.~ There was a thoughtful hum before she spoke again. ~How are these built? We got distracted with the doors.~

Toni could almost hear the mental shrug. ~There are machines that help. The plan is decided on, though most are one of about ten plans, and the machine lays out the house according to the plan using the various materials needed.~

Huh?

Toni couldn't figure out what she meant, though it was obvious the house had multiple types of materials in it.

~Wait. Rarz, have you seen our 3D printers? Like that but with multiple products.~ Cass asked and that caused it to snap into clarity for Toni.

~Very similar, though our machines are more complex. But yes, they are built at a few separate plants. We do have factories, but where you need electricity to generate heat or cold, we tap into the sun or space. Asteroids are harvested via the paths also. After your conversation about the ship and portals, I checked with others.~ His voice came a bit shame-faced. ~That is how we harvest elements. We snap off chunks of asteroids and bring them down. It never occurred to any of us we could do that to Elentrin ships.~

~Well that explains a lot. I feel better, I could even see living here. But what about the rest of the city?~ Toni asked, but part of her mind was already starting to go through what to keep and what to get rid of.

With a fade out and in, they found themselves standing in a town square. The layout reminded her very much of the wharf area of San Francisco or

FAMILY

small-town art fairs. There were stores and booths, Drakyn walking everywhere.

~What are those large white squares on the corners?~ Perc asked, as Toni turned in a circle trying to see everything. The buildings were colorful and now that they had talked about power, it occurred to her there were no powerlines anywhere. The change this could make for everything astonished her.

~Those are designated areas for path creation. That way you don't create a path in front of someone walking. You can tell it is your path because it will resonate for you.~

~Your world is wonderful. So many problems that we have are taken care of. Honestly, I think entertainment will be the biggest issue. You don't use the internet or TV?~ Toni asked, trying to figure out what she would need to bring to keep kids busy in the evenings and on rainy days.

~Yes and no. Your moving stories have captured many people. We have never been fiction writers, so your stories fascinate us. The idea of all the books you have is amazing. There are many who could support themselves just on telling stories. All our stories are of times past or the great old ones. Most of us have what you would call hobbies. But remember, we also create most of our own necessities. While there are those of us that run the great farms, we often will travel there to pick what is needed for dinner with the same amount of effort as you expend to walk out your door. Then there are the math games. Many of us spend hours a day playing those.~

~It sounds like a paradise. What's the catch?~ JD asked, his voice doubtful. ~Storms? Tornadoes? Asteroids?~

~Besides our neighbors trying to kill us?~ Rarz's comment started another round of laughter and JD's embarrassed amusement tasted like kiwis for some reason. ~I suspect our economic system may create the most problem. I will try to explain, but understand I am not an expert. Those are the ones called to office.~ He paused and she could almost hear him marshaling his thoughts. ~This will be a huge oversimplification and may even be wrong in some aspects, but this is how I understand it. For the most part our government has the only employees. Everyone is expected to give some amount of time to support the needed portals for neighborhoods, but for cities, the government pays in what are called *maka*.~ An image of a small round silvery coin appeared in their mind space. ~They are the only currency used. For those who work in the machine plants the government runs or helps with setting up new worlds, warriors like me, we can exchange those disks for anything we need. Most of the time they are traded around for when you need something but have no time to barter or do it yourself. We had an economic system closer to yours a long time ago, but it became too difficult and most people prefer to deal with their own needs. While farmers will gladly trade food for *makas*, most would prefer cookies you baked with your honey, or bread, or even repairing his machines so he can focus on harvesting and keep the land happy. Our scientists work for the thrill of discovery and for every new technique or advancement, they receive credit. Housing, *makas*, other needed things. Many of our greatest spend their lives discovering new and better ways to do things.~

FAMILY

~So mostly a barter system? What do you store up your *makas* for? Most worlds have saving needs. What about winter or low harvest?~ Cass and her ever-inquisitive mind asked.

~Often works of art you would save up for, as the artist might take months to create it. Or for a new coldbox unit. Large purchases. For most day to day items, trades are made. Warriors, like I am, are the few groups that rarely barter. We're never here enough to create things to barter. Clothes for new nestlings, or to hire an *emeryx* to assist if you were very lucky with your hatching.~ Rarz listed all these things off casually, but it was clear that most needed little.

They don't have the greedy nature more humans do. How badly will humans corrupt them?

~Excuse me. What is winter?~ Alinis asked into the lull.

Chapter 22 - Cultural Differences

Funeral parlors around the world are busy as people are finally getting to mourn the family members killed in the attacks. Many religions are offering free services and finding exceptions to the religious tenets that govern body disposal or timeliness of the rites. While the fate of those not returned when the alien ship was crashed is still uncertain, people are trying to move on with their lives. Most cities have opened counseling centers but almost no time off is being given for funerals. Many businesses are on the edge of failing as it is. The bright side is more businesses than usual are hiring, but there is a marked difficulty for those who are known Shifters. The tide of welcome for differences is very slim, given the suffering most have faced. ~ TNN Economic news

"Wait, what?" The shock was enough that it pulled them out of the shared world and Toni found herself staring at Alinis and Rarz in astonishment. "You know, when it gets cold and snows?" Toni's voice held confusion and amusement.

Rarz shared a puzzled smile with his oppy, then turned back to them. "You mean the white frozen water falling from the sky in multiple places in your world? That wasn't one of your make-believe stories? Not just at your poles?"

"No. This is summer, well, late summer early fall. It will start getting colder soon. What was the temperature for where we were?" Toni asked her eyebrows raised.

"About 78 of your degrees. It varies from low seventies to high eighties during the year. The nights usually fall in the mid-fifties. The occasional ocean storm might bring rain that would lower it below the fifties. During an active solar flare it might hit the nineties for a few days." Rarz said, looking back and forth between all of them.

Toni figured they looked like idiots, but the idea of a world always at a tropical temperature. Her list of things just decreased.

"Does that mean you don't have any snow?" McKenna asked and Toni didn't know if that was longing in her voice or not.

"Well, there is ice and what you call snow at the poles, but we never build there, only in the middle of the planets. The planets we have colonized, and our home planet, have very little axial tilt. This makes season changes almost nonexistent and elliptical paths around the sun are rare."

"Huh." Was the general reaction from everyone as they tried to process what they had witnessed in the Drakyn's world.

It does sound perfect, but how will humans screw it up? Can they vet people well enough that only the good ones get through?

Silence reigned for a bit but if there was talking going on, it was close and personal.

"What was your other idea, Kenna? If this works, I mean." JD was still nibbling on the honey. While Toni enjoyed it, he and Cass seemed to find it addictive and were all but licking the container clean.

"Oh. Well. Okay." She paused for a moment as if trying to redirect her thoughts.

Toni took the opportunity to grab another slice of the *lasm*. The stuff was so good.

"America, well Earth as a whole, has a fascination with aliens. We've always wondered if there is life out there. We've talked and dreamed about it for centuries. The Elentrin proved there was, and they are stunningly beautiful. I suspect Thelia will be treated like a superstar for a long time to come, but there are only what, five or six others?"

[I believe there are at least eight. Thelia and the seven crew members that escaped from the ship alive to the planet. Not all of them survived.]

Alinis jerked her head up and hissed. "What speaks?"

Toni fought back a snort of laughter. For some reason the AI's 'voices' rubbed everyone the wrong way. The consistency was amusing.

[That was the AI called Wefor. I am known as Elao. We are being hosted by two of these humans. In exchange and in appreciation, we are doing everything we can to assist them. The sudden violence by humans towards Kaylid is disturbing to both of us. While we comprehend the Elentrin ingrained pogrom, we do not understand this drastic swing in attitude.]

"Welcome to humanity. Our name is inconsistency." JD's voice held mocking humor and resignation. "Our history is like that. Loved one day, reviled the next. All too often the scapegoats died."

The two Drakyn looked worried and McKenna shrugged. "We are not calm and logical. We try, but most of the time emotion and fear drive us. You need to be aware that we are a fractured world and few of us manage to live in harmony."

"But you have worked so well with others. I have seen little fighting among you." Rarz had his puzzled look.

McKenna shrugged. "Threaten us and we come together excellently. But once the threat is passed, the minor differences become more important." She waved her hand, brushing away the worry. "That is something for you to consider. Some of it can be dealt with. My idea was that if you stay looking like Alinis here." She nodded at his mother, her smooth scales reflecting the late summer light. "People will see you as aliens, not like us. I don't think your shifting has really gotten out, not with any proof. And people want aliens, friendly aliens. If more of you come and set up embassies, you can create gateways to any world. You'd be able to make sure you want to let them through, verify they understand what they are walking into. And do it all on what is legally your land. At least that is how we do embassies here."

Toni just looked at her. Her mind locked on that idea. Simple, elegant, put controls on, and it would allow them control.

"Hell," Perc said slowly. "You spin it right, and the governments will make it so they encourage people to go what, populate other planets? Migrate? Not sure what it would be called but it makes it open, logical and legal. Speed and enough of your people would be the only issues."

"You would be able to lure the people you really want or help stagger the immigrations so planets get the right types of people: scientists, builders, etc." Cass suggested, her eyes bright at the idea. "It might work. But still we need to talk to more people first."

"Yep. And building them, talking to the governments. We might need the Secretary of State's help, but that would be on you. You do have ambassadors, people who do this, right?" McKenna asked a bit of panic in her voice.

"Yes. We have," Alinis said. "This idea. It is good. We can build fast. We have machines and templates and can put up full buildings in days. Other countries like that?" Her speech was improving as she spoke.

They learn fast. I hope we learn from them as quickly.

McKenna shrugged. "Given what we are seeing, if you offer immigration options, they might leap at it. Or they might not. I'm guessing here. Let me call the reporter and see what he can do, see if he knows of people we can go talk to and start getting a feel for it. Then maybe we see what living would be like there."

Toni loved the idea of going there, feeling that breeze on her face, but a niggling idea pulled her attention away.

"I think we're going about this slightly wrong." Toni said breaking the thoughtful silence. She felt the eyes directed towards her as she resisted nibbling on the pieces of *lasm* she'd saved for the kids.

"What do you mean?" McKenna asked.

She looks exhausted. We all need a break.

"Anything that we are involved with is going to be tainted. We're all famous, we're Shifters, and anything we even look like we support is going to make people shy away from it. The reporter might be able to get the word out, but I don't think that's what we need." Toni talked slowly, feeling out what she meant even as the words slipped out.

"What are you thinking, Toni?" JD asked. Toni opened her eyes to see everyone focused on her. She swallowed but pushed forward.

"We've just been attacked by aliens. Gorgeous aliens that reach into our media and fantasies. Right now, Shifters are the enemy because we're easy to find, while the Elentrin are mostly under government control. Only a very few people know Rarz exists. Nothing was filmed at the Target really, and in it, for all the grief it is has caused me, most people haven't seen Rarz. If the Drakyn want this to work, it needs to be splashy, attention catching." Toni paused and smiled as it finalized in her head. "It needs to be competitive theater."

The others nodded, intense looks on their face as they listened.

"Keep going, Toni. But I think I see what you are getting at," Perc nodded, his hands stroking down McKenna's arm in a comforting gesture.

With a grin and a sparkle in her eye Toni leaned forward. "Look, the world is reeling right now. Dragons are exotic and exist in most of our mythologies. Play on that. You will need multiple ambassadors and you'll need to hide, or at least not reveal, the fact that you can change shape. Humanity will be cautious about that for a while. But dragons? We almost can't resist them. Look, right now you have the US,

Britain, Japan, India, maybe Egypt, Brazil, and Mexico that have huge hubs of people. All these have embassies for other countries. Send a delegation to each of them. Make it splashy. Fancy colors, elegant gowns and tell them the truth." She knew most of the Drakyn disliked lying; it didn't fit with how they viewed the world.

"The truth?" McKenna blurted. "What good will that do? Everyone will just hate them and start to attack them also."

Toni shook her head, still smiling. The years of psychology courses were finally becoming in useful for more than just manipulating her kids. "The truth. That they are here to offer an alliance to resist the Elentrin. Then ask if they can build embassies – show off the machines that tap into the asteroids. Then, build inhumanly gorgeous buildings. Trust me, pull out the best and most glorious designs you can pull off, but every embassy should be different. Then when everyone is clamoring for your attention and science, mention you have worlds you need help rebuilding, but it could be dangerous with limited medical facilities. They know what the Elentrin do and would be honored to offer their victims homes. Then you start the immigration process."

Everyone stared at her, jaws open as they processed what she said. "It would work," Perc said slowly. "You'd be able to vet everyone, make sure of the type of people they were. Let them know they could bring families. We get some people to go over first, people we trust." He nodded at Toni. "Like the parents and start small. But if this keeps going the way we fear it will, the government will throw money and supplies at us to help encourage the migration."

He took a drink of water, continuing with that idea. "People like me sell our homes, spend all the money on supplies we need - planting, animals, anything else we might need, and walk through the portals to a new world, a chance to start over."

"Holy shit." McKenna murmured with her eyes wide. "It could work. It could let people escape and you could have auditions in other cities. If you put out that any violence against Shifters would prevent you from going to that city, it would help cut back on it. After all, those that hate us want us gone more than anything so the last thing they want to do is prevent you from coming."

Alinis looked from one to the other, her scaled ridges pulled together creating a deep vee between them. "If understand correct. We have your Shifters come to us? What mean by vet?"

JD sighed. "Humans are not as similar as your people seem to be." That elicited an odd sound from Rarz, but he ignored it. "We are more violent, selfish, fearful, and prejudiced than I've seen in your people. Even the Elentrin aren't as problematic. They treat anyone not Elentrin as lesser, regardless of their species. Humans? Humans find multiple reasons to hate. While I don't want to bar people in fear for their lives, neither do I want you to pull in people with these attitudes. I don't think your people could handle it and the way your cities are set up, we will need your help for a very long time."

"You would? If you can manage portals as Rarz say?" Alinis was confused.

"People, well humans, aren't as static as I think your people are," Cass said trying to explain. "We have moods and we vary a lot from person to person, day to day, even minute to minute." Her mouth quirked up a bit. "And our teenagers are even worse."

Rarz nodded. "From what I have witnessed, humans are amazingly changeable. Where one of our people would take decades to be diverted from their course of action, humans adapt and adopt different strategies in minutes if not seconds. We would need to make sure the ones we have are of a good heart. It might be worthwhile to have an empath on each interview team to ensure those that come to our worlds are not harboring dark hearts. While we are not perfect, some of the traits humans have don't really exist in Drakyn."

McKenna perked up at his comment. "You mean like what you said Nam might grow into?"

"Yes."

"One of your children is empath capable?" Alinis had gone rigid either with excitement or attention.

"If what Rarz said was true, yes." McKenna replied with a lift of one shoulder. "But speaking of the kids, I think they'd like to taste the few remains we have and meet you."

"I would be delight. Is rare meet other beings' nestlings." Alinis seemed excited and she fumbled the words more than normal. Toni couldn't help but glance at Rarz, a question in her eyes.

"Nestlings are relatively rare. Your world has incredible fertility. I am one of three children."

Alinis nodded. "Eggs not hatch, nestlings die. We try but so few live to hatch, then make it to two leg form."

Chapter 23 - Pivot

A record number of business have declared bankruptcy in the last few weeks. While some are expected given the damage and deaths in some areas of the country, most Shifter specific enterprises have seen a loss of customers to the point they say it is no longer viable to have their economic model be based on a small unimportant subsection of the population. While some are redirecting their efforts and aiming at a wider audience, most are just changing into a new startup idea. The main business model that is exploding is anything related with cremations and ash disposal. Funeral urns and memorabilia have taken off. ~ TNN News

Toni felt her heart contract at that. She remembered how many people told her how long they'd tried to get pregnant and she and Jeff had made twins within months of her going off birth control. She'd always known she was lucky, but maybe she was luckier than she thought.

"Many are never hatched and the first year or so, our nestlings are fragile and can die easily. After that it will take significant physical damage to kill us. The one planet where we seemed to have a high ratio of living nestlings," he swallowed then continued, "the Elentrin killed every Drakyn there and destroyed all our nests. We lost over twenty-five percent of our total population."

All of them winced at that, the sheer magnitude of deaths. "Then definitely kids. Ours are pretty great." McKenna said, glancing at Toni.

~Kids. There are some people we'd like you to meet.~ Toni sent it as McKenna arranged a platter with what was left, specifically the *lasm* she had also set aside.

~Everyone?~ Jamie asked, a half-distracted tone.

~Yes.~

There wasn't a response, but a moment later they heard and felt the running of feet up the stairs and through the kitchen. The pounding slowed and she could all but feel them peeking through the door to verify who was on the deck. Paranoia had become a way of life. Toni didn't know if that was a good or a bad thing.

The door opened and Charley walked out first, his eyes locked on Alinis, but the other three were right behind him.

Does he look like a king leading his followers or the guard protecting his charges? Or both?

The contrasting image between Charley's white blond hair that didn't seem to be getting darker, and the three space black heads following him had an odd composite. Toni shook her head. With her Peruvian genes, both of her kids would always be tan with dark hair.

Unless they become dragons.

She shivered at that thought, but was it from fear or excitement? Toni pushed away the thought and focused on the kids.

"It's another dragon," Nam whispered. She'd darted to the side and climbed up next to McKenna. Toni noted McKenna's arms were already around the little girl and a soft smile turned up the corners of her mouth. But what was more interesting was Perc petting her hair lightly and Nam leaning into it.

"Yes. This is Alinis. She is Rarz's mother," Toni told them watching her kids like a hawk. Jessi was Jessi, as always.

"Cool. Hi, Mrs. Rarz. Is that fish?" Her head tracking to the table.

Toni fought the roll of her eyes, reminding herself the kids had no idea how odd it was to have alien beings sitting down to eat with them. At this point it would seem almost normal. Jamie, however, tilted his head, looking at her, eyes narrowed. But his thoughts, whatever they were, stayed in his own mind. Or at least weren't shared with her.

"Food?" Charley had followed Jessi, deciding the strange dragon wasn't that interesting. He slipped in between McKenna and JD looking at the offerings.

"You guys act like you're never eaten." Cass protested. "But yes, this is food from another planet. Want to try it?"

While the largest amount of saved food was the *lasm*, there were small amounts of everything left, enough for the kids to try a little bit of everything.

"Is that an insect?" Jessi didn't sound outraged, more curious.

"Yep. From their world. Tastes like vegetable snacks really." Cass offered. The three older kids all stared at it dubiously, but Nam picked it up and crunched into it.

They all looked at her. "Grasshoppers are a treat. This is yummy."

The three kids gave her side eye glances but all of them tried it with much fewer facial gyrations than the adults.

"Oh, it is crunchy. These are good." Jamie declared. The *lasm*, fruit, and honey all met with equal approval. The *lasm*, as expected, was the most popular.

"I guess this solves any worries about the food not being compatible though I can tell you, one of the first things people will do is learn to make beer. Humans love their brews." JD grinned as he said it and Perc nodded, a smile on his own face.

"Heck, maybe I'll start a small home brew thing or mead with the honey."

That started a whole new conversation where they needed to let Rarz and Alinis try various drinks. Rarz could see the enjoyment, but Alinis preferred the wine they had.

The kids had left after waving at the 'dragon lady.' She had watched them go, her eyes greener and bluer than before. "I see you cherish them."

"Yes. Most humans are protective of kids. But ours are pretty great." McKenna piled up the now empty dishes and looked at the two aliens. "So are we going to do this? You come to major cities, all pomp and circumstance, dazzle them with bullshit and we do this quiet?"

Rarz glanced at Alinis, then he dipped his head down.

"Yes. We will go talk to our leaders, but they have heard much of this as we talk. They are discussing the idea. But we would like to rely on your clan to

FAMILY

find us people to go see our cities and decide if they think it will work. Live there for a few months and make sure there isn't something we haven't thought about, before people immigrate in volume." Rarz glanced at his mother and tilted his head. "But overall, we are in favor of the idea and may adopt it with other worlds."

"There is an aspect we haven't addressed, you know," Perc said as they were processing what Rarz said.

Toni glanced over at Perc, frowning. It seemed like they'd been talking for hours, or maybe just the world sharing took forever in subjective time.

"What would that be?" JD had settled back down, though he kept glancing with a wistful look towards the empty honey jar.

"Families."

"What about them?" Toni asked, a bit confused as that had been what they'd been talking about. Why was Perc saying they hadn't talked?

"What about those who can't change? Lots of siblings, parents, spouses? Do we change them? Is it required? Can we change them without McKenna?"

Everyone fell silent, looking at each other. Alinis broke the silence. "I do not understand. Why is families not being Kaylid an issue?"

Rarz heaved a sigh this time. "*Oppay*, humans age. The stories of old people were not fiction." She tilted her head, frowning at him. "They age, get frail and die. The average life span is about eighty." He glanced at Toni for verification and she nodded.

"Eighty? Cycles of the sun? Eighty!" Alinis seem shocked and almost horrified by this information.

215

"Yes, it is a short time. So any spouse or family that is not infected will die while their family lives on after them." Rarz's voice was heavy with a strange weight. The colors in Alinis's eyes spun in rapid changing colors.

"Not realize," she broke off and shook her head. ~This is too important to risk using incorrect or inaccurate words. No one should suffer due to cellular decay. Our old ones only get larger and wiser. They pull back from society and live in the math games and off the stored energy in their quantum spaces. We would never expect you to leave your families behind, or require them to watch their loved ones die. Can something not be done? This is not acceptable.~

Whereas before Toni would have pegged Alinis as mild, even meek, the power and intent in her voice ripped that idea out of her head completely.

After the shock, Cass spoke up a bit shaken, hesitant even. "Your people basically grow larger and retreat? Don't you ever die of old age?"

Rarz and Alinis looked at each other and she rotated one shoulder. ~In a way yes. Some of our older ones live for thousands of your years. But we have noticed, as our means of staying in touch have improved, about after eight or nine hundred years, they retreat and fall asleep and don't wake up. Though more and more lately they say they are going to travel to other worlds, even if they never have before, and we do not hear from them again. Whether they die or simply do not return is unknown.~

"There is a limit on your Speech?" McKenna asked.

"Of course. If there is a path open it can go down it but for practical matters, unless you access a quantum space area, it is limited to a planet or solar system."

"Elaborate?" Cass responded, her gaze intent as if trying to extrapolate more data with her eyes.

"We can create a quantum space for specific conversations. Like your group, but on a quantum level. They usually are only used for elections or the math games. One was created for me to pass information to. But they require someone to maintain it at all times, so they are used rarely. The concentration overhead involved in keeping a quantum space open outside of your personal one can be draining. One of the elders volunteered to keep it open. He said he needed something interesting to do." Rarz shrugged.

"So you don't really die of old age, but more just let go of life. The idea of people growing old horrifies you. Your speech has limits, but micropaths or quantum spaces keep it possible across great distances. You don't really have winters, but live in mostly spring/summer conditions. And you live static quiet lives." Toni recapped looking at the two aliens.

Rarz tilted his head. "Those are the essentials."

"Then here are the problems we need to overcome. How do we allow people to change without McKenna having to bite everyone? Do you want people that don't want to change? Are you okay with our idea about the show with multiple portals? And what do you want us to do?"

Silence fell and Toni waited for someone to add to her list, or pull apart what she said, but everyone just sagged a bit and sank down.

"I have been asked to come back and talk to my people in person. It may be a few days before there is an answer." Rarz voice sounded almost apologetic, but Toni shrugged.

"Makes sense. Though I guess we're stuck here until you get back and I'm both happy and sad about that. Though I just bought groceries dammit."

"I will keep a micro path open. If you contact me via Speech I will hear you. Depending on the level of discussions, I may or may not be able to respond."

"Thank you. But in the meantime, you still want us to find some early adopters?" The two Drakyn looked at McKenna and Toni had to resist a snicker at their identical expressions. McKenna clarified her comment. "Do you still want us to find people we trust that would be good fits to start intermingling? On a small scale I can turn people. Wefor has verified she can ensure they transform. We've been working on it, well since Carina." McKenna didn't look at Toni and Toni could feel the avoidance.

~It's okay.~ She whispered tight and low, sending her love and understanding, maybe a bit of forgiveness.

McKenna tossed her a small smile, but she remained focused on the Drakyn.

"Either way, yes. The offer is still open to you and those you want to bring. Even if, as a planet or species, you decide not to take up the offer, it is there." Rarz finished speaking and rose. "It is best if we leave now. They are anxious to talk." He gave them a shaky smile. "It is exciting."

A few minutes later the silver swirl of the portal closed behind them, leaving Toni with the rest of them.

"Well, I hope you didn't give my bedroom away. Looks like I'm staying."

Chapter 24 - Imprint

Africa is under more turmoil than it has seen since the British expeditions to expand their empire. With some areas all but in ruins and others untouched, the religion that has held such sway over the continent for centuries has found its hold just as shattered as the country. The depths of Africa are not safe places for anyone that isn't a Shifter while the cities have signs and graffiti posted that Shifters aren't welcome. This continent, more than any other, is polarizing into Shifter and human and the two aren't playing nice with each other, as evidenced by the dead on either side. ~TNN News

Toni found herself wide awake early the next morning. With nothing else to do and needing to feel productive, she went downstairs to start coffee and breakfast. She found herself sitting outside, watching the sky lighten, as the sun pushed its way up over the edge of the Earth. The gray sky turning to blue pulled at her.

I wonder if I'll miss these colors someday? If I'll forget what this world looks like.

Sipping her coffee Toni focused on seeing everything around her, the colors, shapes, smells.

"Whatcha doing?" The low rumble of JD's voice pulled her out of her intent fixation on the essence of Earth.

"Imprinting? Remembering? Mourning?" They were all right and all wrong, but she couldn't find the word that explained exactly the need to absorb everything that drove her actions right now.

"Ah. Is it different there?" She could smell the coffee in his mug and thought about getting up to get some more, but that would take effort.

"How would I know? I've never been to that planet." She didn't look at him as she replied but instead, focused on the clouds turning a soft pink as sunlight caressed their fluffy edges.

He didn't say anything, but she could feel the weight of his disbelief surrounding her like a weighted blanket. Toni caved after a minute.

"Really, I've never been. But I've had dreams and shared visions. Much like what you saw." She paused, drinking the last of her coffee. "Did you see the sky?"

"Sky? Nope. Paid more attention to the buildings and the machines. No cars. That might be hard to get used to."

"Or super cool. The sky's purple. They have two moons. It feels like home sometimes, especially when here lately it feels like there are enemies on every side." Looking at him would be dangerous so instead, she memorized the color of the leaves, just starting to fade from green to yellow.

"That would be interesting." They sat there in comfortable silence. After a while Cass came out.

"Here, more coffee," she said refilling Toni's mug.

"Thanks." Companionable silence fell again with all of them enjoying the simple presence of the others.

"So are we doing this?" Cass asked, and Toni wanted to laugh at how neutral her voice was.

"I don't think there's any doubt about that. But is it just us running away to a hidden resort or Shifters, well Kaylid, starting a new world? That's the real question. As for me? I don't really have a reason to stay. I would rather go out there and see what's available. Hell, this is a dream I never thought I'd see come to reality." Toni tried to keep the emotions out of her voice, but the wistful bitterness seeped out.

Toni turned her head to see McKenna leaning in the doorway. She should have heard her, but right now Toni wanted to pay attention to the colors the sun painted everything, to make sure they remained crystal clear in her memory.

"Then I guess I need to start making a list of what we need to do." Cass stood, heading back into the house, her stride brisk.

"List? Do? Wait! You have a plan?" Toni blurted out the words and then felt very grateful she didn't show the wave of embarrassment that went through her.

"Plan? Not so much, but it isn't hard to see what we need to do, though the one thing I can think that we will need to do is set up ways to communicate. Email, phone calls, things like that. Once we've been gone a while, having family that doesn't need to change, visiting occasionally won't be an issue. Or even us coming back here. If we change our hair and get called by a different name, it should be more than possible. Especially if what Rarz keeps hinting at, that we, or at least some of us, can learn to create and control portals – well that puts the universe at our feet, doesn't it?"

Toni closed her eyes and focused on her coffee, the scent, the taste.

Huh, never thought about coming back but then who would I come back for? Everyone I love would be with me.

But that didn't apply to others. Perc had his parents, Cass her sister and family. Even people like Sarah and the other parents. What price would they be willing to pay? Would they change? The idea of creating a new society? Find new worlds?

Portals? Us? We could explore the universe. She's right. Hell, my kids could go places no human would find otherwise. I wish I knew if that excited or terrified me. Guess I'll find out. I seem to be in the middle of it.

The shiver that ran across her shoulders and down her arms made her laugh.

At least I won't be bored.

Cass worked on the lists while the rest of them made food and started to pack up. JD was going to stay with Cass for a bit. He'd decided to repair his house as it put most of them in the same area. Once done, they'd either move there or he'd sell it. Perc was putting his place up for sale and moving in with McKenna. Toni knew the kids would whine at sleeping apart and foresaw lots of sleepovers.

Everyone remained wrapped up in their own little worlds, even the kids seemed subdued or maybe exhausted. Toni suspected they hadn't slept much last night and fully expected to find them in an animal pile in a few hours, sound asleep.

The knock at the door came as a surprise.

You know having sharp hearing doesn't do any good if you don't pay attention.

The amused self-castigation made her smile as she rose from the chair. "I got it," Toni called out as she headed to the front door. Cass, McKenna, and Perc were all working on the LIST as Cass was calling it. Toni had been working on a list of Shifters she knew who were parents that she thought could handle the whole alien world and living with aliens. Sorrell was at the top of that list.

She glanced out the window first and was and wasn't surprised to see Secretary of Defense Doug Burby with Christopher next to him.

"Doug, Christopher. Thought you government types were all done with us?" Okay. so maybe McKenna wasn't the only one feeling a bit abused by the government. Money didn't solve everything.

"Not my idea. I fought for you. I'm just the messenger," Burby sounded exhausted as he protested her accusation. Behind him Christopher nodded, giving him unseen support.

"How long until you retire?" Toni asked as she stepped back so they could enter.

"Not soon enough. I'm counting the days, by next week I'll be counting the hours." He shot her a serious look. "While there are lots of things I regret in my life, know I don't have any regrets about how I fought for all of you."

His words caught her heart and mind. Toni turned and looked at him; she took in his hollow eyes, dark circles, stress lines around his eyes and mouth, and the honesty in his face and words.

"I believe you. Come on in." She didn't bother to announce him; everyone was already looking at them as they walked int.

"Doug. What brings you to darken our doorstep? We getting kicked out?" McKenna sat looking at him and Toni felt more than heard JD come down the stairs. He'd been upstairs actively packing everything hoping for a move back in the next few days. If they were still here in a few days, Toni would need to make a clothing run. She hadn't brought a bag back, though some of her stuff had been left behind.

Burby stood there looking at her, a frown on his face, then he shook his head. "Oh, no. Sorry. You're still good. I'm looking for Rarz. We have questions for him and the phone we gave him just goes to voicemail each time."

"And you drove all the way over here instead of calling us?" McKenna gave him a look and Toni fought back a laugh. That woman was so tired of everyone's shit and Toni couldn't blame her in the least. They all were.

"No. I used it as an excuse to escape." He sank down into one of the dining room chairs and to Toni's surprise, Christopher did too. The normally placid agent looked just as exhausted as Burby, if not as aged.

"Escape? They after you now too?" McKenna didn't give him an inch. A twinge of guilt got Toni heading into the kitchen and coming back out with bottles of water for the two men.

"Not in the way you mean. But the fallout at that level isn't fun." He nodded, taking the water and drank some, his eyes closing in evident pleasure. "They aren't happy with anything and trying to cover their asses so they have a job this time next year. And I don't give a damn. They're getting the truth from me and they don't like it but that's why I'm here. People on the Hill want to talk at him. Or lecture him, or something. I don't think they'll get what they want from him, but I was ordered to bring him there."

"Ah." McKenna frowned for a moment. ~Rarz, can we tell them you are working to bring ambassadors here, just neglect to tell them your people will be having ambassadors in multiple places?~

They hadn't heard from him since he left for his world. It felt odd not to have him around, his gentle questions and all too easy presence.

~Acceptable. Ambassadors in one week. We are discussing which cities and where now. Creating the portals will require work, as we will not have a transponder to home in on, so lots of micro paths until we decide for sure.~

Toni could feel Cass wanting to ask more questions, but the woman scribbled intently on the back of her pad of paper as McKenna spoke again. Toni took a seat on the couch, at an angle to the others.

"He went home."

"Home? You mean another planet home?" Burby sat up straighter and Toni wished she could see his face clearly to see his reaction.

"That's where he lives."

"Oh, hell. Is he coming back? Please tell me he's coming back. Those idiots will try to arrest him if he doesn't come the next time they have a question."

Perc snorted. "That should work well. Arrest the alien that can create portals across galaxies, not to mention planets."

"I did say they were idiots, right?" Burby snapped and then sighed. "Not your fault. Has he abandoned us because of our stupidity?"

McKenna paused, then sighed. "While he isn't happy about how Earth is reacting to Shifters, he went home because formal ambassadors are coming to talk to us."

~Really? Not going to twist the knife a bit more?~ Toni asked, as she pretended to be wrapped up in her phone.

~He's not the cause and we know that. Torturing him is a bit petty of me. Get me in front of Congress or the senate and I'd twist so hard they'd need a surgeon to remove the damn knife. Shifter crap is hate speech and they should have stomped down on it hard. They didn't want to because it let people blame someone else other than them.~

The amount of bitterness in McKenna's words surprised Toni, but then what she said sank in, and Toni almost dropped her phone.

She's right. And they didn't. Those sons of bitches.

Rage flared through her. Not red hot, but white, burning away what was left of her love of Earth. As far as Toni was concerned, they had lost her. They could have done something, made it clear it wasn't tolerated and instead they were turning a blind eye. If she didn't move, she might explode and as much as she wanted to lash out, she had no doubt the man in front of her had done nothing to ignore the problem. And the odds were, he had fought to try and help.

"Excuse me," she didn't even stop to see if anyone cared or noticed but went out on the back deck and tried to calm. She fell back into trying to see every little thing. The details that she always took for granted.

"You okay?" She'd heard Cass come out, and the gentle question didn't surprise her.

"No. But I realize it isn't my problem anymore. This isn't my home any longer."

And I really wish saying that made me feel sad.

Chapter 25 - Paths Chosen

Curves and fluff are the new sexy. Across the world the super toned, muscled, lean bodies characterized by Shifters is fading from popularity. More and more people are saying they find the curves and a generous booty are much more attractive than the perfect body most humans can't obtain without the infection that made people Shifters. Already Sports Illustrated is talking about having an entire swimsuit issue next year that is dedicated to the more voluptuous body. ~ TNN Entertainment News

Toni didn't know how long she stayed outside. Cass had left after hugging her. To Toni's relief, she didn't push her to explain or even justify her anger. Cass always seemed to know what to do and when not to push too much. The kids were still playing, more wrapped up in their own world than the adults.

I swear if it wasn't for food, they would have no need for us at all.

The urge, the need, to pull her kids close and make sure they knew she loved them swamped her, but she pushed it off and rose.

Sitting out here and sulking does no good. Might as well go back in. We need to go back and start working on all those lists that Cass has been creating.

Stepping back into the house, she went to find the others. The four of them were all sitting in the living area talking, but Burby and Christopher were gone. McKenna looked up as Toni walked in.

"They took off. Asked us to let Rarz know to call when he comes back. But that's all I'll do. He needs to decide how they're going to handle their interactions with humanity with all its flaws."

"Agreed. But speaking of that, we ready to leave? I don't know if Rarz will be back in time to let us do this the easy way. But either way, I'm done with this place. I want to get started on the next chapter. Besides, I have people I need to contact and feel out. I don't know how excited or wary people will be. The one thing I need to know before I say anything though—do I let them know we can change non-Shifter family members?"

Her question caused them all to go still. McKenna bit her lip, then stopped herself. She glanced at Perc and JD before looking back at Toni. "I'd prefer that we just said plans were under way to support non-Shifter family members, but I'll leave it up to your judgment. The Drakyn can claim to change them all they want. They will be aliens with unknown abilities and skills. They won't face the backlash that we will because we don't really want people to think of the reason they can change as tiny computers. Much safer to think of it as a virus than something you can't actually turn off." Cass started to stay something, and McKenna rolled her eyes at her. "I know, I know. Technically you can make a virus go dormant, but do

FAMILY

you really want to try to explain that to the billion or so people affected by this?"

"Fine. But yes, I've been talking to Wefor and Elao in the background and there is a way to shut off the nanobots, in that they wouldn't let you shift, but the organic improvements, better cellular division, rapid healing, healthy body weight, none of that would go away. So not sure it's even worth mentioning it. The main reason people would fear and hate what we are is still there. Just no more fur."

Toni listened to all of it and shrugged. "Okay. Well the next issue. Kids."

The adults all broke out in laughter at the understatement. Separating that group had become almost impossible. They were all but joined at the hips and the stress it caused everyone to try and get them apart wasn't worth it. "Shared custody? Scheduled sleepovers? Cause the one night almost had me ready to strangle both of my darling children."

"Charley and Nam weren't any better. You would have thought they were being punished. We'll work on it. But it would be easier if we could create portals."

"Agreed. But from what Rarz said, we could learn but over years not days. Either way, we can set it up, shuttling them back and forth if needed. And don't forget you need to think about Nam. Making that legal."

"Ugh," McKenna groaned. "But yes, I do."

Toni laughed. "Have fun with that. I'm going to go herd the children in their den and get them to pack up everything neatly. Then maybe tomorrow we can schedule a truck? How the hell did we get so much stuff when we came with a few suitcases?"

"Weapons, tactical gear, clothes to meet important people in," McKenna rattled off as she looked around. "Buying all the crap we forgot to bring. And we've been here for well over a month. Almost two."

"Ugh. Fine. Cass, your lists take into account all the stuff we'll need on another planet? It occurs to me that while food and basic things like pots and pans probably have equivalents there, I doubt things like shampoo and other stuff does. Though with no periods and, per Wefor, all the nanobots ensure no conception unless you specifically request it, that means we don't need some hygiene things. But other things probably don't exist."

Cass nodded and scribbled on her notes. "I have thought about that, but not to the beauty and hygiene products. But I must say, no tampons is very, very nice."

Toni and McKenna responded with 'Amens' while the men just looked vaguely uncomfortable.

They went their own ways and Toni headed to the basement. The kids had created their own play area. Books, some construction blocks, and a TV with approved video games. The four of them were in a pile, each with a book. Nam was coloring in her coloring book, while Jamie's looked like something she'd expect a high schooler to read. Charley and Jessi were reading the same book, it looked like one of the magic school ones. If nothing else, his craving for the stories had made Jessi's reading level up in leaps and bounds.

All their heads jerked up when she came down the stairs. The immediate tension in Jessi and Jamie made her cringe.

FAMILY

"Do we have to leave?" Jessi blurted and Toni wanted to cry and scream at the same time. Instead, she focused on remembering they were healthier and happier than she had ever seen them.

"That was what I wanted to talk to you about." They sat up looking at her, wariness clear on their faces. Exasperation washed through her, but she made a concerted effort to not let it get into her tone. "We are planning on going back to California as soon as possible." She sat down, not liking the idea of looming over them as she talked to them. Treating them as if they had no say so in this would only make it more difficult for all of them. "Kenna and I discussed it and we understand how much you like to stay together. And we are okay with it." She placed specific emphasis on those words and saw all of them relax. "That being said, we may need to move you between houses occasionally and as McKenna works to get custody of Nam legally, you may need to sleep in your own rooms in separate houses."

They instantly began to protest and Toni raised her hand. "I know. But you two," she nodded at her kids, "want to make sure Nam can stay, right?" They all looked at each other and nodded slowly. "Then you will need to work with us and help us do it right. But we will work very hard to make sure you spend most nights together."

A sigh of relief ripped through the room. "Okay, Mom," the twins chorused.

"Good. Now, if you would, pick up and pack everything you can. Yell if you need help from anyone."

The nodded their agreement and Toni went back upstairs. She knew she needed to get the information to the parents about the option she had for them, but she thought it might be bigger than that. But she needed to be back in California to really do anything.

~I would like to return. Is that permissible?~ Rarz's voice rang in their shared mindspace.

Huh, he must have opened a micro portal to talk to us. We really need to learn how to do that. Most useful thing ever.

~Sure. Actually that might make it easier for us if you're willing to do some portals for us.~

~Of course. I can start teaching you how to use the paths if you wish.~

Toni blinked at the parallel of her thoughts.

~Oh, that would be wonderful.~ Cass's excitement bubbled through the mindspace and Toni fought back a smile.

Toni felt the creation of the portal and glanced out to the back and saw the silver swirl appear. Unable to resist, she watched him stride out of the portal and it slowly collapse behind him. With him here it opened a lot more possibilities. The urge to be out of the house and to make it more difficult for even the good guys in the government was nigh irresistible.

~What do you think about going back tonight? All of us. I'm thinking we shouldn't be so easy for them to find. Granted, we'll be home but they can't just drive over anymore.~ Her question hung in the mind space for a long moment.

~Yes. I think that would be best. Besides, I want to talk to my parents about this in person, not over the phone. I'm a bit paranoid about any of these things being talked about online or over the air. I don't know if they would try to stop us, but I'm not sure I want them to know we are part of what the Drakyn are going to present. Oh, they'll guess but they won't know if we don't tell them.~ Perc's calm logical voice put into words the feeling that kept Toni uncomfortable and feeling like something bad was about to happen.

~Agreed. I guess we're packing hard and fast tonight.~ McKenna matched actions to words as she rose and by the time Rarz walked in the back door everyone was moving with a purpose, even the kids. They seemed excited to go home, though at least part of it probably related to getting back to their obstacle course and being able to really stretch their animal forms in McKenna's back yard. If they were going to stay, a fence might be needed but for now the adults would always be around. And they would be carrying.

In two hours everything was packed. Toni had the least and the kids were going with McKenna, at least for now.

"Rarz, can you do a portal to my house first? I have a lot to do there." She'd only been gone a day, so she knew nothing major would have happened but from the emails Sarah had sent her, the level of stress seemed high.

"Of course, Tonan."

Hearing her full name in his deep voice caused ripples down her back she didn't want to address. She remembered when she told it to him. The dream world had called to her the night she started her period and her mom had told her she was entering womanhood. The dream offered an escape. Being a kid was hard enough, she didn't know if she could handle being a woman, but either way she had told the dragon man she was a woman now, so he could call her Tonan, not the little girl name of Toni.

She laughed to herself. That conceit had lasted about a week and she'd gone back to Toni, and her full name remained something private and rare to hear from anyone.

The portal let her out at her front door and the three boxes and duffel bag followed. She felt it snap close behind her and she already missed the scent and sound of the others.

Enough. You have people to call and a what? An escape? Migration? Wonder if this is how the Irish or the Pilgrims felt? Persecuted and hounded. Not knowing if where they were going was going to be better or worse? I have a lot more empathy for the early settlers now than I ever did in school.

Shaking her head at her own silliness, she lugged all the stuff inside, dumping the laundry and getting it going first. Then she sat down and called Sarah.

"Toni, do you have any news?" No hello, just the desperate question. It caused whiskers to ache, whiskers she didn't have in this form.

"I have an option. How about a potluck at my house? Only Shifters or their families. If you need someone to watch your kids, McKenna said they could come over and play with our kids."

"Done. What time and what do you want me to bring?" Immediate acceptance, not even hesitation. That bad feeling got worse.

"Food, something to eat. About six? You need Kenna's address?" Toni passed over all the information then repeated the call to Sorrel, and all the other parents on her list. Ones that she thought would care. She didn't bother calling the Bara's.

Tonight is going to be interesting. Wonder if they'll believe me.

That struck and she thought. ~Rarz?~

~Yes?~

~Would Alinis be willing to let me have some more *lasm* and your honey? I want to prove to people that there is another world with edible food. It will help hammer home what I am talking about.~

A minute of silence and her mind filled in the calling his mother, asking the question, the reply. She rubbed her face. When had her world gotten so weird?

~*Oppay* says she would be delighted. I'll bring it to you in one of your hours?~

~Perfect. Thank you and thank her for me.~

He agreed and signed off. She could tell McKenna and the others hadn't made it back to the house yet. The lights still felt far away.

Now to get ready for a house party I guess. And try to convince people to leave this world.

Chapter 26 - Dinner Display

The study of the weird virus has reached a fever pitch with people wanting to know if they have this disease as more people shun the very idea of being a Shifter. With the backing of some very religious corporations, all who have taken the stance that anything of alien origin is not in "God's design," the research is advancing quickly. Rumor is that within the next month or two there will be a test to look for the virus in anyone. Is this a wave of testing like they do for drugs? Where everyone tests to see if you are a Shifter as part of the job application? ~ TNN Science

The first knock on the door made her jump and glance at the clock. Ten minutes early, but that would be about right. She didn't know for sure who would come. She had called Sorrel, Sarah, Pearl Chun, Don Hauff, Mariposa Juarez, the Williamsons, and the Harnens. Toni thought about calling the Baras for all of six seconds, but if their daughter was worth so little, she didn't care about them. As Sorrel said, the Morzovs had moved, which she felt bad about. Ivan Morzov had been an impressive man. He also changed, but into a wolverine while his daughter became a spectacled bear. Some had seemed enthused, others wary and suspicious. At least two had asked if they could bring others.

This might be good or a complete disaster. I'm glad I bought extra whiskey.

Pulling open the door, Pearl Chun, the mother of Ping, stood there. A small woman, round face, her hair was in a tight bun that only accentuated it. Her normal placid expression had cracks in it. Her daughter turned into a panda, as did Pearl, something that had been regarded with great favor. At least it had when they met.

"Pearl. I'm glad you could come."

Pearl looked at her and took a deep breath before she stepped in, a large container in her hands. "I almost didn't. But it came out that we could change when those aliens came after us. My family in China hasn't been heard from since they attacked. At this point we may have no more choice." She hefted the dish. "Where should I place this?"

Toni gestured to the counter. She had bought a bunch of chicken fingers, easy to eat things with various dips. Cooking wasn't something she had the energy for right now. Before either of them could say anything the bell sounded and people kept arriving. By 6:45 she had a full house. Most of the people were the ones she had known, parents of children who shifted. In most cases at least one of the parents also shifted except for the Harnens. Their oldest son also changed. He was seventeen and trying to decide what to do. The new people were both single parents of a Shifter child. Laurel Otto, whose eight-year-old turned into a wolf, she was in the same class as Charley. And Joseph Kilian. He was a huge light-skinned black man, with sharp eyes and graying hair. His grandson was the one who changed, his daughter long out of the picture. At thirteen Luke didn't know how to feel about the mix of popularity for shifting followed by the hate. Joseph had agreed to come when Sorrel mentioned it.

When everyone had food, more to give them something to play with, Toni set a covered box down on the small coffee table but didn't open it. The eyes of everyone present snapped to her, then to the box. The silence seemed tense, as if the wrong word would cause it to explode.

Here it goes. Either they'll believe or storm out calling me crazy. And I wouldn't blame them for either reaction.

"For those of you who don't know me. I'm Toni Diaz. My twin kids and I all shift into black jaguars. One of my best friends is McKenna Largo." One person inhaled a sharp short breath, so at least one person hadn't known who she hung around with. "I'm sure all of you saw the crash of the alien ship?" It had been broadcast on damn near every network. The cameras at White Sands had captured the entire thing, though the resolution had not been good enough at the distance they landed to show anything of the burial except the smoke billowing into the air. The crash had broken the Neilson ratings.

When everyone nodded, she swallowed and continued. "Now what I'm going to tell you is, while not classified information, is stuff that we really don't want to get out. If it does and anyone asks me about it, I'll deny everything." She waited until they all nodded. "I was involved in helping the ship land. Trust me, compared to what might have happened it was a landing. Also involved was an alien from yet another planet. They have made an offer to my friends and me. They authorized me to extend the same to you."

Everyone went even more still, looking like prey animals hoping the predator wouldn't see them.

"If you want." Toni shrugged trying to not appear like a salesman. "They have cities, buildings, homes, from where the Elentrin killed their populace, and they are willing to offer them to Shifters who are willing to move there."

The silence stretched on for so long, she wondered if they had heard her. Sara broke the quiet. "Are you telling me aliens are offering to let us settle on another planet?"

"Yes."

"Bullshit," the word exploded out of Joseph Kilian's mouth like a bullet. "You trying to tell me not only are aliens trying to kill us but more aliens are offering us homes? Why the fuck do some freaking aliens give a damn about us?" He'd risen, his large bulk intimidating, but Toni just looked at him.

"Yes. The food there is edible, the climate temperate, and they have houses we can move into on multiple planets."

"How do we know they don't just want to use us too? That this isn't a trap. Hell, how do we know we won't starve to death on another planet." His belligerent tone and stance screamed fear to her, and that allayed any worry.

"You don't, but I trust him and I trust his people. As to the food," She reached down and took out what Alinis had provided. This time she laid out the container full of raw *lasm*, her mouth watering as the strange sweet scent hit her. Then the honey. The *lasm* lay in what she might have called glass, but it glowed with a light her eyes struggled to translate, while it was bound in fibers that didn't match anything she'd ever seen on earth. The honey lay in a jar made of something akin to ceramic yet picking it up it felt like you lifted air. Even the containers screamed strange and foreign.

"That is food from another world?" Mariposa sounded excited and scared at the same time.

"Yes. This is a fish they call *lasm*. I prefer it raw, but I'd say an entire market on ways to cook it would spring up. From what little we've discovered they don't have many varieties of cooking styles or seasonings. This is honey from their version of bees. It is probably the best thing I've ever tasted. I'm a predator so my craving isn't as much, but for a bear and wolverine I know, they licked the jar clean."

Joseph blustered out, "You think some food will prove it to us?"

Toni shook her head. "No, but you can taste it and you'll know this didn't originate on Earth. What I have here just tastes different, but something in it calls to me."

All of them, even Joseph, gave in and tried the various things she had provided for them to taste, Sorrel being the bravest.

"Oh wow," Sarah breathed after she ate the honey. "That is good. Makes me want to make baklava with it."

Toni had been watching her the closest, as being a non-Shifter she'd had a moment of worry about it, but none of the food caused any issues. The *lasm* disappeared as did the honey on the bread she'd purchased to put it on.

"I'm not saying we'd be pioneers, but life would be different than what we have now." Toni waved her hands around the place as she spoke. "It might be hard or even dangerous. But it is an option."

The parents looked at each other but it was Sorrel who spoke. "Life is dangerous. Americans get spoiled with easy access to food, clean water, housing. If you are offering a planet where we won't be hated for the color of our skin, the fact that we can change, letting us have houses to live in? Why would I turn that down?"

Everyone had fallen silent while he spoke and Toni wanted to hug him, but she needed to level with all of them. "The Drakyn don't think the same as we do and it will be living in another world, literally. But it will be a world where we can make it good or bad. We've asked them about vetting people, but for now they are trusting me to help pick people to test this out. The next part is up to you."

They talked back and forth and unfortunately most of their questions about the planet and living conditions were met with shrugs or 'I don't know' responses from Toni. But she did keep a list of the questions and promised to get them answers to their questions.

At the end she looked at them, not speaking, just asking.

"You know I don't shift. If we go, will humans be accepted?" Sarah asked, her voice tiny. All of them looked tired and stressed. The Shifters, while healthier, still looked exhausted.

This question had been one Toni knew would be asked. "Arrangements have been made that if you go to the planet with your family, you will be provided the option to convert into a Kaylid if you wish. While it will be mandatory for no one, the overall benefits may be worth it to you."

A strange hush filled the room as people looked at each other. Too many emotions for her to tell what the reaction was, but Sarah gave a short sharp nod to her husband.

"I want to believe. A world with no drugs, no gangs, a chance for my grandson to grow up and put his mark on the world the way people once did? But it seems almost unbelievable. Then you mention that maybe we can shift? Yet..." Joseph Kilian trailed off and shrugged. "Let me think about it? This is a big decision to make."

"Of course. This isn't a now or never. I'm expecting this to be rolled out slowly over the next while. I'd watch the news. You'll recognize the next big thing when it happens." Toni refused to say anything else.

Eventually people left, exchanging numbers and talking. She noted that there was a bit of hope, but a lot of concern. Concern she couldn't blame them for. The idea of moving was one thing. Moving to another planet with aliens? The idea thrilled and terrified her. And she didn't know which one was greater.

Sorrel lingered, helping her clean up. Everyone had eaten what was brought, enough Shifters in the mix to not have any leftovers. The *lasm* and every drop of the honey had been eaten too.

If nothing else, a thriving trade should be able to be reached with those two items, though don't know how the insects would go over? Vegan food?

"Toni?" Sorrel's voice pulled her from her odd musing as she dumped trash. She looked up at him, lifting an eyebrow in encouragement.

"I am more than willing to go first. My son has few friends his age and would think this all a grand adventure. I already know multiple languages and cultures." He gave her a wry smile. "Life as a refugee will do that to you. Let me use these skills to be the vanguard of this. Besides, I always wanted to be an explorer like the old stories. This might be my only chance."

Toni blinked, surprised at his words.

I thought a few might take me up on it eventually. I didn't think I'd get any solid answers except "no" today, though I didn't get any of those either. Maybe it's worse out there than I realize. I've been a bit sheltered, even with what happened to Carina.

"Okay. I have a list of things we were thinking it would be best to do. We will have the ability to travel back and forth between here and there. Do you want to go over what we thought and see if you have anything to add?"

"Please? I have about an hour." He seemed eager, almost excited and that helped her, and brought her family back to mind. What wouldn't she do for them?

Toni grabbed a notepad and the list Cass had been working on. Sorrel didn't own a house and had few belongings, so the need to sell things was low. He'd need to sell his car or put it in storage for a while. Cass had been very thorough, talking about freeze-dried food and supplies, and even bringing starter plants to see what would or wouldn't grow on that planet. Cass had tons of tests she wanted to run. They were still trying to figure out what equipment would be needed and if, with the generous government payouts, she could rent a lab with the right equipment to verify everything.

Sorrel's face lit up when she mentioned the number of starter plants they wanted to play with. "Oh, I would enjoy that. Gardening is relaxing and watching your effort turn into food. I would gladly buy many plants." He frowned then shrugged. "It is late fall, most plants won't be available, but I can get many seeds and starter pods. That way we will be able to test almost immediately."

"That's a great idea. Is there anything else you can think of?" The list was comprehensive and involved spending a large amount of money over the next few months.

"I don't see toilet paper or bidets mentioned, and have you tested the water?"

Toni looked at him blankly. "Bidets? Water?"

Sorrel smiled a flash of white. "Again, most water on our planet isn't drinkable. Is theirs? If Shifters can drink it, can non? It would be a very important aspect."

"Oh shit, you're right. Give me a second." She refocused on the mindspace. Everyone was busy, packing, moving, talking to family. ~Rarz? Cass? We need to test your water and make sure we can drink it or what needs to be done to it so we can and make sure our plants can drink it. And figure out an option for toilet paper or bidets.~

~Oh crappola. We didn't think about that. Most water isn't drinkable and that's important. But those are tests I can do with the local lab here.~ An odd cackle that tasted of burnt popcorn filtered through. ~I'll rent lab space from my old job. That will be entertaining. And they'll have everything I need. Not sure why I hadn't thought of that before. But the revenge will be delightful.~

~You can do that?~ Toni hadn't realized you could just rent labs like that.

~Yep. I'm certified so I can request lab time and have access to the machines. It will cost but since I know exactly what I want to do and will bring in all the samples, and lock them up, it shouldn't take me much more than a week.~

~Ah, yes. That can be arranged, but I have no reason to believe the water will not be sustainable. What else in the way of samples would you like me to bring?~ Rarz's calm voice filled the mindspace.

~I'll let you two work that out, going back to Sorrel who is here talking to me.~

~Give him my number. He's got lots of practical thoughts about necessary supplies that I'm missing. ~

~Will do.~ Toni disconnected and blinked and looked at Sorrel. "We'll make sure. Thanks for pointing it out. I'll give you the number to the scientist who is running all the tests and she'd love your input."

Sorrel frowned but didn't say anything about it. "Then I shall start making plans. This will be fun."

"Running away?" Toni flinched at the bitterness in her own voice.

"No. Moving towards the future. You can't live your life in the past. We aren't time travelers, at least not backwards. The future is infinite, now more than ever. Call me when you're ready. I need about a week."

With that he was gone, leaving Toni there thinking about his parting words.

Maybe he's right. A future living on other planets, with other races? That might be a better way to look at it.

Chapter 27 - Offer Made

The downsides of a global economy are being more evident as the weeks pass. The devastation in Australia, China, Argentina, and France are showing how linked economies are: industries such as cell phones, auto lubricants, medical supplies, and computer parts. While most people only think about food when thinking about global trade, the impact of having so many links in the chain shattered is staggering. Factories that just opened again are closing, laying off employees with no indication when they will reopen. People's tempers are fraying with this on the back of the invasion and most of the resentment is being turned towards those that are the root cause, Shifters. ~TNN Aftermath

The next day Toni headed over to both check in, see her kids, and have dinner. She'd spent the day trying to deal with employment paperwork and frustration made her snappish.

~Want me to bring anything?~ Toni asked as she got into her car.

~Nah. But Kirk and Anne are coming over. Wanted to talk to them and get a feeling for what's going on.~ McKenna replied, a bit distracted and Toni figured she was experimenting with food again. Ever since Colombia, McKenna had focused more on food and flavors and Toni suspected she'd gotten some Drakyn food to play with.

~Okay. See you in a bit.~ Toni wanted her kids, but they seemed to have entered the "adults are boring" stage. Only Nam still sought out active adult interaction, but the kids were always in cuddle piles, either in human or animal form, and it seemed to solve their touch needs.

Yeah, but it doesn't solve my touch needs.

Toni pushed the thought away. They were happy and healthy and that mattered more.

I need to improve my mood. Things are going well; we just need to wait for their big appearance to occur. At that point we can get it moving in the right direction.

Two cars she didn't recognize were already parked at McKenna's when she got there. JD's Hummer was there, as was Perc's car. Which meant a full house. Toni got out, a small overnight bag in her hands. Anne and Kirk stood there talking to McKenna. They both looked worn and exhausted.

"Hey," Toni said. Greetings were exchanged and Toni dropped her bag in the bedroom hallway. Where she slept depended on Perc and JD, but it really didn't matter. Even the couch would be fine. Following the sounds of kids, she headed out back where JD and Cass were talking and manning the grill. It smelled good and she nodded at the two adults, but her attention was on the chatter of the kids.

The vocal sounds meant human and she picked up her pace. She'd seen them less than twenty-four hours ago but after weeks of having them there every day, she missed them. And Carina. That thought brought a pang to her heart, but she moved down the steps to the obstacle course they were enhancing yet again.

"MOM!" Two voices yelled and they came barreling to her. Twin impacts on either side of her, heads buried in her waist. The tightness in her chest eased as she hugged them back.

"Hmmm, I seem to be missing two kids hugging me." She looked up to see Charley and Nam hanging back. At her words they sped forward and were all wrapped in the group hug. "I love you all. Remember that."

And I do. They really have become our kids. Maybe that's been my problem. I keep trying to focus on just mine and forgetting ours. Group families? The wave of the future.

The idea had merit. Everyone helping made parenting much easier and the kids were never lacking an adult if they needed one.

"We know, Mom. We do miss you."

Hmm, sounds like someone has been whispering in their ears about me feeling unwanted. Wefor probably.

Toni didn't know if she felt annoyed, upset, or grateful the AI stuck her nose into her personal feelings. But then it wasn't like the AI couldn't know. The mindscape probably reflected or shared more than they always paid attention to. Either way, by communicating via the mindscape all of them exposed more than they ever would normally.

"Wanna see what we built?" Jessi asked as they released the death grip on her.

"Of course," she said as they grabbed her hands and pulled her over to the newest addition to their obstacle course. This time they had things to jump over and apparently climb up. And Toni admitted it looked like it would be fun to run in cat form. Even Nam was helping, though all the kids watched her with sharp eyes. She glanced over to see JD and Cass watching them just as carefully, for all that the adults seemed busy with the grill.

Family indeed. All of us.

Toni laughed and spent the next hour helping the kids make their course even more fantastic and promised to run it with them later.

After dinner the kids disappeared to play a video game. She could hear the sounds from their bedroom and the adults sat out on the deck. Toni took the time to really look at Anne and Kirk. The two she'd met barely a month ago past the point of caring about anything.

"So we've been avoiding the subject. Wanna tell us how bad it is?" JD asked, leaning against the railing, his voice level and serious. McKenna had settled down next to Perc, a glass of whiskey in her hand.

Toni envied Kirk as he took a swallow of his drink, at least he could get some distance with the alcohol. She supposed she could tell her bots to not filter it, but she needed to practice that level of control more and besides, right now she probably did need to keep a clear head. Which was why she had iced tea so she wouldn't be tempted to let the alcohol smooth the edges.

"Crimes against Shifters are up. Way up. And the official stance is if you can ignore it, do so. Otherwise do the minimum." The way he said the words made her think they tasted bitter on his tongue, or at least on his heart. "I've been asked to take an early retirement. I'm seen as too 'pro-Shifters' for the current administration. Marchant took a new position to fill out a vacancy and the new police chief has no like for Shifters, hence my retirement."

Anne sighed. "I haven't seen his level of retribution, but I wasn't as visible as he was. What I do know is all the Shifters have been quietly dismissed, either issued medical retirement or their position was removed." She sighed. "And there isn't anything we can do about it. Right now, people are so upset and scared even the ACLU hasn't done more than file a token protest. People are still trying to get lives and jobs back together and money is tight everywhere. But more telling, no one has the energy to get upset about Shifters being mistreated. They need someone to blame."

"And the Elentrin are too pretty," McKenna replied with a sign of defeat. "Nothing you said really surprises me. What are you going to do?"

Kirk shrugged. "Retire, go someplace quiet and I guess keep my head down. Not sure what else I can do."

"I'm just going to stick it out a bit longer. I have another five years before I can retire, maybe by then the social pendulum will have swung back and we can start mainstreaming again. But if no more Shifters will be born, not sure that will happen. It's a limited population." Anne sounded exhausted and dejected. "Which means eventually there won't be many left."

"Really? This immortality thing won't cause issues?" Perc asked, leaning forward, curious.

"Oh it will, but unless I'm misunderstanding what information has been released, you aren't immortal.

You can still die, get hurt, get killed. You just aren't likely to get sick or die from old age, otherwise known as cellular decay." Anne shrugged. "With the way the courts are going and with how stupid people can be, I suspect a lot of people will push the envelope on what can be done with their 'healing' factors. Which means dead people." A sip of whiskey. "But we'll be fine. Waris sends you his respects and apologizes, but right now people are looking for reasons to attack anyone in the public domain, though in our area most people are happy with the way we were ready. But trying to convince them it was thanks to you guys? Well that isn't what anyone wants to hear."

Toni struggled to place the name as McKenna nodded. It finally clicked, he'd been her Lieutenant in Narcotics. She sighed internally, too many people. With deliberation she scanned the faces and they all nodded. They'd talked about this and agreed.

"Then assuming you can keep information quiet," McKenna's voice had a teasing tone and Kirk snorted, while Anne just gave her a flat look, though her lips twisted a little bit. "I have some information to share and an offer to make."

Kirk took a longer drink of his whiskey. "I get stressed whenever you say stuff like that. It is NEVER anything I expect or even want to hear." One more mouthful and he steeled himself. "Go for it."

"Allies that helped us defeat the Elentrin have offered us new homes on their planets. They would assist us in moving to another world." The shocked looked on Kirk's and Anne's faces made Toni hide hers in her glass. Laughing right now would be a bit mean. "Also, if you want, I can make you into Kaylid, well, Shifters."

Anne and Kirk looked at her, stunned. Anne's mouth opened and closed a few times while Kirk closed his eyes.

"That I didn't expect, and I thought I had prepared myself. But that one wasn't in the list. There's another alien species involved?" Anne asked, and as a group they explained about the Elentrin, Drakyn, the war and the portals. They explained that the Drakyn were going to make their appearance very public in the near future and that they would be trying to get as many Shifters as wanted to migrate to these other worlds. By the time they were done, a full hour had passed and they sat there. Kirk's glass had been refilled once but neither of them said anything for a long while.

"Is there a time limit on this offer?" Kirk asked finally. He looked rather like a man who had been overloaded with information. Toni knew that feeling all too well.

"Nope. It's there. Granted, once we leave, communication will be much more sporadic, but we've already thought about checking in regularly to get email, buy things. I doubt we will reach a point where we don't need Earth and all that it has. At least not for a very long time."

"I need to think on this. I can't tell you how honored I am by the offer but this will take a lot of thought on my part." Kirk's words were slow and the frown that creased his forehead seemed more than just personal consideration. "Is this offer open to everyone? The changing part I mean," Kirk clarified.

"Not really. It will be open to any family members that are part of Shifter groups that migrate over. But for the most part we aren't mentioning it can be done. It's going to come from the Drakyn, not us. We're going to try really hard to make it seem like all of this is from these 'new' aliens."

"However," Perc said after McKenna finished. "We are going to talk to our families about it. My parents and Cass's sister's family. But otherwise all our family is here in this house."

Toni hid another smile as McKenna reached out to take Perc's hand. They really were just as cute as JD and Cass. The thought that Rarz should be here rippled through her, but they had agreed he should stay in very human form and remain at the house in Baltimore until everything was public. If they were lucky, no one would talk for a while and mention that Rarz had been the Drakyn to arrive on Earth. The military had been given orders to keep their mouths shut. If it worked, great. If not, well, he was very hard to trap anywhere.

"Good to know. I need to think, but it means a lot you made the offer." Kirk looked down at his drink and finished it. "With that, I think I've had enough shocks to the system tonight and I'm heading home. I feel the need to get very drunk, and that was just enough to tell me I can't have any more if I don't want to stay here." He rose and Anne followed him.

"I'm about at the same point. It's been a rough two months and I'm ready to go home and just think." Her comment held worlds of emotion that Toni didn't even try to unravel.

McKenna saw them off and Toni leaned out, looking at the mountains.

Someday I'm going to be having a drink and looking at a different world. It isn't so scary anymore. I'm just tired of waiting.

Chapter 28 - Circus is in Town

I don't want them here. They aren't human, not anymore. We tried to send the blacks to Africa once. Why don't fix up that damn ship and send all these furry animals away. It might work this time. Off our planet. Then no more aliens will come. Good Christian humans won't die and we won't have those abominations in our midst. ~Caller on Harvey Klein Talk Show.

In the days that followed, they kept waiting for the Drakyn to show up. The news was always on so they would hear the second anything happened. But while they waited, they all planned.

Toni worked with parents, asking questions and sorting out her own things. She cashed out her 401k and sold everything in the house she didn't need. It was odd going through your life and realizing how little really mattered. For her memories she bought a nice weatherproof tote. Nothing sexy or pretty, but durable and would survive almost anything. In it she put things that had nothing to do with living, and everything to do with her past. Wedding photos, things that reminded her of Jeff, baby books, important jewelry, pictures, and the little reminders of her parents. When she was done, she didn't know if she wanted to sob or laugh. The mementos of her life didn't even fill it halfway. The emptiness mocked her, as if the lack of doing anything the last few years was a mark of failure.

No. I have two wonderful children and that was worth the time. So I wasn't party girl traveling the world. I've made a good life. I have a good family. These are just things, and in the end, they can't replace the memories or life I have.

With maybe more force than necessary, she shut the lid and rose. She needed to finish cleaning to put the house on the market. The kids were staying at McKenna's. Toni would be moving into the other bedroom if the house sold before they left. Sorrel had thrown himself into planning with a vengeance and constantly sent emails and new thoughts to the entire group. He was proving a well of information and pointing out assumptions they had made.

If nothing else, letting McKenna deal with the kids while she dealt with putting her life into boxes made it less stressful on her. And she refused to think about asking Rarz over. He found human homes so odd.

~Toni?~ As if summoned by her thoughts, McKenna pinged in her head.

~Yep,~ she replied while sorting through clothes. At least half of the kid's clothes were too small. And that brought up another question, how to get more clothes. Maybe they would never get away from Earth. The mile-high list of complexities threatened to overwhelm her.

One step at a time, that's all we can do. One step. The Drakyn wear clothes so there must be a way to make them.

~Were you eating here or there tonight?~

Toni lifted her head and surveyed the disaster of her kitchen. She was trying to pare it down to only what she thought she would use and create a box of 'Once we have electricity figured out' she would to take. At least this time she had remembered to pack a can opener to open all the cans they were planning on bringing.

~There. My place looks like it's been ransacked, which I guess it has been. How can kids have so much junk they never use? Am dumping pretty much all the toys and just hoping the TV and video games will still work there.~

~Oh, I really hope so. But then lately they never want to be inside. Their store of games they come up with seems to be never-ending. But Jamie might miss books.~

~Yeah, thinking e-readers and occasional microportals to buy and download, which just tells me more and more that we will never really leave Earth behind. And we need to make sure we have some money here we can use.~

~Maybe.~ McKenna didn't sound as sure as Toni had expected.

~What does that mean?~ Toni paused in her sorting to focus on the mindspace.

~Mind you, I don't think Rarz has been lying to us. But if there are all these other planets, don't you think there has to be some trade going on?~

~Huh.~ Toni sat and thought about it. ~You know, I bet there is, but it's probably small scale. Look, even their shops are small. Remember that one vendor we watched. They had three or four of five or six different fruits. A customer walked up and pointed at one. A portal opened and what she pointed out came tumbling out a minute or so later. They don't have to worry about making things and waiting for people to buy. When they buy, they pick it, make it, whatever. I don't think they trade or think of stocking up like humans do. And with no winter, they don't have non-growing seasons. They always have things growing. All they need to do is take care of the land. I think if we move in, humans will change the way they interact with the rest of the universe.~

~True.~ McKenna's sudden laugh filtered through the space. ~I wanted something new and challenging. This is going to qualify. Hell, I'm trying to believe that Perc asked me out. Me dating a football player?~

~Enjoy this, it's the fun part of dating. You two are good for each other.~ A flicker of something caught her attention on the TV that had been playing on mute. Toni turned and looked, trying to make sense of what was showing. ~Shit, McKenna! It's started. They're here.~

She dove for the remote and clicked unmute.

"The strange swirl has been hanging in the air on the front lawn of the White House for over thirty minutes. There are reports of similar effects at the lawn at Westminster, Tokyo's Imperial Palace, New Delhi's Secretariat Building, the national Congress Building in Brazil, European Parliament, and Parliament House in Canberra." A reporter's voice played out over the image as people with guns surrounded it.

~Yes! They listened and are giving everyone time to witness everything. Though I suspect Tokyo might be a bit slower. Has to be damn near the middle of the night there.~ McKenna's voice held worlds of

FAMILY

emotions, and Toni understood all of them as she looked at the image on the screen.

~Let's hope this works, I'd hate for anyone to get shot.~ Toni couldn't help but worry. So far, she liked all the Drakyn she'd met. Any of them getting hurt or worse, killed, would crush her.

The screen cut to show similar portals hanging in all the places they had spoken of, each of them surrounded by military personnel, all with weapons aimed. ~Damn I didn't think about this. We did tell them some of our customs?~ Toni asked, worried. ~And warned Rarz to have them make their skin relatively tough? 'Cause I'd think in Warrior form they could withstand a bullet, right?~

She didn't know why she was seeking reassurance, but what had been excited morphed into terror filled as she tried to watch all the images at the same time.

~Yes. Cass and Perc have been working with them and providing information on the different cultures. And remember they have done this with multiple worlds. They are just being much more showy and direct with us.~

This is what you get when you purposefully distance yourself. You're out of the loop and then stress over things that have already been discussed. You're going to need to figure out your mixed feelings about the Drakyn, and Rarz specifically.

The castigating thought didn't really help, but she tried to settle down and just watch what was about to unfold.

"Look, something is happening!" the reporter said, his voice spiking with either excitement or fear. The screen still showed all the portals and in a strange harmony, figures stepped out of the openings. The lead figure in each image was slim and elegant, the image of serpentine grace and beauty. They wore robes of vivid colors that flowed and caressed the body, their hands held outward, palms up and empty. The scales matched the colors that surrounded them. They weren't wearing the bright vivid colors of the Elentrin, but in colors of nature that made you smile with memories of childhood wonder. The main figure didn't have wings, but the tail was obvious as they strode forward. They were followed by three others. The next being was large, imposing with wings fully displayed in warrior form. These figures wore robes of a somber dark blue that highlighted the massive wings that flexed up and down as their head swiveled to scope out the surroundings. That one resembled Rarz, massive and intimidating, but even now, hands were held open and hanging by their side, with no weapon in sight.

Toni inhaled sharply at the third one that stepped through. She wanted to protest, to tell them now, but all she could do was watch and try to remember to breathe.

Dressed in cream colored robes similar to what Rarz had shown up in, a child the size of a nine-year-old danced through, ribbons tied to wrists as the various children danced across the multiple screens and they tried to look at everyone, everything around them. The large eyes, delicate build, awkwardness, and the wonder, made it clear this was a child, not an adult. The final was another Drakyn, but rather than the slim elegance of the lead figure, or the massive bulk of the warrior, this one seemed almost average. Dressed in simple robes of light brown and pulling a wagon behind, it could be ignored when compared to the bright colors, massive form, or curiosity of the child.

They came to a halt, all the weapons pointing at them. In the various reports on the screen, people tensed, waiting for orders, everyone keyed up. Toni thought she might shatter as she watched, learning forward to not miss a moment.

"My name is Sorleia. I am an ambassador from the Drakyn. We come offering trade and to seek alliances between our peoples."

The words were identical, except for the names, repeated in multiple languages across the world. Toni couldn't breathe as she watched, her heart beating so hard each beat felt like it might crumple into a ball of stress. In a weird harmony that could not have been planned, people emerged from the crowd around the Drakyn, approaching them carefully as they clustered together. Toni focused on the one with the wagon, the one everyone didn't look at. She wondered if he was another warrior. With their ability to store mass there was no telling. Or heck, maybe he was one of the elders Rarz had mentioned.

Across the world, relayed through the cameras of reporters, she watched world leaders welcome the Drakyn, saw weapons be put away, and more subtle protections slide into place. But the biggest hurdle was completed, and everyone remained unharmed.

~They did it.~ Cass's soft voice acted like a splash of cold water, yanking Toni out of her absorption in the drama playing out across the world.

~They did. Now to finish our part in this play. How are your tests going, Cass?~ Toni was determined not to focus on stuff she couldn't control.

~Really well. The soils aren't that different than ours. While the first few crops may be thin, I suspect with selective breeding the planets will modify themselves to create viable versions for each planet. I'm not sure if I'm surprised or not that the soil is so similar. Would make an interesting paper. Maybe once things settle down, I should apply for a doctorate in Xenobiology.~

Toni rolled her eyes. ~I'm still trying to figure out what our society will look like. We're going to be very much like the wild west for a while. Focused mostly on living, not really jobs for the most part. And I suspect the Drakyn will be better teachers than most humans. But we do need to think about school for the kids.~

~No worries. It's on my lists.~ Laughter from just about everyone rippled through the mindspace. ~What? I like my lists,~ Cass protested. Toni shook her head, smiling.

Leaving the TV on low, Toni rose. She needed to finish getting ready to sell the house. Her phone rang and she glanced at it.

~Gotta go guys. Parents calling me. I guess they know what the big secret was.~

~Yeah, Kirk is calling me. Talk to you later.~

"Hey, Sarah. I take it you saw?" Toni kept her voice light and happy as she answered the woman's questions, but her eyes kept being drawn back to the TV and the gathering of Drakyn exposing themselves to the world.

To a brighter tomorrow and the hope of a future for all of us.

Chapter 29 - Wrench in the Works

The world has exploded with speculation about the new visitors. The showy entry, stepping out of what looked like portals hanging in mid-air has fueled the fire about these new arrivals. But when you add in the fact they look like human dragons? Social media has become nothing but dragons. Between memes, questions, images of them, no one has enough information. The various countries have ushered them into restricted areas, and no one can get in close enough to talk to them. The ones that appeared on the lawn of the White House haven't been seen since and even the insiders aren't saying what is going on. ~ TNN News

Raymond looked at the documents on his computer. The Shifter committees were being formed and while their rights wouldn't be taken away, the committees were working on new restrictions. After all, people with epilepsy or other dangerous diseases were regulated for theirs and others' good. It would take a while to get a coherent plan of action laid out, but already the idea of identifying Shifters and restricting them had gained traction. There were motions in several states to have it listed on driver's licenses. There were a few reasons for this. With the revelation that they would not age, there might be a problem in the long run with the preconception of what a fifty or eighty-year-old should look like. While it wouldn't be an issue immediately, a few pointed comments at a luncheon or two had started that effort rolling. The other advantage was in an emergency situation if you had two badly injured people and one was a Shifter, you could focus on the other with the knowledge that the Shifter should heal most things in a few hours.

A grin split his face as he worked on other plans. His long-term plans. By the time this personality retired, and a new rising star appeared, the groundwork would have foundations that would be very difficult to destroy.

His desk phone beeped as the intercom came on. "Sir, there's a news alert you should probably see."

Raymond sighed, he had asked to not be disturbed but Shelia had a fine touch of when to interrupt him and what wasn't worth the disruption. Otherwise she wouldn't still have her job.

"Can it wait, Shelia? I'm in the middle of things." He didn't try to keep the annoyance out of his voice. After all that was why you had employees, to take your annoyance out on them and not the people you needed to use.

"I really think you should see this, sir. It's important."

Her voice had a high squeaky note that stopped him. He rarely heard her sound that rattled. Well, if you didn't listen to the employees you had, why bother having them.

"Thank you, Shelia. Channel?"

"It doesn't matter. It's on every channel." Her voice sounded even funnier and he became a bit more curious. He put down his burner phone, the only thing he used to work on his future plans. He woke his computer up and tuned into TNN.

"Breaking News – a portal has opened in front of the White House and two beings that look like something out of a Peter Jackson movie have stepped out." The camera zoomed in on the lead being, the robes in so many colors you couldn't concentrate on just one of the swirling colors. Raymond couldn't take his eyes off the lead being. They looked like something a CGI specialist had thought up for the next movie, but better. The curved neck, the flowing clothes, and the tail, who the fuck could make a tail look so elegant.

Then when it spoke, he felt all his plans shudder as if something hard had hit them. Something that could make or break everything. The next hour he watched every bit of information and noted them speaking in the language of the country they landed in. He watched the child that tagged along charming people. In every party, one of them had wings but the rest didn't. Did that mean something? Was it as simple as blue eyes versus brown or was there something there that wasn't obvious?

Raymond watched as they talked, as officials surrounded them, always with security in the background. As he did, he scribbled thoughts, ideas, and more, on a piece of paper on his desk. If you didn't use a notepad then there were no impressions left behind. You never knew what could be used against you. When the screens changed back to a reporter, the aliens all being ushered into restricted areas, he sat back and thought, his mind racing.

What do they want? Why are they here? How can I use their agenda to further mine?

The initial news report told him nothing about the ultimate goals of the Drakyn, but he could learn more. He rewound the live feed, buffering was wonderful, and zoomed in on the people who escorted the aliens away.

Aha. I know who you are. And I know who controls you.

He made quick notes, people to call, arms to twist. No matter what, he needed to be involved with these discussions. The idea of yet another race of aliens coming on the heels so close to the others, and with apparently benevolent intentions, set his teeth grinding. The unknown had a very big chance of messing up his plans and he wouldn't tolerate that.

Leaning back in his chair, he stared at the replay, watching the similar scenes unfold at multiple governments.

It's very choreographed, very guaranteed to hit our weak spots. There is no way this is just a random guess on how to approach us. Make sure the reporters had time to get in place. Someone coached them.

The idea rang of truth and he started digging through his memories. Trying to find the trail of clues that might give him an insight into how this had come about. Another splash of color on the screen had him looking at the scene in Japan and he noted this group was predominately dressed in red and vivid blue. If you interacted with different cultures, you were usually given a debrief as to cultural mores and habits. In Japan color meant a lot, and the visitors were dressed in red and blue, two of the most favorable colors.

Oh yeah, someone from here coached you. But who?

He dug out his phone and hit a number. Three rings, and his temper started to twitch when Higson answered.

"Yes?" The voice sounded like he'd been asleep. Some people didn't know when to take the opportunities they were offered.

"Enjoying your new position, Walter?" Raymond inquired silkily. "I thought it was a job you'd enjoy."

"Sure am. Best job ever. We had a late night yesterday. Today's my day off, but I'm enjoying the work, that's a definite."

Raymond smirked, getting him a position as the attaché for one of the more playboy generals in Washington would get him in a position where he might overhear interesting tidbits, and keep him otherwise distracted with the general's cast-offs. They were always young, pretty, and morally flexible.

"I wanted to ask a question. You had mentioned something about a big lizard guy with a tail and that he made what you called a portal? You remember that?"

"Sure, he was the talk of the whole group of people that were coordinating that entire thing. They made us sign this NDA thing, saying we wouldn't talk about it." He sounded drowsy and tired.

"Hmm, can you tell me who he worked with the most?"

"Oh sure, he was totally fawning over the Largo chick and the other Indian type woman. She was the one with the kids, I think." Another yawn that had

Raymond frowning. "But yeah. He's the one that they looked at and asked to do stuff with portals, so that was him. I mean I think so. I saw him turn into something with wings and a tail. Apparently there was more, but the reports didn't make sense. It was like he turned into a dinosaur or something else. Mass conservation would refute that, so whatever, But I haven't seen or heard of the dude since the ship crashed. Maybe he died?"

Raymond looked at the frozen image on his screen. The large hulking figure, wings hanging out to the sides, and hands that looked like they were made to rip and tear.

"I doubt it. Did you ever get a name?"

A long, drawn-out yawn that made Raymond want to reach through and shake the man, but right now he needed his good will. "It was something funny. Maybe I heard it wrong, but it sounded like Roars or Rares, something like that. Don't remember if he called himself anything else. Had too much other stuff going on." A beep sounded and Walter cursed. "Sorry, got to go, that was my thirty-minute warning. Time to get up and go get the general. Talk to you later."

Before Raymond could ask another question, Walter hung up. Growling, he tapped his fingers on the desk, thinking about trying to figure out who was involved. A vague memo sparked his memory and he dug back in the archives of the government system. Something small, a bill passed with a rider no one paid attention to because it was so small.

It took him fifteen minutes, but he had the bill up and the reference information he needed. Another few minutes of accessing various systems and a list of names lay in front of him.

McKenna Largo
Percival Alexander
Cassandra Borden
Tonan Diaz
Jessi Diaz
Jamie Diaz
Charley Davis
Joseph Daniel Davidson

He stared at the names. Nothing there was obviously anything that resembled what Walter had mentioned. Either way they would know this man, and he could easily justify it as information about the newcomers.

Ten calls and an hour of ego stroking, fear mongering, and highlighting the risks of making deals without information on these aliens, he got exactly what he wanted, though it would take another few days to be processed. He had time. The process to get subpoenas issued had been started. They were required to appear before Congress to discuss the exact nature of how they got onto the alien ship and who assisted them, with an interest in finding out if they knew anything about these other aliens.

When it got issued there wasn't any place on the face of the Earth they'd be able to hide. They'd be on every no-fly list and their licenses would ping if run.

And I'll finally get rid of these annoying bugs in my plans.

Chapter 30 - Tipping Point

Breaking News: Multiple explosions have occurred at six locations around the world. Shifters United, a global entity, that has been pushing the whole Shifters are People first attitude had arranged multiple meetings for people to get together and talk about the current attitude towards them worldwide. While there is no government approval for this movement, people do have the right to legal assembly. They had rented multiple venues and their primary speakers were being televised across all the venues. An anti-Shifter group associated with ISIS has claimed credit for the bombs. At this time reports of over two thousand beings at these various meetings have been reported dead. Even the vaunted Shifter healing hasn't made it so everyone survived. ~ TNN News

It was done. Her house was sold. The money in escrow and she had a storage unit with what she needed to keep. Which really wasn't that much, more of it was being used to stack up what they thought they might need in their new home. But the majority of the money wouldn't be spent until after they were there and had some time to assess. A safety net as it were.

I'm just glad this is over. I'm tired of this place. Tired of the hate.

She had loaded up her car and locked the keys inside her house when McKenna pinged her.

~The government guys actually came through.~ McKenna voice all but bubbled with relief and excitement. That, more than her words, pulled Toni's attention fully into what she was saying.

~Why? What happened?~ At least it wasn't something negative. They had enough bad things of late, none of them needed any more in their lives.

~They arranged for me to get full custody of Nam. Her parents signed away all rights. They did something funky where I'm declared as having diplomatic immunity. I'm still not sure, but Doug said it was his way of saying thank you. Tomorrow is his last day. But either way, I don't have to worry about her getting taken by CPS.~ The exultation in her voice filtered through tasting like cotton candy.

~Excellent. Have you told the squad yet?~ It was what Toni had started calling the four kids, as they had formed their own little squad that no one else could seem to understand.

~No. Was thinking a party tonight? To celebrate?~

~That sounds great. I take it you'd like me to stop at the store on my way there?~

~If you don't mind.~ They chatted as Toni started up the car, heading for storage first, then she'd hit the store. The ringing of her phone surprised her.

~Hey Kenna, Sarah's calling me. I'll talk to you later. I'm not sure what was up, she talked to me yesterday, and they still haven't decided on anything.~

"Hey, Sarah, what's up?" Toni prepared to listen to the woman babble, so far everything she'd come up with they'd already thought about and prepared for, but you never knew. After all, Sorrel kept pointing out holes in their plans.

"He's dead, they killed him," her voice came out in hysterical sobs and Toni almost ran off the road as she flinched back, pulling the car towards a ditch.

"What are you talking about? Who's dead? Who killed who?" Pulling over into a strip mall Toni focused on the conversation even as dread swirled around in her stomach. She couldn't handle any more dead kids, she just couldn't.

"My brother. He was at the Shifters meeting in Denver. Someone planted a bomb. He's dead. They hate us. They want us dead. Get me out of here, I'll do anything, but I don't want to see my son get killed for something he takes such joy in." She sobbed and stuttered the words coming out in rushes.

Toni closed her eyes trying not to lose control. "Okay. I'll send you the list and let you know when we can start moving people."

"Soon. I'm done. All I have left now is my son and my husband. I refuse to lose them too. We'll be ready." She didn't say goodbye, just ended the call.

Toni pulled up the news on her phone and felt one more support get knocked out from under her as she saw the information about the attacks scrolling on the screen.

Gods, so many dead. People killing us because of what we can do. I can't let my children grow up here. Surrounded with so much hate.

The very last vestiges of resistance or even concern vanished. A difficult life was one thing, but a life where so many people around you hated you? She'd do almost anything to prevent her children from growing up in such an environment.

~Rarz?~ She'd avoided reaching out to him for so long but now all her concerns seemed silly. No matter what, he'd never lied that she had seen, and he offered her a chance.

~Yes, Tonan?~ The sound of her name again ran along her spine in an odd way. The instant answer soothed something in her.

~I know the Drakyn are still working through the embassies and the long-range plans. But are you ready to start taking people? Things have changed here, and I have people that I think are ready to go now.~

~Define now.~

Toni had to blink and think about that. ~In the next week or two? We will probably need a Drakyn to help us go back and forth between the worlds for a while, but at least two families are ready, maybe more.~

~That I can do. We have one of the planets the Elentrin abandoned after killing most of my people. It has ten small-sized towns. They can easily support about twenty thousand with existing houses and business structures. There is a small group of Drakyn that are willing to go there and set up businesses to provide access to the various farmers and fisher groups on our other planets. A week is more than enough time.~

And she thought she had been thinking about all the aspects of this, it looked like everyone took this seriously.

~It would probably only be about ten people or so first. But the numbers may change.~

~Small or large we are looking forward to having your people here. Cass has asked to come and get samples to finish running some tests. That is scheduled for tomorrow. Unless there are results that indicate danger to humans, there should be no reason this can't happen.~

~Thanks. I'm headed over to McKenna's. The house sold today. So,~ she trailed off not sure what to say.

What do I ask him? Take me now? Tell him I don't want to be here. Or maybe, can I come visit now? Breathe in the world of my dreams? All of them? None? You know we aren't going to his home planet.

~While the homes we have set up for the McKenna Largo clan are not on my home world, I would enjoy getting to show you the world of my home.~

The parallel to her private thoughts made her jump and she didn't know if he really was reading her mind or something else.

Probably just coincidence. We've met in his world often enough.

~Thanks. I'll try to get people ready. Do I contact you? Or is someone else doing the portals?~

~I will be your primary point of contact.~ He paused then continued, ~Unless you no longer wish that.~

~Huh? No. That is fine, I just didn't want to waste your time.~ She started up the car and continued driving to McKenna's.

~Excellent. Goodbye for now.~

Toni arched a brow at that but shrugged, concentrating on driving to McKenna's, but the phone rang again, and she stared at it.

I've gotten so use to people just talking to me that I regard the phone as an imposition.

The number wasn't in her contacts, but she answered it, never could tell lately.

"This is Toni," she said as she turned down the street to McKenna's.

"Ms. Diaz, this is Joseph Kilian."

It took her a split second to place him, but then she nodded. The one who'd come on strong but mellowed out a lot.

"Ah, yes." She decided not to say anything else, to give him the chance to lead the conversation. She wasn't sure if it would be a good or bad one yet, his tone had been too neutral.

"I discussed it with my grandson. We want in. Or he does, and I'd rather get him away from here. I'd like him to not end up like his mama, my daughter. I'll go. If I need to watch him live forever to give him a safe life and start without drugs or gangs, I'll do it. I can't lose him to the new dangers. I won't. I'll die first."

His words caught her, but the grief and desperation in his voice yanked at her throat making it hard to speak. "What's happened?" It could be related to the bombings, but this seemed too personal, too immediate.

"New gang member initiation is to get a Shifter to change and bring them their pelt. So far two kids, young ones have been killed. Samantha was twelve." Rage and bleak grief twisted his voice. "I'll do anything."

If she started crying now, she wouldn't be able to talk. Toni tamped it down. "Okay. Sorrel and Sarah want to go to. We are planning to go in a week. I'll email you a list of things to get and put money in a bank account. We can come back later and get it if needed to buy more things."

"I don't have much, I'm not rich," he sounded desperate and Toni felt nails clawing to coming out.

"You don't need much. Clothes, toiletries, games, blankets, and a computer, though we still don't know how to work the internet. The rest we'll figure out and can come get it if needed. "

"I can do that. A week?"

"A week. Give me your email and I'll send you the lists now." He did and after hanging up Toni sent off the email to him and Sarah, then in a preemptive move, included the others. The list by itself might point to them being preppers. There was a tendency for the government to monitor preppers, but she didn't really care about that anymore. After the invasion and the shortage of supplies, being thought a prepper was a good thing.

Blinking back tears of frustration and horror, she dragged herself into the house. At least McKenna would be in a good mood. She wouldn't tell them about this. Not tonight. Tonight they'd celebrate Nam's officially being part of their family.

Chapter 31 - Green Light

Breaking news: The benefits of trading with the Drakyn are being highlighted by watching the machines building an embassy for them in a small lot in DC. From insider sources, when the government told them they wouldn't be able to supply funding or even materials to build a place for them, they said not an issue, they would provide their own materials. Currently we are building a machine building, a two-story structure for them. It is like a 3D printer in the same way a clay tablet is like an e-reader. If this is some of the tech they have to trade, we need to make sure we are very nice to these visitors. ~TNN News

The last few days had been crazy busy. The only people not snapping at everyone else were the kids. Cass had a screaming match with her sister that had JD over at her house consoling her. Toni still hadn't figured out what it was about, but it had to do with Cass leaving and a disagreement about if she should. She really wasn't sure and wasn't going to pry.

Perc was busy getting his house sold but he hadn't even told his lawyer friend Laura Granger about the plans to leave the planet and most of the 'friends' he'd thought he had faded once his contract with the NFL had been terminated. Add the fact that he was the public face of sports Shifters and no one wanted to talk to him lately. Even Laura had been getting enough death threats that she was seriously worried. More and more it wasn't safe to be a Shifter. He had not said anything to her about his parents' choice, and she didn't want to pry. From his drawn looks, she suspected it had not gone well.

They had withdrawn the kids from school, citing home schooling, which would be true in a way. The kids had been warned not to shift in public under any circumstances. Glancing at Nam, they all agreed with no argument and Toni wondered what she had said.

She was at the breakfast nook in McKenna's. Sorrel and his son were scheduled to come over today. They had everything ready to go and for now were going to limit it to one truckload and put everything else in storage until needed. Eliah seemed excited the one time she'd met him to discuss this move. The gang killing had shaken up a lot of people and a few more names had been added to the list.

Sarah and her family would be there in two days, as they were still working on selling their house and most of their belongings. Toni thought McKenna was a force of nature when she had decided on something but she had nothing on Sarah Johan. The woman was a general and had gotten more done in the last few days than Toni had thought possible. It gave her hope and there was a spring in her step, so Toni wasn't going to argue.

McKenna was working on her computer, trying to finish purchasing freeze-dried food. It should be here tomorrow if they paid the extra shipping.

"Why is the meat so expensive? And Cass did get all the water tested from the wells and faucets, right? We can drink and cook with it?" Toni knew all of them felt overwhelmed and a bit scattered as they tried to double-check everything. "We need more meat than veggies or pasta, and we don't know how hard getting the *lasm* will be. Alinis did confirm there was no immediate risk of over-fishing, right?"

Toni smirked at McKenna's babble. "You need to pause if you want me to answer your questions."

McKenna jerked her head up and laughed. "True. So any answers?"

"Yes. Cass has tested all water sources, and she says it is exceptionally pure and we'll love it. As to the fish, you know how it looks and kinda reminds you of salmon?" McKenna nodded, a frown drawing her eyebrows together. "Well, apparently they're closer to the size of sturgeon here on Earth. Like Beluga sturgeon that can reach up to a ton."

"Oh. That might explain it, but still no risk of over-fishing?"

"They reach that size in two years and they have managed to transplant to other planets. And they don't have any natural predators, so they are growing like crazy. So if we practice some conservation, it should be easy. They also mentioned maybe setting up a few planets for nothing but farming, both animal and plant."

"Oh. Huh, that might solve a lot of problems." McKenna signed. "Neither of us can solve or fix everything but at least I think we have the most important stuff accounted for."

"All we can do. The kids are excited, but I think it is more than they are hoping to find new animals and things to chase and eat."

McKenna wrinkled her nose. "Which I understand, yet it still kinda makes my stomach turn."

Toni laughed. "That doesn't bug me. I'm too used to them putting anything in their mouths. This, at least, is animals and I'm pretty sure the nanobots will solve any issues. Poison might be an issue, but I figure they'll yell if there's an issue. Then we can deal with it. I'm not going to stress over something that I can't control."

"Fine, fine." McKenna threw up her hands and pushed back from the computer. "Now, we just need to finish up and then go. It should be fun. Or at least different." She looked like she was about to say something more when her phone rang. She arched a brow as she answered it on speaker. "Doug. I thought you had retired. Shouldn't you be out enjoying the relaxing life?"

"I should be, but I needed to warn you."

Toni felt her stomach churn, pushing all food thoughts away.

"About?" McKenna sounded like Toni's stomach felt.

"Someone put some pieces together and subpoenas have been requested for you to appear in front of Congress to talk about the alien that helped us bring down the ship. All of you, including the kids. The only person not on that list is Rarz and that's probably because we didn't issue him a check or ever write his name down. We only referred to him as an unspecified ally. There are rumors that you might be charged with treason if you passed information to the Drakyn that is meant to destabilize our government. At the least, it would be aiding and abetting an alien species that may not have good intentions towards us. A few other countries have chimed in also about wanting to be in on the questioning. No one wants to offend them as their house-building machines alone are game changers, but humans and Shifters are fair game right now. I don't know what you can or can't do, but you deserved that much." His voice sounded exhausted and like he just wanted to sleep for a month.

"What does that mean?" McKenna asked, her voice thin and tight.

"It means you'll be considered guests of the state and will be under intense scrutiny by everyone. Everything you did, the way you knew it, who you contacted, everything will be torn apart and probably ninety percent of it will make it into the public space. Which means the court of public opinion will then tear you apart, too."

"I see. How much time do we have before they come for us? Not like our addresses aren't in the database system," McKenna pointed out.

"Probably two to three days. They have to finish getting a few signatures. There's enough pressure that I'd expect to have federal marshals knocking on your door twenty-four hours after they sign it."

Toni took in a shaky breath, watching McKenna's head drop down. "Thanks, Doug. We won't be here. I'll send you an email address that we will check occasionally, but we'll be gone."

"I had hoped that might be your answer. Whatever they want with you, it won't be good for you or the country, to be honest. Stay free and good luck." He hung up before they could say anything in response.

McKenna looked at Toni, a bleak look on her face that Toni knew was on hers as well. "He was there when Rarz made the offer. He isn't stupid. He knows we have an option or he already suspected what we were planning on. So we move everything up?"

"Only option. Instead of leaving next week, we leave not tomorrow, but the morning of the day after. We need to tell the others to be ready to leave tomorrow. All of them. They can come back later and finish up what is needed."

McKenna straightened her shoulders. "Then let's go." Her eyes unfocused and Toni heard her in the mindscape. ~Okay people, plans have changed. The government has decided we might know something about the Drakyn showing up so perfectly and is calling us in for questioning. We want to be gone before that. So instead of leaving next week, I want to leave in two days and go over with Sarah and her family. If we get caught here, we'll never get away. From what Doug says, there is a chance we might be charged with either aiding and abetting or interfering with a government investigation. Worst case, treason.~ The word sounded hollow in the mindspace.

~Crap. Okay, I'll finish up in the lab today and shut everything down. All samples will be removed or destroyed. But it means I need to get there now. JD, I'll be very late to get everything done today.~ Cass's voice wrapped around them.

~Okay. I'll finish with Cass's place. We had it almost done. I found a developer to buy my place for less than asking price, but I'll take it. Not like I need to buy a new house. The storage unit is rented and half-full with everything we've talked about. It's the largest unit they have, and we made sure to map out an area for portals to pop into. It's paid for five years in advance, so we can get in and out without needing to be visible outside.~ JD responded, and Toni could almost hear his thoughts kick into gear.

~Parents have decided to stay.~ Toni flinched at the pain in Perc's voice, but she understood. His parents had a life here and didn't want to walk away from it. No matter how much they supported their son they weren't ready to walk away. With Perc gone though, the focus of his being a Shifter should dissipate and he could always come back and visit.

~Rarz, did you hear all that?~ Toni asked. She felt the tension of everyone waiting for his response.

~Yes. I apologize if our actions have caused you harm.~ There was a tentative tone to his voice and she didn't understand it.

~This isn't on you, just slightly unexpected. I just want to make sure you don't have any issue with this change in timelines.~

~It is not an issue. I will be there when you need me.~

~Can I ask another favor?~ Toni hesitated to ask the next question.

~There is much we owe you. There is little we would not do for you~ His voice calm and rich.

Guilt swamped her but she asked anyhow, it was little enough to ask. ~Can you ask everyone to not mention our names or that they have talked to any humans. We don't want there to be anyone that people can point to. Keep it to the microportals that you gleaned information from. Please?~ It shouldn't be possible for your voice to break in mental communication. But her voice broke anyhow.

~Of course. We had already decided not to mention that we had any prior interaction with humans.

Everything we know was backed up by our research, so it should not cause any questions or concerns.~

~Thanks. We'll see you tomorrow. Sorrel?~

~Yes.~

Toni turned to McKenna who had a funny look on her face. "What?" Something about McKenna's face set off alarm bells in her mind.

"You're all ready to go, right? Everything taken care of, supplies purchased?"

Toni gave her a sharp look. "Yes. Right now, I'm just the liaison between the Drakyn and the families that are going to go there first. But no, all of my things have been taken care of." Her tone wary.

"Good. Can you go tomorrow and take the kids? All the kids?"

McKenna's words hung in the air as Toni looked at her, unable to breathe, to think.

"You want me to go, tomorrow? To be the first there?"

"Yes. They might be here tomorrow. I want to make sure that no matter what happens, the kids are safe. From what I've seen, the Drakyn would protect them always. Please? Will you? Will you make sure my kids, our kids are safe?"

Toni blinked and then forced out a laugh that sounded torn from her heart.

"Yes. I'll go and yes, I'll keep them safe."

Everything snapped into place, all the planning, the preparation, no longer was it something in the future, it was tomorrow.

I'm leaving this planet. Holy fuck.

Chapter 32 - Trouble

Dragons are in. These new aliens are taking the world by storm and no one can get enough. When contrasted with our last encounter with aliens, no one is arguing at the peaceful way they are reaching out, though some grumbling about wishing they were only coming to the US has arisen. While negotiations in all countries is very hush-hush, the idea of new trade opportunities and new markets that might open is enough to make even the bleakest outlook for our future seem brighter. When you add in the rumors that they are willing to trade medical knowledge, maybe what caused Shifters can be cured completely. ~TNN News

Morning dawned early, and Toni was already up, her bags packed, the kids' packed, and it was still hours before anyone was scheduled to go. She made breakfast and listened to the news. An article caught her attention and she hissed out in annoyance.

~Wefor? Elao?~ She asked. The two AI's had been quiet of late, but everyone had felt their presence with subtle suggestions and answer to questions they hadn't thought about.

[Yes, Toni?] The reverberation was Wefor, but she could tell Elao had focused her attention on her also.

It felt strange—not bad, just odd. Like a magnifying glass had centered in on you.

~We know that Shifters here on Earth will be in danger for a while. They were talking about tests that will detect the virus which I assume is the nanobots and how they look under a microscope?~

[For your current level of technology, that is as accurate as they can get. The nanobots have a specific pattern that would resemble some of your more deadly viruses, such as the Ebola shepherd's crook pattern. So while they are unable to see the actual programming or individual parts, they can see the structure when they associate with other bots.]

[Correct, though the information in the databases from the *Forlin* will provide them the ability to isolate them within the next few years.] Elao added into the conversation.

[Is there a reason for your questions, Toni?] Wefor chimed back in and the strange focus intensified.

Toni shivered and tried to focus on stacking up the pancakes she was making. They'd keep warm in the microwave until people got up. ~Yes. They are coming out with ideas on how to ID Shifters, even those who don't shift. If they manage to do that, they can identify and make it into another way to discriminate against people. Is there anything we can do? A way to make them... I don't know, disappear?~

A humming sort of silence. She got the impression of electricity zooming back and forth on a line between two buildings. As they talked, she worked on cooking. It gave her something to do and was both occupying and letting her mind free to roam, going over all the things that needed to be done. But no matter how much she fretted, twisted or thought, everything else she came up with had been addressed.

[Toni, Elao has a possible solution, but it would require McKenna to assist in making it work, and Rarz. And while it should work, there is no guarantee.]

~What are you thinking or what is the solution you have, Elao?~ Toni finished the last batch of pancakes. She could hear people moving about and Sorrel should be here in about an hour. The place was mostly packed up. The rest would follow tomorrow and they had arranged for a management company to rent the house. McKenna didn't want to sell until they were sure they would never return to Earth.

~I'm sure McKenna will help.~ Toni said.

~Help with what?~ McKenna asked walking into the kitchen. Still dressed in her rumpled sleep T-shirt, she headed straight to the coffee maker.

"It's already brewed, just grab a mug." Toni said with amusement. JD and McKenna still needed it every day to function.

"We have arranged for this wherever we end up?" McKenna asked, pouring the cup.

Toni held back a laugh. "Yes. We have French presses, large ones, ready, so as long as you have the ground coffee and hot water you will be fine."

[This addiction to a drug is not real. The nanobots ensure that you have no need of chemical additives. This apparent addiction is chosen, not based in chemical needs.]

"Shush. I'm keeping my addictions, thank you very much. You already made booze unpleasant, let me keep my coffee." She took her first sip, sighing a bit.

Then she opened her eyes and looked at Toni. "What do you need my help with?"

[Toni raised the issue about Kaylid being identified after we are left by the nanobots in their blood. There is a way this can be prevented, but your assistance will be required to do this.] Wefor's voice still rubbed across the nerves in her mind, but by this point it almost felt normal, familiar.

"Ooh. Yeah. I'd rather those we can't get this offer to, those who choose to stay here and live as normal, not be mistreated because of what we can't stop. So yes, I'll help. How?"

"They said they needed Rarz too. It might have to wait until he gets here."

[Toni is correct. It will take a bit of juggling to pull this off, but Elao is sure it will work.]

A bubble of humor washed across the mindscape. [Yes, I am sure. It is programming I've been working on for *reyans*. It will work within a 94.325% success.] Elao responded with that same gentle amusement.

"Then we'll do it. Let me take a shower and get Perc up. I hear the kids moving. They are super excited and Charley is still trying to convince me to let them go over in animal form."

"Ha, they tried that with me. Didn't work." Toni smirked a bit at the memory as she put bacon in a pan. Might as well enjoy what would be harder to get very soon.

"Oh? Share. How did you derail that plan?" McKenna had paused on her way back to her bedroom, a cup of coffee in her other hand for Perc.

"I pointed out if they did that, they would have to wear backpacks in cat form and carry their suitcases with their mouths and I would make sure to record it for my future entertainment. They decided maybe they would go over in human form."

McKenna looked at her with a serious look. "You are a cruel woman. I think I may have to worship you."

Toni laughed as McKenna headed towards the bedroom. The clock said six, everyone was moving early this morning.

~Kids, I have food ready. Clean up and finish packing. We'll leave as soon as Sorrel gets here.~

~Yes, Mom.~

The food pantry held enough food to last them one more day and then it should be mostly empty. They had scheduled to eat the last of it tomorrow before they left. Everything should be taken care of by then. She didn't know if she was excited, anxious, terrified, or just wanted it over with. Waiting had always been the worst part. She was completely ready to go. Her suitcases waiting, her boxes in the garage. After that, they would have to see what was in the storage units that would be needed. They really weren't sure, but then that was why she was going first with the kids. To help see where the weaknesses were and what they needed to think about.

The soft rumble of a vehicle came from outside. Toni grinned. That had to be Sorrel. She went and opened the garage and sure enough, he was getting out of his four-door blue sedan. A young man she recognized from the zoo, and from visiting his dad to discuss this, got out on the other side. Almost as tall as his dad at fourteen, Eliah looked like him with the dark skin, curly hair, but his face looked more sullen, more cynical than his father. It struck her as odd given everything his dad had been through. Maybe this would be good for him, a new world, new options.

"Heya. Bring your stuff into the garage but stay out of the taped-off square. I've got food inside if you're hungry," she said as a way of greeting. They were trying to keep everything hidden, just in case someone was watching. The warning from Doug was hanging heavy in their minds. For all that they still had days.

They nodded at her, and in a few quick minutes had all their stuff inside the already crowded garage. She closed the door and ushered them inside just as Perc and the kids emerged from the back rooms.

[Toni, have you asked Rarz yet if he is willing to assist? This will take a while to initiate.]

~Ack, sorry. Got sidetracked. And what do you mean initiate?~ Toni had finished most of the breakfast prep and multiple plates of pancakes sat in the oven and microwave. She needed to clean and then...leave? The idea made her swallow so anything to delay sounded good.

[This is not something that can be just done. The nanobots will need to be instructed. Just as information could be exchanged between the command module and the drone nanobots, this information will need to be disseminated the same way.] Wefor told her in a way that Toni suspected was condescending, but never crossed the line.

~Rarz. You free to come over? We need to see if can protect those that don't end up coming with us.~

~Yes. The space we designated?~ His rumble of words delighted her as always.

~Please. Sorrel is here, so not sure which form you're keeping.~

~For the time being it was decided looking pure human would be safer. If someone sees us, they would see, in Cass's words, a big-ass human, not a monster from the movies.~

Toni choked on the sip of coffee she'd taken. Everyone looked at her as she moved over to the sink and washed her face. ~That makes sense. Then yes, please.~ She switched channels in her mind. ~McKenna, you ready?~

~Yep, coming out now.~ Actions matched words as McKenna emerged, hair in a ponytail, jeans and a t-shirt, empty coffee mug in her hand. Perc followed her out, also freshly showered. "Was making sure everything was packed. I know we aren't leaving until tomorrow, but I don't see a reason to spread out and have to repack everything then." While she wasn't bouncing on her toes, there was a spring in her step and a smile on her face that implied a lot had happened in the thirty minutes since she went back with the coffee.

Before Toni could tease her, the strange pressure change feeling rippled out of the garage. Sorrel and Eliah were off in a corner watching them with wide eyes. Toni followed their gaze. With the four kids chowing down on food, McKenna, Perc, herself, and then Rarz walking in from the closed garage, it must seem a bit odd.

JD and Cass were finishing up at her place, selling his car, and loading up the secondary storage site before coming over tomorrow. Either way, today was Toni's last day here. She took another swallow of coffee so as to not think about that.

~So what do I need to do?~ McKenna switched to mental as she focused on food, and let the kids chatter away at Eliah.

[Rarz will need to open a microportal to one of the satellites circling the Earth. Then with the help of Elao, a message can be sent, bouncing off satellites and leveraging the transharmonics of the communication wavelengths to change the programming of all nanobots.]

Toni listened with interest, zoning out the kids babble to Eliah, even though they'd somehow pulled Sorrel into their discussion. It kept them occupied and she would worry about the mischief they were hatching at a latter point.

~Change the programming how? To what?~ McKenna had her eyes closed in her concentration expression when the people talking weren't corporeal. Toni didn't know if she realized she did that. Or heck if they all did it. It was odd to try and talk to someone you couldn't see but heard, like they were in the same room with you.

[The nanobots that remain inside the body need to stay as they are. But after discussion their programming should be able to be updated to instruct them to break down into their component parts which would be indistinguishable from the basic cell detritus for at least another twenty years. By that time, your people will no longer have any proof that there is anything biological that links to people shifting shape.]

~How many nanobots are in what our scientists are seeing?~ Toni couldn't prevent the question, it all sounded so crazy. Make something tiny break down into even tinier parts and they wouldn't see it. She always saw the pieces of evidence when the kids snuck cookies. Crumbs everywhere.

[A few hundred. The resulting pieces should not be recognizable to most scientists.]

Oh. I swear, magic might make more sense than some of their science.

~That sounds valid. So what's our part in this?~ McKenna asked, finishing up her coffee.

[Once Rarz opens the microportal, we will need you and Perc to be standing in front of it. Wefor and I will need to focus to get the right frequency to hit the satellites and then make sure it starts a loop bouncing from one to the other. We must not stop once we start, because if the entire program command isn't finished, their internal routines will regard it as a hacking attempt and refuse to acknowledge all further commands.] Elao's voice had a stern quality.

McKenna shrugged. ~Sounds good to me. Perc, you ready?~ The man in question had a plate of bacon and pancakes.

~Yep. Will I be able to eat while we do this or need to concentrate?~

[You may find the experience is a bit overwhelming,] Elao said, a hint of apology in the AI's tone.

~So be it.~ He took three large bites of pancakes, then shoved in two pieces of bacon. ~Go for it.~

Toni rolled her eyes. No wonder the kids' table manners sucked.

~Wefor, if you would assist with the location of the satellite that is closest? This will require intense concentration to keep the portal moving with the satellite without disrupting it or causing it to fall out of orbit. I don't know how easy this will be. Ships and planets are much larger than satellites,~ Rarz said and Toni tuned them out. This wasn't anything she could help with. She headed into the kid's bedrooms, picking up the little things they hadn't grabbed, and searching out a brush and elastic to deal with Jessi's hair.

"Mom, I don't want my hair braided," Jessi whined as Toni worked the brush through the explosion of snarls that Jessi had collected during the night.

"Fine. Do you want a ponytail? A twist? What do you want? We can leave it loose, but then you'll have it in your mouth and catching on everything. A braid is the easiest if you want to go in and out without it tangling on things." Toni provided in a logical list of options. This fight had happened more than once over the years.

Jessi heaved a sigh, one that seemed to come from the bottom of her soul. "Fine, braid it. But no silly scrunchie at the end."

"Okay." Toni took advantage and braided her daughters long black hair in quick efficient movements. The jangle of McKenna's phone grabbed her attention as she wrapped the elastic to finish off the braid. She rose to grab it, glancing at McKenna and Perc. They were like frozen statues, strangely unmoving. If it wasn't for the occasional blink and slow breaths, she might have worried.

The caller ID said DB Sec. Frowning, she answered it. "McKenna's phone."

"Get out now. They had people waiting. They signed the order to appear twenty minutes ago. If you aren't gone in the next thirty, they'll be there. I think it got signed faster than they expected, so everyone isn't in place. They were expecting another day or two but you need to go now." He paused and signed. "Toni. They have a rider to put the children in supervised houses, to make sure they aren't being brainwashed by their parents' deviance. It's a small section but you'd never get them back if they get your kids. They have your home addresses, names, and jobs, but not much else. They were still researching. Get out now while you still can. Run. All of you, run." Fear and worry created acid grooves in his tone.

It took three full seconds for Toni's brain to catch up to what Doug Burby was all but shouting through the phone. "Oh fuck. Got it. Thanks." She hung up, dropping the phone in the pocket of her shorts. The curse had everyone looking at her. Kids with wide eyes and Sorrel confused.

"Everyone grab your stuff; we're bailing now. They're coming for us. Get to the portal area." She snapped out. The kids looked at her for a heartbeat then sprang into action. Sorrel wasn't much slower. Toni spun to look at the frozen figures on the couch. Rarz stood next to them, frowning a bit in concentration.

~Guys, Wefor? How much longer?~ She didn't stand there waiting, instead she went through the house like a whirlwind grabbing everything and stuffing it in bags. The boxes would have to wait, but the suitcases and important stuff needed to go now.

Shit. Portals. Rarz is busy and we need one now. Dammit I knew we should have fought to learn how to use them. If I could create them now this wouldn't be an issue.

[At least another ten minutes. This code is complicated, and the satellite moves out of range quickly.]

Elao sounded distant and preoccupied, which she probably was. Literally and figuratively.

~Bad things incoming. We need out of here ASAP or everything is going to be for naught. Move it as fast as you can.~ Toni rattled it off even as she finished grabbing McKenna and Perc's stuff.

[Understood.]

~JD, Cass. We're burned. Get out. Take what you need and bail. They know the location of Cass's house so get out of there and don't go back.~

~Got it.~ JD didn't say anything else, but she could feel the panic spurt from Cass before it was shut down.

Portal, what do I do about the portal?

The rest of the people in the house were headed towards the garage, the kids with their backpacks on and their suitcases being dragged behind. Sorrel and Eliah had grabbed all their other bags and were quickly moving everything left in the house into the garage.

Argh, what a time for those three to be unavailable.

Toni stared at McKenna and Rarz, her thoughts spinning in a frantic circle. The idea of those government idiots taking her kids, of anyone breaking up that group made her want to rend flesh from bone. Granted, they would be gone in the first hour but still, it wasn't something that she would ever allow to happen. She'd see them on an alien planet first.

Alien!

For some reason Rarz didn't register as 'alien' anymore, but his mother had. And she had tapped into their little mindspace group. Toni reached for that light in her mind. Since that day it had been an odd purple color. Toni hadn't thought anything about it as the female Drakyn had never spoken to them again, but now everything rested on that. She hit that odd light with a mental finger and all but screamed into the mindspace.

~Alinis!~

A heartbeat, a breath, the sound of sirens in the distance approaching as she jacked up her ears.

Shit, shit, shit, what else?

~Yes?~ The voice sounded distant thin.

~Alinis, we are found out. We need off our planet now and Rarz is occupied. Can you help?~

Please for my children be willing to help.

The voice suddenly became strong, clear. ~Show me where to open the portal. I will bring you into my home. How many?~

Toni thought her knees might buckle, but she pictured the carefully taped area in the garage. ~Four adults, five kids, plus Rarz and all our stuff. We need to get through asap. I can hear the people coming for us getting near.

~Opening the path now. You were lucky to get to me. There was a tiny path open from one of the embassies to our world, otherwise you would not have reached me. As soon as the path is established, I will come to your world. Then you can start moving your belongings through.~

Toni looked at the space with everyone around her as they watched the swirl of light, a paler pink gold than Rarz's silvery light snapped into place and Alinis stepped out. Eliah muttered under his breath, eyes wide, but they had no time.

"Sorrel, everything through fast. Kids, your stuff, move it. We need to get all the supplies on the other side. They'll watch this place for weeks." Toni and Alinis helped. In under two minutes they had all the boxes, duffels, and suitcases tossed through the portal. The last one had been tossed through when they could all hear the cars and sirens coming to a halt outside the garage.

"Eliah, help me grab them, I want them here at the portal." Toni ordered while she ran into the house towards the others on the couch.

Alinis followed them into the house. "What are they do?"

"Too long to explain. Sorrel, can you grab the other side of McKenna? We need to get them right on the edge of the portal."

With Alinis helping, they got all three of them into the garage just as the banging on the front door started.

"McKenna Largo. Please come to the door. We have a subpoena for your attendance at a hearing." The voice was loud, male, and not very friendly.

"Yeesh, since when do they do this crap for a subpoena. What happened with 'Hi, you've been served' and disappearing." It was obvious something else was going on. This was coming across like a scene from POLICE!

Toni made a decision. "Sorrel. Go through. We'll follow. I'm sending my kids after you." She caught his eyes in a glare that was half terror, half determination. "I'm trusting you. GO!"

With a shaky nod he headed through, Eliah following. Toni turned to her kids, Nam, and Charley with wide panicked looked on their faces, standing near McKenna, their bodies trembling. "I love you. Now get. I'll be along in a minute."

Jessi and Jamie's lips started to quiver, and the banging came again. "We don't have time." Toni reached down, hugged Jessi, then threw her into the portal. Moving with a speed born of terror and need, only Charley wasn't caught off-guard as she tossed him in.

"This is your last chance. If you don't open this door, we will break it in." The bellowing came again. Toni crept over and shut the kitchen door. It would give them one more minute she hoped.

~Alinis. Go. I'll wait here and pull them in.~

~Can we not move them in now?~

~Not without risking what they're trying to do. Go, I'll follow and bring them with me.~ Toni assured her, hoping that she wouldn't prove herself a liar.

~Very well.~ With a nod of her elegant head she stepped into the portal and disappeared.

~Hurry up!~ The desire to shake them, to pace, to run, to do something ate at her, but she stood, as silent as possible.

[Forty-five seconds,] Elao sounded like she was slurring, but Toni held her breath, listening, her hearing jacked.

"Okay. No answer. Break it down. Everyone, get back."

Please have reinforced the door. Please make it take them more time.

Toni didn't know who or what she was praying to, but she held her breath, every second, one more gained in the race against time.

SLAM
SLAM
SLAM
CRACK

Toni could hear the door splintering on that last hit.

"Back! Clear the place." The voice again.

Shit, shit, shit. We're out of time.

Toni turned. They had positioned the three of them in their weird trance to be in front of the open portal.

Rarz, sorry. But I'll leave you if I have to. You can get home from anywhere.

"Living room clear. Check the kitchen and the bedrooms."

~Guys?~ Toni held her breath, her body shaking with tension.

[Done!] The exultation of joy barely registered as Toni shoved with all her strength and Perc and McKenna went flying into the portal. Someday the startled looks on their faces would probably make her smile, but for now she just hoped they didn't land hard.

"Checking the garage," a voice said. Toni grabbed Rarz. She tugged and dove into the portal at the same time, her mind screaming out to Alinis.

~Close it, now!~

The world spun and she landed hard on her back, what little air she had was knocked out of her. Toni lay there, breathing hard. She listened to the voices and the chatter in her mind, McKenna and Perc were exclaiming and being brought up to speed. The kids were babbling. Sorrel was remarking on things softly and being very gracious to Alinis.

She sensed more than saw Rarz crouch over her.

"Are you well, Tonan?"

"Just recovering from the excitement." She opened her eyes to see him staring at her. "It got a bit intense there at the end."

"So it seems." He stood and offered her a hand. For reasons she didn't understand, she took it and let him pull her up. "While this was not the original plan, you are now in the home of my birth. Would you like to see my world?"

She could tell the kids were already outside, and since no one was screaming in pain or struggling to breathe, the odds were there wasn't anything that was going to kill them.

"Sounds good." She moved towards where he had pushed open an arched door, the scene seemed more Moroccan than anything she'd seen much in California.

"Welcome to my world, Tonan Diaz." His voice rumbled, but it seemed to take place far away and in her head as Toni stepped out onto a paved walk and looked up at a lavender sky with two moons hanging it in. "Welcome to my home."

Home. I'm home.

Epilogue

The news that is setting the globe on fire, the Drakyn have announced they are looking for settlers for many of their planets. They would prefer Shifters or what they call The Changed. When asked why, they responded as follows. "Drakyn do not age as you do, and our worlds are significantly different from yours. We would prefer those with the ability to heal from smaller injuries and be willing to create something that will last their lifetimes, not the short lifetimes of humans." When pressed for details they said they would allow family members of Shifter families, but at this time are not accepting any all-human families or individuals. ~TNN News

"What do you mean you can't find them?" Raymond wasn't mad, but he was concerned. In the three weeks since the orders to appear had been issued, not one of the Shifters had been found.

"I don't know. We've inspected all their houses and they're empty. Most of their homes were already sold before the orders had been issues. The marshals can't find them, neither can the secret service. We have them on watch lists and actual warrants are out as persons of interest, but nothing. It's like they've disappeared. " The senator sighed with annoyance. "At this point we've had to shelve the hearings arranged for them, as we can't provide any estimate of when they will be found."

"I thought we had arranged emergency pick-up the day the orders were issued?"

"We did. They arrived at ten in the morning. There were even pancakes still in the microwave, warm. But they were gone. Now I will say this came up as a surprise. The original agents on scene noted suitcases and boxes, food, little things like that. They stayed there for about three hours, then left the house setting up a watch for anyone coming in. They watched for a full week and never saw anyone or anything, yet when they went back in to clear it out one more time, the place was empty."

"Yes, you already said that. They weren't there," he bit out the comment, hating when people said the obvious.

"No," this time the senator sounded a bit annoyed and Raymond pulled back on his attitude. "I mean it was clean. All the suitcases and boxes were gone, the food cleaned out and there was no sign of anything left that the original team reported."

"Oh. What about their vehicles?"

"Still sitting there. Including one for a Sorrel Narrio. But we checked and the vehicles had all been sold in the last week. The keys were mailed to the dealer after the house went under watch. The house has been handed over to a management company, the keys dropped off a few days ago. That company is planning on furnishing it next month and renting it out. They've prepaid for five years of management. If they are still in the country, I have no idea where they are."

The newest news story, the immigration offer from the Drakyn, was the headliner of the day and hung on the screen of his computer.

"Yeah. I might. Thank you for your time, Senator. I think you're right. We need to shelve it for now and see where we can gather other information. I'm starting to think the that this new Australia might be the answer to all our concerns about the Shifters."

"New Australia?" The Senator barked a laugh. "That's an interesting way to put it. Maybe we can get a tax on anyone leaving, make some money off it?"

"I wouldn't mind, but we'll have to move fast to get it done before most of the people leave. Maybe we don't say anything to encourage them to get out?"

"Either way, it's not like they can take their money with them. They can't actually spend it on another planet."

Raymond didn't respond that there were ways. If you included cutouts, proxies, there were more than a few ways for anyone to still spend their money, but it might not be a battle to fight right now. "True. Well, we tried. We'll have to make sure any deals we make with this group of aliens are profitable. But think of how much better our world will be with this problematic element gone. It will be better for everyone. The dregs of society are leaving because of their own choice. It sounds like the perfect solution to me." He kept his voice light and positive, knowing the senator would respond to it.

"True. With that, I guess the New Australia is accurate. Getting rid of the dregs of our society and we don't even need to do anything. They'll self-elect to go. This sounds perfect to me."

He ended the phone call, leaning back and looking at the screen. "So somehow you set this all up, didn't you, Largo. I guess Willard was correct about how much of a pain you are. But..." he trailed off still staring at the alien dragon on the TV talking about the opportunity they would offer Kaylid. "You aren't my problem any longer. But if I'm really lucky, something out there will find you very tasty and you won't be anyone's problem anymore."

With a final sigh, he mentally checked that one off and moved on to other problems, making sure he never got tagged as a Shifter and prepping his fictional identity in a few years. He planned to be president in about forty years. The world would never see him coming.

Authors Note:

I hope you enjoyed the Kaylid Chronicles. This will be the last book in this series. In the future I may come back and write further about the fight against the Elentrin and give the kids their own series.

Visit my website at www.badashpublishing.com to sign up for my newsletter and find out about the next books coming out for BAP. Or follow us on Facebook - https://www.facebook.com/badashbooks/

If you enjoyed this book, please leave a review, it makes a HUGE difference. Thanks!

Miss a book? Find them all here.

No Choice is available now!
New Games is available now!
Commander is available now!
Home Alone is available now!
Decisions is available now!
Incoming is available now!
Trust is available now!
Allies is available!

Happy reading!

Mel Todd

ABOUT THE AUTHOR

Mel Todd has three cats, none of which can turn into a form with opposable thumbs, which is good. If they could they wouldn't need her anymore. Writing and trying to start her empire, she decided creating her own worlds was less work than ruling this one.

Printed in Great Britain
by Amazon